CHINA STRIKE

ALSO AVAILABLE BY MATT REES

FICTION

The Damascus Threat

A Name in Blood

Mozart's Last Aria

The Fourth Assassin

The Samaritan's Secret

A Grave in Gaza

The Collaborator of Bethlehem

The Ambassador (with Yehuda Avner)

NONFICTION

Cain's Field: Faith, Fratricide, and Fear in the Middle East

CHINA STRIKE

AN ICE THRILLER

MATT REES

CROOKED
LANE

NEW YORK

Published in the United States by Crooked Lane Books, an imprint of The Quick Brown Fox & Company LLC.

Crooked Lane Books and its logo are trademarks of The Quick Brown Fox & Company LLC.

Library of Congress Catalog-in-Publication data available upon request.

ISBN (hardcover): 978-1-68331-134-8
ISBN (ePub): 978-1-68331-136-2
ISBN (Kindle): 978-1-68331-137-9
ISBN (ePDF): 978-1-68331-138-6

Cover design by Craig Polizzotto
Book design by Jennifer Canzone

Printed in the United States.

www.crookedlanebooks.com

Crooked Lane Books
34 West 27th St., 10th Floor
New York, NY 10001

First edition: July 2017

10 9 8 7 6 5 4 3 2 1

TO MATTHEW KALMAN
AND
HANS-JÜRGEN JANSEN AND MONIKA TRAPP

The obstacle is the path.

—Zen proverb

PART 1

CHAPTER 1

The bastards fired him at the end of the graveyard shift, after he loaded the last pallet of blank paper and ink cartridges onto the truck and waved it into the night. Gibson pulled on his Knicks jacket and shivered out into the parking lot. On the overhead line, the A-train carried the first comatose office workers toward a tense new day of bitching around the water cooler and fielding calls from people who were almost as mad as they were. He laid his hands flat on the cold roof of his car and squeezed out a pinch-mouthed whine of frustration that seemed to match the squealing wheels of the subway train on its elevated tracks. Those people were heading into a new day, but day wasn't coming. Gibson dropped into the driver's seat of his Darien Focal and tried to slam the door. It shut almost noiselessly, as if it could handle all the pressure he couldn't. He pulled through the gate in the chain link fence onto Atlantic Avenue, turning on the wipers against the drizzling rain.

The plastic freshness of the carpets in the car taunted him. It was the clean scent of the indulgent life he would never have. He pulled up at a red light. If he hadn't bought this car, he'd only be halfway screwed now that he had lost his job. He had taken out a loan to finance the new car instead of picking up a used vehicle at a price he could afford. He got the new car because he deserved it. He deserved to sit in a cabin infused with the smell of success. Not the dusty scent of the old Saturn he remembered his father driving when he was a kid. The pristine odor of this car was part of a picture he had of himself in which he would drive it home each day to a nice house out on Long Island with spotless rooms and the bouquet of fresh paint. He would come through the front door to greet his wife and their new child. Sure, he had figured he deserved it. Now he knew what he really deserved. To be all the way screwed. Yeah, what he deserved.

He took out his phone and thumbed through to his wife's number.

"Hey, asshole." A man in a tan trench coat hammered the hood of the Darien. He opened his arms wide in outrage and glared at Gibson.

Gibson dropped his eyes back to his phone and shoved his foot down on the brake. He had been creeping into the crosswalk. *Don't kid yourself,* he told himself. *You're not moving forward, no way. Not even that slow.*

The man came around to the side window. He thumped it. His cheeks were red with the morning cold and a recent shave. The belt of his trench coat was cinched tight over the kind of bulk that signifies an athlete gone to midlife seed. Gibson was accustomed to this shit. Heading home from the night shift, and everyone else grumpy on their way to work, half asleep and ready to rumble. It didn't matter to most of them that they were mixing it with a six-five African American in his twenties. *They* were supposed to be scared of *him.* But when a New Yorker was pissed, he got pissed beyond all reason and all fear.

Gibson dropped the window. "I'm sorry, sir. I apologize."

The man had his fingers over the rim of the window, holding tight, knuckles pale. "You could've damned well killed me."

Only if you're one of those guys who bleeds to death after a gentle poke, Gibson thought. Trench Coat didn't look like a hemophiliac and Gibson had been moving slower than the guy was walking. The light changed. Half of New York leaned on their horns behind him. "Yes, sir. I'm sorry."

The man in the trench coat stepped back. He kicked the rear door of Gibson's Darien. Gibson heard the metal dent. The man walked away quickly toward the Ralph Avenue Station. Gibson knew he was looking at about two hundred dollars of damage to the car. He could work that off in two days. Except that now he had no work. For an instant, he imagined everyone on the street dead by his hand. Then he remembered Miranda, and he shut the window.

He eased onto the gas. He put Miranda on speakerphone.

"Hi, honey. You on the way?" She was still sleepy. She never let him come home and find her in bed, though. She would wake up and brush her teeth and take a shower and dress for work, and she would welcome him and feed him and tuck him in between the sheets before she went off to the Pioneer Supermarket and ten hours of standing behind the meat counter for eight dollars an hour.

"I got fired." He watched the cars and trucks overtake him on the inside, weaving around him. He drove carefully in his new car.

"Aw, damn, baby."

"I didn't do nothing. It's just cutbacks, you know?"

"Sure, sweetheart."

He listened to the silence. He was a man, and a man was supposed to have a solution. But he had nothing to say. How about this? "Don't worry. I'll get a new job, and we'll make the down payment on the house in Freeport anyhow." Yeah, how about it? He could no more fill the silence than he could buy that house, now.

"We'll be okay." The streetlights went out. Look at that, the world didn't end. The day was starting anyway. "I guess."

"No guessing. We will be okay. Little Anthony is *not* going to grow up in a rental right here next to the sewage treatment plant and the airport."

"Don't forget the expressway." He smiled.

"Not next to that, neither. The only way is up. Hey, you didn't complain about the name. I called him Little Anthony, and I didn't hear you say a thing."

"I'm going to let you call him Anthony. It's okay. I give."

She laughed low. "Deshawn is a dumbass name. You think I'm going to let you give our son a dumbass name?"

He smiled. "Okay. I said I give. I love your name, Anthony. I want our baby to have your name too."

He teared up. Every time he failed, she reminded him that he hadn't failed *her*. He turned south onto Rockaway Boulevard. A Lufthansa jet lifted off at JFK. Briefly it seemed to be heading directly at him. Then it canted its wings toward the ocean.

"We still got the payments on the car to make," he said.

"Sell the car. It doesn't matter. It's just a car."

"But in Freeport—"

"In Freeport they've got busses and the Long Island Rail Road. I know you loved getting that car. But we're okay without it."

"If we even *get* to Freeport."

"We are *going* to Freeport."

He crossed Woodhaven Boulevard. "You know what? I'm going to sell the car right now."

"Anthony, come home and let me make you breakfast."

He knew she had heard the fakery in his voice, the fragile enthusiasm cloaking a desperation that could only lead to disaster. "I'm going to drive it right back to the dealership and sell it to them. Whatever they'll give me."

"It's six AM. The dealership won't be open."

"I'll wait in the lot for them to open. Soon as they do, I'll sell the car, and I'll go out to find a job. Not on no night shift, neither."

"Just come home."

"You go on ahead to work now. I'm going to take care of this."

"Anthony—"

"I said go to work." He was driving too fast. He lightened his foot on the gas. He made his voice soothing. "Miranda, hell, I just—"

"It's all right. You do what needs doing, Anthony, and you do it your way. I trust you."

"Okay. I'll come by the market later."

"I'll see you then."

He hung up. He turned south to skirt around Aqueduct. Amid the concrete of Queens, the grass of the racetrack and the bright white rail gleamed between the stands, a sliver of another richer world. The Darien was a simple family sedan, but when he drove it, Gibson was a jockey on a sleek thoroughbred, pounding around the track. He bought the car from a dealership in Ozone Park, barely five minutes away. He'd have an hour or two to enjoy just sitting in the car before he gave it up.

He inhaled *that* scent. It was never going to last. Soon enough he'd have a baby, and the car would smell of diapers and discarded morsels of food. Well, he'd have enjoyed that too.

The sound system. That was sweet. He turned on the radio. An orotund Midwestern baritone boomed out at him, telling him the news like the world was about to be over. "Secretary of State William Kurtz faces off against Chinese trade negotiators at a new round of talks in Vienna this week. Kurtz says Beijing is pushing the talks to the brink with demands for big concessions on Chinese imports to the United States." The secretary of state's patrician lockjaw tones cut through the clicking of a photojournalist scrum. "We're prepared to negotiate in good faith, and we're hopeful that the Chinese delegation will approach the talks in a similar manner. We all have to walk a careful line here. Threats are not constructive. When you issue a threat to get the upper hand in negotiations, you never know when someone's going to hear you out there and misunderstand and take irreversible action that's harmful to both sides of the issue." The newsman came back in. "Trade talks are expected to conclude in early July. Next up, traffic from—"

Gibson tapped the control on the steering wheel, and the radio zipped through to a jazz station. "The Sidewinder" hit the riff twice, and then Lee Morgan went into his solo, the triplets fast and just enough off the beat to be irresistible. Gibson reached his right arm over the top of the passenger seat and spread himself out in his fine automobile. Lee Morgan was a phenomenally talented trumpeter who died young because of his heroin addiction. Anthony Gibson lost his job in a warehouse and was giving up his car, but he had his health and his life and another life that was growing inside a wife whom he loved. Maybe the people riding the subway into Manhattan had it right. It was a new day, after all.

The sole of his right sneaker suddenly dropped. He frowned. The resistance in the accelerator pedal had disappeared. The engine revved. The pedal was stuck, flush to the floor. The car jolted ahead, picking up speed.

Gibson stamped on the brake. He felt only slackness and the speed of the car forcing him back into his chair. He glanced at the speedometer. He was doing sixty on a narrow suburban street.

Ahead of him, the street met the feeder road for the expressway. He yanked on the hand brake. The Darien fishtailed a little, but the acceleration continued. Gibson cursed and jammed down on the foot brake again.

As he sped toward the end of the road, a blue car came across the junction at high speed, blaring its horn so loud Gibson couldn't hear the sax solo on the radio. The driver shimmied around a Ryder truck and went right into the back of a Toyota sedan.

"What the—?" Gibson howled. He couldn't see what was entering the junction from the south, and he couldn't stop to find out. He might make it across the feeder road and come to a halt in the long grass on the other side. But he might just plough straight into another car.

A silver Darien Cayuse flew into the junction. The driver tried to cut left. He was going too fast. The SUV flipped onto its side and rolled into the back of the Ryder truck.

"Oh, shit." Gibson entered the junction. The speedometer said 110.

The cab of a massive semi rolled in front of him.

He wrenched the wheel to the right. He almost passed the semi. Then a red Darien Venturan came out on the other side of the truck, fast as the jet taking off from JFK. It struck Gibson's car right where he sat.

He lifted out of his seat and felt the entire universe break over him at once. He landed in the long grass and tumbled with the sense that some parts of his body were detaching, snapping away. When he was still, he looked up at the sky. It was dark and then darker.

He couldn't see the road. But he heard the crashes, one after the other. On the expressway beyond the grass too. Engines whining, racing too fast. Cars tumbling, bouncing, and crushing with the sound of a plastic food container in the hands of a petulant child. Everyone was crashing.

A tall man ran over to Gibson and knelt beside him. "Sir, do you hear me?"

Gibson squinted. Hard to see anything, but he picked out the blue eyes and the black hair, and then he saw the pistol in the shoulder holster. "Don't shoot." His voice was barely a whisper.

"I'm here to help you, sir. What's your name?"

He couldn't think of his name. His brain was shutting off. The only names he remembered came to him. He wanted to say Miranda. Then he said, "Little Anthony."

"Anthony, I'm going to help you. My name is Dominic Verrazzano. I'm a federal agent. I'm going to get you help."

Federal agent? What happened to me? Gibson stared and blinked. *What'd I do?*

The agent made a call on his cell phone. He yelled above the chaos of the pileup, the screaming people, and the keening car alarms and wheezing radiators. "Not all of them. It looks to be only Dariens. But they're crashing. Every one that I can see. I need an ambulance. I have a guy here who's—"

A guy who's good as gone, Gibson thought.

"I'm going to get you an ambulance, Anthony." The agent leaned close. "It may take some time, though. The roads are going to be jammed. Can you hang in there with me?"

The ejection from the car and the fall had shredded Gibson's Knicks jacket. His phone slipped from the jacket pocket. The agent grabbed it. "Is there someone I can call who can talk to you while we wait for the ambulance, Anthony?"

Gibson snorted like a horse running out of steam on the track at Aqueduct.

The agent worked the screen of the phone. "Miranda?" He had found the last incoming call. "Who's Miranda? I'm calling Miranda. Anthony, you're going to talk to Miranda for me. Stay with me, now."

He leaned in close as he spoke into the phone. "Miranda? I don't have time to explain. I need you to talk to Anthony. He's been in an accident. I just need him to hear your voice now, okay?"

The phone was at his ear, but Gibson heard nothing. The agent's face was inches away. He saw compassion in it.

"Say something to Miranda, Anthony. What do you want to tell her, Anthony?"

Tell Miranda, he thought, *that car killed me.*

CHAPTER 2

After Verrazzano closed Anthony Gibson's eyes, he surveyed the highways and boulevards, jammed with totaled vehicles wrecked in impacts with Dariens. People gathered in small groups around the victims they pulled from the chaos. Others stood about hopelessly, peering through crushed bodywork at someone trapped or dead. It was curious, Verrazzano thought, the perplexity these onlookers displayed. So many people died on the roads that these New Yorkers ought to have sauntered blithely on to their destinations, stepping over the corpses on the blacktop. Their shock was less at the carnage than at the realization that this had been going on every moment of their lives and that they had never once paused to sense the pain that they could inflict with one moment of inattention or aggression behind the wheel. The pain that could end them in the split second it took to glance at a cell phone or to fumble for a better radio station.

Unlike them, Verrazzano understood. He was a former Special Forces guy, "special" because he was trained to survive in an environment so hostile it would fry the average soldier in a matter of minutes. He could track and neutralize a target anywhere in the world. Most of all, he had inflicted death so often that he had learned to look beyond it. For him, a body on the road was nothing to gawk at. He had long ago considered where the soul went and concluded that it was free and clean and that it left all its suffering on the one who had been the instrument of its death.

He bent over Gibson and placed the dead man's hands across his belly. Someone out there had Gibson's afflictions and a whole load more laid at his feet right now. "I'm going to find them, Anthony," he murmured.

His cell phone rang. He picked up. "Hi, sis. You okay? I'm going to have to take a rain check on dinner. I'll have to work on this—whatever it is. Tell the little princess I'm sorry to miss her." He hung up.

The roads were jammed. Any cars that hadn't crashed were nonetheless going nowhere. Verrazzano left his ICE cruiser at the side of the highway feeder and jogged past the racetrack toward the A-train at Aqueduct station.

A half hour later, he came out of the subway onto Eighth Avenue. Even on the steps out of the station he knew everything was wrong here too. The sirens of motionless ambulances wailed in the halted traffic, professional mourners at a funeral. Subway passengers stood at the top of the stairs, stilled by the sight that met them. Verrazzano looked up and down the canyon of tall buildings along the avenue. Everywhere the huddles around the dead, the injured on the curb, and the cars squeezed into the shape of discarded toothpaste tubes.

He sprinted along Twenty-Sixth Street and into the redbrick building that housed the New York field office of US Immigration and Customs Enforcement. On the sixth floor, he saw Noelle Kinsella striding across the Homeland Security Investigations area, her loose red hair flowing behind her and the bangles beating a rhythm at her wrists.

"Jesus Christ, Dom," she called out. "What the hell?"

"Is the SAC here?"

Kinsella tugged off her purple overcoat and tossed it into her cubicle. She headed toward the conference room in the corner of the floor next to the office of the Special Agent in Charge. "He called a meeting with FBI. Should have started about five minutes ago."

"I didn't get anything on that." Verrazzano waved his cell phone. Within minutes of the crash, everyone had hit the phones and the network blew up. "System's down."

"Everything is down, except my blood pressure."

Kinsella pushed open the door and entered the conference room. Verrazzano followed her. There were three people, backlit by the big window and the bright sunlight off the Hudson. The head of the field office, Jim Callan, paced, his hand raised and brushing the wall nervously. In the quiet room, the Glock in his ankle holster ticked gently against his short boots with each step. Special Agent Roula Haddad, the computer specialist on Verrazzano's team, sat at the end of the table. A woman in her early forties stood behind her, surveying the newcomers with hostility. That was sure to be the FBI agent. Her hair was light brown, cut to fall over her cheeks as if she wanted to hide behind it.

Callan greeted his agents. "Dom, Noelle, take a seat."

Kinsella dropped into a chair. Verrazzano stayed on his feet. He rarely sat for anything, whether it was typing on his computer or drinking a coffee. He wasn't about to start now, when he was buzzing with adrenaline.

Callan wore a shirt the same off-white color as his face. His tie was the faint blue of a vein viewed through pale skin. It was as though you could see inside him and pick out his spinal column—except that *his* backbone went directly from his head to his gut. The SAC gestured toward the woman behind Roula Haddad. "Guys, this is Special Agent Gina Jahn, FBI, New York field office."

Jahn carried a little extra weight, but only so she could throw it in your face. She pursed her lips and glanced at Verrazzano like a very disappointed mother. Her neck crooked to the right. For

Verrazzano that was a tell—a ploy to control the adrenaline that jagged the Fed's neck muscles.

Callan swept his hand to take in the new arrivals. "Special Agents Kinsella and Verrazzano."

"I'll be liaising between ICE and FBI here." Jahn kept her arms folded. "You guys pass on whatever you get to the Bureau through me."

"You're going to pass information back the other way, right?" Kinsella's sarcasm was as thick as her eye shadow.

Jahn didn't appreciate that. "FBI is lead on this investigation. We have a major incident with potential to develop into a terrorist investigation. Or possible criminal negligence by an automaker or one of its suppliers. That's FBI jurisdiction, and we don't have time to argue."

Immigration and Customs Enforcement was an agency with a broader mission than its name suggested—even if the FBI agent wanted the ICE guys to cede everything to her. ICE was the second-largest law enforcement agency in the Federal government after the FBI, though it didn't have the long history of the Bureau. It was put together from other agencies under the Patriot Act after 9/11. Anything that crossed US borders was ICE jurisdiction, from trafficked people or drugs to cybercrimes committed through the Internet. Kinsella was about to take another shot at Jahn, but she caught Verrazzano's eye. He shook his head a little, and she held her tongue.

"If we're going to pass anything on, we'd best know what the hell's happening. Roula, give us the latest," Callan said, "so Dom and Noelle are on the same page."

Haddad pushed a wisp of black hair away from her dark eyes. She pecked through a few screens on her laptop.

"The pileups are enormous. We don't have a figure on how many cars are involved so far, but the bulk of the damage is to

Darien Motor Company vehicles. Other makes of car have been involved, but it looks like that's only as collateral damage. The cause of each crash appears to be a Darien vehicle speeding out of control." She glanced down the screens on her laptop. "First reports from NYPD and law enforcement in Jersey and Long Island are that they simply accelerated and wouldn't stop. We don't have a casualty number. But the hospitals are all jammed."

She turned her screen around. The browser showed a collection of grainy surveillance cameras, five columns across and four lines down, all running live. "Sixteen shots of the highways in the city, as well as bridges and tunnels to Jersey and the Island. Every one of them is just chaos. Totally shut down."

Even from the other end of the conference table, Verrazzano noted the unmoving dashes of black on the screens, the dead laid out flat in the roadways, like minus signs representing their subtraction from the sum of the living.

"NYPD just can't get through to where all the accidents happened," Callan said. "Because they happened everywhere. It's the same for the ambulances. If someone's hurt too bad to be treated on the spot, they're—well, they're dying right where they are."

The FBI woman drummed her fingers on the back of Haddad's chair. "Why would all these Dariens suddenly go out of control?"

"I witnessed a big pileup out in Queens, and I was able to survey the streets from the elevated line of the subway on the way toward Manhattan," Verrazzano said. "There were plenty of Dariens that didn't crash. The older ones, I think. The ones that *did* crash looked pretty new to me."

"Does that seem right to you, Roula? Is that confirmed by what you're seeing?" Callan gestured for Haddad to scan the screens. He leaned over her as she tapped her keyboard. "Continue, Dom."

"If we want to know how big this might be," Verrazzano said, "let's see how many Dariens have been sold in the Metro area over the last year or so."

Callan nodded at Haddad. She tapped at her computer. "About one hundred fifty thousand. In New York, New Jersey, and Connecticut."

"This thing happened at about six AM. That's pretty early for commuters and too early for people taking their kids to school. Let's say thirty thousand of those cars were on the road and went out of control. Even if only half of them were going fast enough to cause a fatal crash, that's a lot of dead people."

The weight of the death toll silenced them a moment. Then Kinsella cleared her throat. "I just don't see why."

The FBI woman hammered her fist down. "It's terrorism. What's so damned difficult to grasp here?"

"If it's terrorism, it's a lot more complex in preparation than anything we've faced before," Verrazzano said.

"Those bastards are getting smarter all the time. Technology makes everything easier. Except stopping them."

"It could be a flaw in the cars," Kinsella said. "The car companies have a track record of detecting a problem with one of their parts, then failing to disclose it. They don't want the expense of a big recall to fix things. They figure it's less costly to allow a certain number of people to die and then pay compensation to their relatives."

"So the terrorists are Darien? One of the biggest motor companies in the world?" Jahn's eyes were violent, then suddenly they were full of satisfaction, so that Verrazzano wondered if she had reached out and slapped him so fast that he had missed it. "Let's get real here. A faulty part couldn't cause this. If the brakes were going to fail or the accelerator pedal was going to jam, it would be random. It wouldn't happen in thousands of cars all at the same time."

"You're right," Verrazzano said. "So it's got to be the software."

Haddad looked up from her screen. "It's possible. We have no idea what's inside the box with a car's internal computer. Remember when it turned out Wolfwagen was programming its cars to beat emissions tests? The EPA didn't figure it out for years because regulators are not computer programmers. They don't go through every line of code in a car's computer to check it, and even if they did, it wouldn't mean anything to them. The government ends up taking all this stuff on trust."

"You shouldn't trust a used car dealer, and I guess you shouldn't trust a new car company." Kinsella laughed.

"Roula's right that we don't know what's inside the box. But we do know it can be hacked from a remote location," Verrazzano said. "There's a small possibility that the company made a mistake in the software. But at least we know where to start."

"We go to Darien," Kinsella said.

"*We* go to Darien." Jahn jabbed a finger at her own chest. "Most of the cars Darien sells in the US are manufactured domestically. That makes this an FBI case."

"Hold on there, Gina." Callan turned his big Texas A&M class ring around the fourth finger on his left hand. "Granted the FBI may be the lead on this case. But there's definitely going to be ICE jurisdiction here."

She rolled her head side to side. "How?"

Haddad spoke up. "If it's a hacker of some sort, it's likely to be a major organization. It isn't going to be some guy out in the woods of Idaho. The car companies have pretty good security on their systems. We might even be looking at cyber warfare by a foreign government. That means there was probably a cross-border element to this." Everything that went through US borders was a case for ICE. Even if it did cross that border in a fiber-optic cable or a wireless signal.

The FBI woman set her hands on her hips and spread her elbows wide. "I'm going to insist on this. FBI leads."

Verrazzano walked down the length of the table and stared into Jahn's eyes. "I don't care about jurisdiction. When this crash happened, I got out of my car and went to the nearest injured person I could find. I reached his wife on the phone before the cellular networks went down. When he died, I told her he was gone. Then I let her talk to me some more."

Jahn raised her hands in frustration. She broke the stare with Verrazzano and looked toward Callan for support. "We don't have time for—"

"His name was Anthony Gibson. His wife's name is Miranda Gibson. She's pregnant with Anthony's child. He'd just been fired this morning. He was on his way to sell the car because he couldn't afford the payments on it."

"Look, Special Agent—"

"Anthony and Miranda didn't have shit." Verrazzano moved closer to Jahn. He lowered his voice. "But now they've got me."

Jahn's face told Verrazzano that she had backed down— for now. The light infiltrated the cover of hair across her cheek. Beneath it, her skin was marked with a deep scar and smaller wounds around it. She saw Verrazzano note the disfigurement and brought her hand up to cover it.

Heavy, fast footfalls sounded across the floor outside the room. Special Agent Bill Todd came through the door. For a moment, the ICE agent was puzzled by the silence. Then he gestured toward the remote control on the table beside Haddad. "You guys need to turn on the TV."

Callan fumbled with the remote, waving it at the television on the wall. The screen flipped to life. CBS showed the chaos outside their studios on Sixth Avenue.

"No, go to CNN," Todd said. "Channel forty-two."

"Why in hell do we need to—?" Callan thumbed through to the cable news channel and halted, staring at the picture. On Pennsylvania Avenue in front of the White House, a double-decker tourist bus tangled with wrecked passenger cars. He peered closer. "Those are Dariens. Is this happening everywhere, for Christ's sake?" He flipped to CNBC. The screen showed the streets of a city engulfed in rioting. A storefront burned, silhouetting the figures running in front of it, carrying boxes looted from the shop. The sun was yet to rise. He scanned the information at the bottom of the screen. There was so much news that morning, it seemed the crawl line was as fast and out of control as a Darien. "It's LA," Bill Todd said. "After the cars crashed, people went out and—and so this." He gestured at the rioting.

"It *is* coast-to-coast." Haddad worked her keyboard. "Detroit, Chicago, Boston, Houston, St. Louis, Philadelphia, Phoenix, Columbus, Atlanta. I don't know if it's everywhere, but it's near enough."

"There's something else." Todd reached out and touched Verrazzano's shoulder. "It's Tom Frisch."

"Tom who?" Jahn frowned.

"A guy who owned a security company. Tried to release poison gas into the UN building last year," Callan said. "Dom arrested him. He's held under special incarceration regulations at our detention center in Brooklyn. He hasn't spilled much, but we think there's still a lot he can help us with."

"Like what?"

Callan glanced at Verrazzano. He knew what the SAC's lowered brows meant: like the name of the man who organized and financed Frisch's attempt on the president's life at the UN. But even Callan didn't know how much Verrazzano wanted to catch *that* guy. Frisch was the only person who understood that.

Jahn folded her arms across her chest. "What the hell does this have to do with—?"

"Darien?" Todd said. "Frisch says he knows what happened this morning. Knows *why* it happened, I mean."

"Let's go," Jahn said.

"He says he'll only talk to Dom."

"No use trying to drive to Brooklyn." Verrazzano looked out of the window, at the crashed cars and the traffic and the meandering pedestrians on the side street. He smiled at Jahn. "Let's you and me take a walk."

CHAPTER 3

The detention center mostly held regular criminals pulled in by city cops off the streets of Brooklyn. A couple of floors were set aside for ICE to pen suspected illegal immigrants before they were processed through to the agency's main holding center sixty miles north of the city. Then there was Frisch. His crime would have been so damaging to the state were it to have succeeded that he was in a corridor all to himself, with no record of his whereabouts even in the general ICE computer system. Frisch hadn't shaved since Verrazzano arrested him. His beard was down past his collarbone, brown with dry strands of gray curling against the grain. His hair had grown out too. He was as unkempt as he had been when he was a SEAL undercover in Iraq and Afghanistan. Verrazzano didn't allow him a razor or scissors, to be sure that Frisch would never be able to slip his guards and meld in with the other prisoners. So too he was denied a uniform. He wore denim pants, a gray T-shirt, and orange Crocs that Verrazzano bought for him at a charity shop. He sat calmly and folded his hands on the table.

At Verrazzano's side, Jahn smoldered. "Okay, Mister Frisch, we understand you have information related to the mass crash of Darien vehicles on the streets this morning." She started the audio recorder on her phone and set it on the table.

Frisch's beard stirred. There was a smile under there. Verrazzano saw it in his eyes. For a man facing execution, Frisch looked very Zen. He reached out with a sudden movement and took the phone. He shut off the recorder. When he thumbed the home button at the bottom of the phone, a picture of Jahn and a man with a shaved head and a goatee came up behind the app icons. They were smiling and hugging close. "That's sweet, ain't it?"

Verrazzano took the phone and handed it back to Jahn. "What do you want to tell us?"

Frisch stretched his arms above his head. "I asked *you* to come see me, Sergeant Major Verrazzano. Why'd you bring the soccer mom?"

Jahn ignored him and wiped the screen of her phone against her jacket. She glanced at Verrazzano. Her eyes said, *Sergeant Major?*

It happened every time Verrazzano came to interrogate Frisch. The prisoner tried to take him back to their days in Colonel Wyatt's rogue Special Forces unit. Back to the hideout in Beirut where Verrazzano found Frisch after it all went wrong. *Sergeant Major* was Captain Frisch's reminder that only the officer class was entitled to have all the information.

Frisch winked to let Verrazzano know he could follow his thoughts. There were teeth showing through the beard now, a broader smile or a snarl maybe.

"What do you have, Frisch?" Verrazzano said.

"A ticket out, Sergeant Major."

"We'll see about that."

"We'll damn well agree on it right now."

"If you have information about what happened today with the Darien cars, it will certainly count in your favor, if you share it with me now."

"It 'counts in my favor' if I pass the salt from the left and say 'please' and 'thank you.' What I've got for you merits a different grade of reward altogether. It gets me out of this hole. It gets me a passport and a ticket to Caracas, where you aren't ever going to come after me."

Verrazzano thought of the streets filled with smashed cars and dead bodies that he passed as he jogged across the Brooklyn Bridge to the detention center with Jahn moving easily at his side. "I'll fly you there myself if you can help me get this case cleared."

Jahn was silent. Frisch watched her, his eyes tracing along the scars, purple and pure white ridges that lined her face from the temple down along her jaw to her neck. He grinned and stroked out his beard. "Someone got you with a bottle. Those scars go back and forth. He dug it into your face and went like this." He jerked an imaginary bottle up and down.

"It's not your business," Jahn said.

"It was a he, right? Of course it was. Was it in the line of duty? Or did your old man get nasty with you?"

Verrazzano snapped his fingers. "Maintain your focus on your request to see me, Frisch."

"Maintain my focus?" Frisch rolled the words over as if they were the smoke from a fine cigar. He leaned forward. "Focus on this—it's Wyatt."

The name was like the sound of all those cars smashing together at once. Verrazzano's mouth went dry.

"Who's Wyatt?" Jahn said.

"Colonel Lawton Wyatt commanded me and Sergeant Major Verrazzano in the Special Forces," Frisch said. "And then some."

And then some. Verrazzano wondered if she'd figure out what that might mean. She couldn't possibly know, but she surely would sense the tension that crackled between the two men. It was alive with the electricity of secret shame. Verrazzano had believed he was in Special Ops, only to discover he had been working as a private mercenary, hired out to traffic in weapons, to assassinate politicians and businessmen. All to enrich Colonel Wyatt.

"You've got a few things you'd best explain to your FBI pal, Sergeant Major."

"You're the one with the explaining to do," Verrazzano said. "What's Wyatt's involvement?"

Frisch resettled himself on the plain chair across the table. "Before the UN job, Wyatt and I disagreed about methods."

"You mean, one of you didn't think it was a good idea to pump nerve gas into the UN and kill the president?"

"That was our target, and we never disagreed about that. I said we disagreed about methods. I wanted to use direct subterfuge to get my people inside the UN building."

"Hiding the nerve gas on some poor schlub and tricking him and his wife into helping you?"

"It was honest and clean, as far as plans go."

"But Wyatt wanted to do it a different way?"

"Wyatt let me do my thing because he always prefers to let the operative on the ground make the decisions. But yeah, he thought we should try something else."

Some people carried evil on them the way rats hosted plague fleas. Wyatt was the very contagion itself, the bacillus of the Black Death in camouflage fatigues. "Which was?"

"'Joy arises in a person free from remorse.' You've studied the Buddha, haven't you, Sergeant Major? Sure you have. Anyone who sees death the way we did ends up in a meditation class, because the other option is to find nirvana with the barrel of a pistol in your mouth. You ever think about being 'free from remorse?'"

"Tell me, what was Wyatt's preferred method? For the UN op."

"Except you aren't free from remorse, Sergeant Major. So you've got no joy. If only you knew how little you have to regret. Wyatt wanted to disable the UN security system for a few minutes so that my hit team could get inside."

"How did he intend to do that?"

"He was in contact with some hackers who could take it down."

Verrazzano felt the connections he was yet to make forming softly and reaching out toward each other. "These same hackers are the ones who infected the onboard computers of all the new Dariens. The ones who caused the big wreck this morning. Is that what you're saying?"

Frisch pointed two fingers and snapped his thumb, cheerfully planting an invisible bullet between Verrazzano's eyes.

"How do I find the hackers?"

"I refused to deal with them," Frisch said. "I liked my plan. I liked my guys. I didn't want some outside dipshit screwing me over."

"Who are they?"

Frisch muttered on. He was smart and tough, but he'd been too long in solitary, talking to himself, fretting over the flaws in the way he had worked the UN operations and damning himself for them. "Like I'm going to put myself in a position where I'd be hung out to dry by foreign agents."

Verrazzano stiffened. He sensed Jahn's heightened awareness. She had heard it too. "Agents of a foreign government?" he said.

"They weren't from a country where a lot goes on without the government knowing. So agents of a foreign government, yeah."

"Which government?" Jahn said.

"Wyatt figured he knew how to deal with them. He'd worked in their neighborhood since he was a lieutenant in Vietnam." Frisch directed his explanation toward Jahn. "The last couple of decades, he'd mostly operated around the Mideast, as Sergeant Major Verrazzano knows to his cost. But old man Wyatt got his start killing and torturing his way across Southeast Asia back in the early seventies. I guess he kept up his contacts there. Either that or he's a sentimental old bastard."

"An Asian country? Which one?"

"Well, it sure ain't Bhutan. Take a guess."

"Wyatt's working with the Chinese?" Verrazzano said.

Another playful bullet from Frisch's fingers.

"How do you connect that with what happened today?"

Frisch stroked his beard. "Wyatt doesn't share much, Sergeant Major. You know that. You have to add things up yourself when you work for him. That's what I'm doing now. The kind of chaos you got this morning could only be the work of a big, big organization. The Chinese Army has an entire tower block in Shanghai filled with hackers trying to bring down US government and commercial websites, breaking into proprietary industrial systems and copying them for their own companies to make the same stuff at cheaper prices."

Frisch was working his way around the perimeter of what he knew, probing, just as he'd have broken into a hostile camp. Verrazzano tried to hurry him. "What's the end game, Frisch? For Wyatt? For the Chinese? Did they intend to create this chaos? Or did one of their hackers mess up?"

"I don't know where it's all going, but Wyatt's in it for sure."

Jahn strode around the table behind Frisch. "This is crap. We came over here because this mope thinks he can squeeze us with suspicions and suppositions. Let's go." She moved toward the door.

"Sit down, baby." Frisch spoke to Jahn, but he kept his eyes on Verrazzano. "Sergeant Major Verrazzano is just about to show you why he's stayed alive all this time."

"Agent Jahn is right. Bringing us over here for what you've told us so far would be dumb, and you aren't dumb," Verrazzano said. "You've got something else."

"Maybe I'm bored? In need of charming company?" He smiled at Jahn as though he had just spotted her across a crowded bar.

"Tell me what it is you know," Verrazzano said. "Something concrete. Proof that Wyatt's connected to the Chinese. Then I'll get you out of here."

Jahn reached for Verrazzano's shoulder. "This guy tried to kill the president. He shot a man dead inside the UN building."

"The UN operation failed. The man who ran it is an unforgiving type. If we free him and Captain Frisch hits the streets, it'll take all his ingenuity to stay alive. We won't have any more trouble from him. But this issue, this case with the cars—we need to fix it right now."

Jahn waved her hand dismissively, but there was surrender in it too. Verrazzano snapped his fingers for Frisch to continue.

"Wyatt knows the way the world's going," Frisch said. "He always did. Always picked out the tilt of the deck, so as he could stay dry and tip the other guy into the water, so to speak."

"The deck's tilting to China?"

"It was tilted very clearly their way until about ten years ago. Then their economy hit the crapper, and that made them desperate."

"Which means they're looking for anything to give them an edge."

"And Wyatt specializes in giving someone an edge." Frisch leered. "During the UN operation, I received payments from the colonel to finance certain arrangements I had to make."

"Storing and transporting nerve gas? Paying off officials?"

"You'll get their names, don't worry. Yeah, so he paid me to do those things. He transferred the money to me in Bitcoins."

"How did you know it was from him?" Jahn said. "Bitcoin is anonymous."

"Because he called me up and said, 'Hey, I sent you the money on Bitcoin, asshole.'"

"Don't call me an asshole."

"I was quoting him. He called *me* 'asshole.'" Frisch waited for Jahn to release her tension. Then he added, "Asshole."

Jahn turned to Verrazzano and raised her palms. Verrazzano gave her the hint of a smile. It said, "You know what this is about. You know he's trying to wind you up until you snap." The flicker of impatience in her eyes let him know that she got it. A female agent had to deal with this more than a man. She was tough, but toughness didn't make it easier.

"Go on. Make the connection," Verrazzano said.

"I got a bunch of payments from him. Bitcoin transactions are recorded anonymously in the block chain, to protect against fraud. Still there's ways around that, sometimes. I wanted to know what Wyatt was doing and where he was, just in case he decided to leave me hanging. To get hold of anything that might help me anticipate his double cross. So I tried to track the Bitcoin payments back. I couldn't trace them. He was using a Bitcoin laundry service that mixes up the payments along the way so that you can't trace the breadcrumbs."

"You couldn't track them, but you did have the address they came from."

"You're getting the idea."

"Then a payment came that *hadn't* gone through the laundry site."

Frisch smiled at Jahn. "Didn't I tell you the Sergeant Major was a smart guy? You're right, Verrazzano. Finally I got a payment that came direct to my Bitcoin account. That meant I could cluster the address with the information from the previous payments. By tying the address to those other known addresses, I could follow it back to its source."

"Which was?"

"The whole time we were planning that operation, Wyatt told me he was in Cyprus. He said he wanted a base close to the

Middle East, so he could make his deals with the Islamic State head cases and all the other gangsters around that neighborhood."

"That's where he was when he sent you the laundered payments?"

"Cyprus is chock-full of rich Russians and dirty banks. Where you have rich Russians, you also have people prepared to offer them financial anonymity."

"And fraud," Jahn said.

"What else do you need financial anonymity for? Rich Russians, fraud, and extreme violence. Those things pretty much always come together."

Verrazzano made a come-on gesture with his fingers. "But Wyatt was somewhere else when he sent you the traceable payment?"

"He sure was. Our friend the colonel was in Beijing."

"So what? He was in China," Jahn said. "You said you had proof of his involvement in the Darien crash. He could've been in Beijing sightseeing for all we know."

"The last time Colonel Wyatt travelled anywhere for pleasure, rather than business, it was when his mom and dad took him to Disneyland in first grade, and he probably moonlighted as hired muscle even then."

Verrazzano restrained the urgency he felt. He didn't want Frisch to hear it, didn't want to give him leverage. "You've connected him to China. Now connect him to the car wrecks."

Frisch smiled broadly through the heavy beard. His posture was expansive. He was like an athlete telling the story of how he made a fantastic play. "Once I traced the address to Beijing, I was able to access the Bitcoin wallet that the good old colonel was using. I still couldn't track any of the payments he made when he used the Bitcoin laundry. But all the payments he made out of Beijing were visible. There were five of them."

"Who got the money?"

"Three of the payments went to Europe. I couldn't find the precise locations. Same with another one that was in North America somewhere."

"The last one?"

"The address on that last Bitcoin wallet was—well, that's the one that's going to get me out of this place. It was in Dearborn, Michigan."

"That's where the Darien Motor Company is headquartered," Jahn whispered.

Frisch mimicked the FBI agent's shock. "Oh, hey, you're right."

"What was the address?" Verrazzano said.

"I'll take you there."

"Give us the address and we'll check it out."

"I'll tell you when I'm outside these walls, man."

"You're going to have to make me certain that I can't do this without you, Frisch, before I get you out of here. You haven't done that yet. What's the address?"

"It checks out, Sergeant Major."

Verrazzano read the smugness behind the beard. He got it. Frisch had sent someone to scope out the address. "How did you do it?"

"Some of the guys who work at the detention center here are a bit more corruptible than you, buddy."

"You paid off an ICE agent in the detention center?"

"Where would I get money for a payoff? Nah, I put a scare into him. A guy should never have a wife and kids if he's going to hang around with people like me and you. Makes you vulnerable. So yeah, I had someone go along and meet the nice couple in Dearborn who got the money from Colonel Wyatt. The husband's an employee of Darien."

"A Chinese computer engineer?"

"You'll know that when you and I have made a deal and I'm out of here. If you leave me sitting in here with my mouth shut, you'll be gambling with time you don't have."

"Is it in the New York area?"

"Nuh-uh."

"If we're flying somewhere, I'm going to have to work some angles to get us on a government flight. Domestic air travel is already shut down because of the crash, in case it's a bigger terror threat."

Frisch hesitated. "Put us on a plane to Detroit."

"You've got a deal."

Frisch watched Verrazzano take out his cell phone. "I'm not doing this just to get out of here."

"You're doing it because you love America?" Jahn clenched her fists.

Verrazzano snapped a photo of Frisch with the phone. "He's doing it because he hates Wyatt."

Frisch laughed. "As Chairman Mao said, 'A journey of a thousand miles begins by stepping on one single asshole's face.' This is the start of my new journey."

"Wyatt's the guy you'll step on?" Jahn said.

"I'm going to need to step on more than one asshole to get where I'm going."

Verrazzano went to the door. "Mao also said, 'It's not hard to do some good. What is hard is to do good all your life and never do anything bad.'" Frisch stared at him. They had both committed some of the worst acts a man could perform. Verrazzano knew they had come out of it with different ideas about their guilt, about who they were and how they could make amends. It wasn't only joy that was missing for a remorseful man. To regret was to be mostly dead, and Frisch's Special Ops training meant that he placed a high value on remaining alive. *Maybe I'm taking Frisch to*

Michigan to give him another chance, Verrazzano wondered. *Everyone deserves one.*

He opened the door. "I'll be back in a few minutes, Frisch. You think real hard, meantime. Make sure you're ready to do some good. Because if you're not, the moment you leave this detention center, you're entering a world where one bad action is fatal."

"Bad or not, I can stay ahead of Wyatt," Frisch said.

"But you can't stay ahead of me." He shut the door behind him.

CHAPTER 4

Verrazzano sat in the corner of the observation room with his laptop across his thighs and his feet on the desk. He kept his back to the wall, his screen angled away from the security cameras. He logged into the ICE system with an anonymous username that he had persuaded Haddad to give him.

He heard the door of the interview room slam and footsteps in the hall. Jahn entered the observation room. "How're you intending to play this?"

The Panasonic's bright backlit screen flickered over Verrazzano's face. He called up Bill Todd's personnel file. "Like a guy with four arms plays foosball."

"Is your SAC going to authorize it? Getting Frisch out of here."

Verrazzano found the template for Todd's ICE identity card. He copied it to a password-protected file on his laptop, logged out of the ICE system, and opened up the identity card template again. "Sure he is."

Jahn's laugh was low and cynical. "I didn't think so. I've heard about you. About how you brought Frisch in. What you tried to pull at the UN. You damned near cost the president his life."

"I damned near cost *me* my life." Verrazzano took his smartphone from his pocket and found the photo he had snapped of

Frisch. He sent it to his e-mail account and put the phone away. "As for the president, any day he doesn't die is a day at least a dozen plots to kill him don't pan out, which means it's a good day. And he didn't die at the UN." He downloaded the photo from his e-mail onto the laptop. He pasted it into Todd's identity card.

Jahn had her hands on her hips. "I can't just show up in Detroit. I have to inform the FBI field office there, work with a local agent. Doesn't ICE have an office there?"

"Sure. They even have one inside the airport. Everywhere you have international flights landing, you have ICE agents on call."

"So what're you going to tell them?"

"I just sent them an e-mail telling them to have a car waiting for me in the pool."

"And they agreed?"

"They're cool with it, sure."

"They didn't ask why?"

"I guess law enforcement in the Motor City is busier than even we are today. They've got other things on their mind."

He locked his laptop and went to the door. "Frisch already got us one step along in figuring out this mess on the roads this morning. As soon as he ceases to be helpful, he's gone. Okay? I'm not going to take any unnecessary risks with him."

"He's a liability. What kind of manpower are we going to need to watch him?"

"I'll hold one of his hands. You hold the other."

His real intention dawned on her. "You're kidding me. You think they're going to let us take that guy out of here with just the two of us as escort?"

"I don't plan on asking them."

"Well, aren't you full of surprises."

"On casual Fridays, I go to the field office in spats and calf-skin gloves."

"You're going to break him out?"

Verrazzano moved close to Jahn. "We. *We* are going to break him out."

"Yeah? Why am I going to do it?"

"Because you're my partner now. And because you know I'm right."

Jahn's eyes flickered. "You're serious?"

"I told you already about the guy who died just after I found him in Queens this morning. If I don't take this seriously, Anthony Gibson's going to come back to life and run me over next time I cross the street."

"When Frisch ceases to be helpful, as you put it, what're we going to do with him then? We can't just walk into an ICE detention center and drop off a fugitive."

"No one's going to know he's gone."

"Get real. They'll figure it out?"

He was pleased to hear her use the word *they*. Despite her scowl, she was on board. Maybe she even trusted him. "I'm *sure* they won't figure it out."

The heavy door at the end of the corridor reverberated as the guard drew back the bolts. Bill Todd walked through and hurried toward Verrazzano.

"He's in there," Verrazzano said.

Todd opened the door to the interrogation room, stripping off his jacket. Jahn followed him inside. Todd took off his tie and shirt. At the interview table, Frisch grinned through his beard. He pulled off his T-shirt.

"You sure you're ready to go through with this, buddy?" Frisch said to Todd. "The food's for the birds and the waterboarding smarts."

Todd kicked off his shoes and handed his shirt to Frisch. "Don't get stains on it."

"Man, I'm not even going to have to break a sweat. I'll leave all the rough stuff to Sergeant Major Verrazzano and Sarah Palin's ugly big sister here."

Jahn shook her head. "You're insane, Verrazzano."

In the doorway, Verrazzano smiled. "So you're in?"

"Do I sound like I'm in?"

"You haven't *stopped* me, which suggests you're kind of into it. Soon enough you'll be an accessory to breaking Frisch out of here. I'd say you're in, whether you like it or not."

Verrazzano slapped his hand on her shoulder and went out into the corridor. He ducked into the observation room to pick up his laptop and took the elevator down to the basement.

Along the corridor from the elevator, he found the staff gym. It catered to the ICE agents and auxiliary staff who watched over the illegal immigrants awaiting a hearing or deportation. It was a large room behind glass doors with mirrored walls and bright white Nautilus machines. At midmorning, the room was empty, except for a trim, middle-aged trainer at the reception desk. He wore a blue polo shirt with the Stars and Stripes sewn onto the left breast like a corporate logo. He stared at a television that was suspended above the juice bar beside his desk, watching with a strained look.

"The president's just coming out." The trainer sounded grateful for Verrazzano's arrival. Something momentous was happening. He wanted to share it.

On the TV screen, the president came to the lectern in the White House press room. "Ladies and gentlemen, good morning. We do not yet know the extent of this morning's massive car crash, but we do know that it has affected every state of our Union. We expect that many thousands of people will have lost their lives and many more are injured. I have asked FBI and other law enforcement agencies to devote their full resources to an investigation." He paused and looked gravely around the room. He lifted his hand, making a fist. The camera lenses snapped, and flashes flickered across his face. "We can already conclude, however, that this is an act of terrorism. It will not go unpunished. Whoever is behind this attack on our way of life, on our economy, on the lives of our citizens, will pay the price. Let me reassure you—"

Verrazzano flipped his ICE badge out of his wallet and flashed it at the trainer. An ID card dangled from the man's neck. He was an external consultant, not an ICE agent. That would make him easier to impress.

"Got to get this done before the lunchtime rush, Kip." Verrazzano gestured toward the president on the screen. "Sorry to interrupt." He took his laptop from under his arm and laid it on the desk. "We've got a breach."

"A breach?" Kip had the guilty look in the presence of authority that only the truly innocent display. He glanced up at the television, seeming to expect the president to reprimand him or order his punishment for joining with the terrorists.

"A breach." Verrazzano tapped Kip's desktop computer. "From this module here."

"No way. I only use that for scanning IDs and issuing gym cards to the private contractors."

"Show me."

"Up here's the monitor, see. Down on this shelf under the desk, I've got the hard drive and a laminator for the membership cards."

"Internet connection?"

"Wireless. But I turned it off." He touched his fingers lightly to Old Glory on his shirt. An unconscious gesture of fear. "You know, for security."

Verrazzano opened his Toughbook. Twice the thickness of most laptops, designed to withstand three hundred pounds of pressure on its closed lid or a drop from six feet, its dimensions made it appear substantial and intimidating. "Would you give me a couple minutes to check it out, Kip?"

"Sure thing, sir."

Verrazzano leaned over the desk. Kip stood beside him, glaring at the monitor of the desktop computer. Verrazzano lifted his hand. "Kip, step away for a few minutes, please."

"Sure, sure." The trainer wandered over to the Nautilus to wipe it down with a paper towel.

Verrazzano unraveled a USB wire and connected it to his laptop. He bent below the desk and slipped the other end of the wire into the laminator. He called up Todd's ICE card on his screen, identified the laminator as his printer, and hit print. The card stuttered out of the laminator with Frisch's photo on it. Verrazzano ran his thumb over the bar code on the front of the card. It had come out clean, without any bumps that might make it unreadable in a scanner.

He put the card in his breast pocket, twirled the USB wire around two fingers, stashed it in his pocket, and shut down his laptop. He knelt under the desk and opened the laminator. He yanked the rollers out of their sockets. "Kip," he called. The trainer came back to the desk. Verrazzano waved the rollers. "The problem was in the laminator. I have to take these. Quite possibly the compromised material could be read from them."

"Wow. Really? How in hell did anyone get access?"

"You'd be surprised what those bastards can do."

"What bastards?"

Verrazzano looked hard at Kip.

"Sure, sure," Kip said.

Verrazzano left the gym. He cut into the men's room and cracked the laminator rollers in two against a washbasin. He wrapped them in a wad of wet paper towels, dropped them in a trash can built into the wall, and buried them under more wet

towels. Documents could, indeed, be read from discarded laminator rollers, but no one would find the doctored ID card on
these. He left the men's room and headed for the elevator.

Frisch was pacing the interrogation room when Verrazzano
entered. He wore Bill Todd's dark-blue suit and pale-blue tie.
Todd was at the table in Frisch's denims, his T-shirt, and orange
Crocs. Verrazzano gave Todd a questioning look.

Todd glanced at his watch. "Ninety seconds."

"Be ready." Verrazzano beckoned Frisch toward the corridor.
He held up his wrist watch and counted off the seconds to the
change of the duty guard at the turnstile. "Go."

Jahn hit the buzzer beside her. Within thirty seconds, a uniformed guard came to the door. He held a cup of coffee and a
white paper bag with his breakfast bagel inside.

Todd stepped forward. Jahn gestured toward him and spoke
to the guard. "Take him back."

The guard put his bagel and coffee on the interview table. "Let
me just set these down here. Sorry, I just got on shift." He jerked
his head for Todd to move. "Let's go." They went along the corridor and through the metal barrier to the cell block.

Verrazzano set off toward the security checkpoint. Jahn came
along behind him with Frisch.

The corridor came to an end at a ceiling-height turnstile and
a bulletproof screen for the guard booth. As they approached the
security check, Verrazzano slipped the doctored identity card into
Frisch's hand. Frisch read the card cupped in his palm. "Todd?
Wait, he was one of the guys who booked me after the UN job
went to hell. That guy back in there?"

"You like the irony?"

"You should've told me. I could've beaten him to death. I'm
an ICE agent now."

"If we did things that way, you'd be at the bottom of the East River right now and your nuts would be in the Hudson." Verrazzano dropped his ICE identity card into the tray under the security glass and gestured for Frisch and Jahn to do the same. The guard stared at Frisch's long beard. Verrazzano wished he had let the guy shave.

"He's going undercover," Verrazzano murmured.

The guard seemed glad to have an explanation for the shabby appearance of the man whose ID said he was an ICE agent. He slipped the cards back into the tray. "You have a nice day, gentlemen."

"I'm having a great day so far." Frisch turned to Verrazzano. "So you don't beat people to death?"

"As long as you're helping me track Wyatt and his Chinese connections, you'll be cool."

"And when that's done?"

"You'll be taken care of."

"I don't like the sound of that."

"Remember what Mao said about how hard it is to do good and keep doing good? You help me do something real good, and maybe you won't ever have to wear those stinking Crocs again."

"You're going to kill me as soon as I can't help you anymore." Frisch appeared unconcerned at the possibility.

"And *you're* going to run off as soon as you get a chance. But not with this." Verrazzano reached into Frisch's jacket and took out the fake ICE identity card.

"What if I get stopped?" Frisch said. "You should really let me hold onto that ID."

Verrazzano juggled the card and gave a thoughtful smile. "Forget it. Okay, now it's time for you and me to go do what we do best." He put the card into the side pocket of his jacket.

"We're going to kill some people?"

"Sure. But only the ones that try to kill us first." They followed Jahn to the elevator.

"Someone *is* going to try, though."

Verrazzano hit the up button. "Count on it."

CHAPTER 5

Haddad dropped a list of names printed in small type and three pages thick onto Kinsella's desk. Kinsella set aside her coffee and took her eyes off the live feed of Eyewitness News she had running on her desktop. The East River was filled with rescue boats searching for a woman whose kids had died in the crash as she drove them across the Queensboro Bridge that morning. Emergency services couldn't clear away the bodies on the roadway, but the mother had refused to leave her children. When the cops tried to carry her off, she escaped and jumped. Kinsella sighed and shook her head. She leaned close to Haddad's list. One of the names was circled in the same lurid purple as the print her lips made on the disposable coffee cup. "Tom Frisch?" she said.

"I have an alert programmed on the name of everyone arrested by Homeland Security in this field office," Haddad said.

"And Tom Frisch popped up?"

"Like a penny so bad it's nuclear."

Kinsella touched the list. She needed to figure out how to free Bill Todd from Frisch's cell at the detention center. It had been two hours since Verrazzano made the switch. She had to get Todd back on the job, but she didn't want Haddad to know what Verrazzano had done. "So what does this tell you?"

"That he's dead."

"How come? He's supposed to be in a cell at the detention center in Brooklyn."

"I guess he must've gotten out of the detention center."

"Well, how in hell would that have—?" Kinsella halted. Haddad grinned at her. "Okay, what've you figured out, smart ass?"

"Dom went over to see Frisch this morning because Frisch claimed to be able to help us with the Darien crash investigation. Bill got a call soon after on his mobile. He told me Dom wanted him to get over there too. All air travel is suspended because of the terror threat, but Dom's got himself onto a government flight to Detroit. Now Bill isn't answering his phone."

"You've lost me."

"If I was Dom Verrazzano and I needed Frisch's help, I'd do a deal. Frisch wants to get out of jail. So that's the deal. I get him out, and he helps me. Bill takes Frisch's place in jail, until someone figures out how to get him released."

Kinsella tapped her false nails on the desk. "So how does this list help us?"

"It's a record of the first confirmed and identified deaths from the Darien crash."

"Frisch was still in jail when the crash—"

"*Our* Tom Frisch isn't dead. He's out there with Dom Verrazzano. *This* Tom Frisch, the guy on the casualty list, was a sixty-two-year-old insurance clerk who got run over on First Avenue by an out-of-control Darien this morning. He was killed right outside NYU Medical Center, which is why he's already officially recorded as dead, unlike thousands of others who're still lying at the side of the road."

Kinsella frowned at the list of the dead. An idea came to her— just the outline for the moment, but enough to light up her features when she turned them again toward Haddad.

Haddad smiled. "Okay, go to it. I've got to track this Bitcoin trade from China."

A half hour later, Kinsella entered the detention center on Atlantic Avenue in Brooklyn. She headed for the office of Special Agent Vincent Lyons. He had the deep fake tan of a pro wrestler and a carefully tended strip of white-gray beard running from his lower lip to his chin. He greeted Kinsella with a resentful pout. At the field office, the Special Agent in Charge didn't think much of Lyons. So Callan had sent him to hold the keys to the cells in Brooklyn, while Kinsella and Verrazzano got the most challenging cases.

"Special Agent Kinsella, what can I do for you?" Lyons didn't stand.

Kinsella didn't sit. "You could try *not* to screw up again. Think you can manage that?" She slapped a single printed form down on the desk in front of Lyons.

He picked it up. The hair on his fingers was black, curled into little pubic triangles above each knuckle. "This is a death certificate. What the hell do you mean, 'not screw up'?"

"Read the name on the death certificate, Vinnie."

Lyons mouthed the words as he read them over. "Thomas Frisch? So what?"

"Thomas Frisch. The guy who tried to kill the president and the entire United Nations at the General Assembly. The guy who's supposed to be in a cell in your detention center—"

"Supposed to be?" That got Lyons on his feet.

"The guy who got hit by a runaway truck in Manhattan this morning."

"How the hell did—?"

"My partner, Bill Todd, came over here this morning to pick up Frisch. To bring him over to the field office for questioning."

Lyons sat back down in relief. "Todd lost him on the way?"

"Todd didn't leave your detention center, Vinnie. He came in. He didn't go out. But evidently Tom Frisch did."

"What're you telling me?"

"Apart from the fact that you screwed up? I'm telling you that Bill Todd is somewhere in your facility."

"Where?"

"Jesus Christ, Vinnie. Well, let's start with your office." She turned a circle, examining the small bare room. "I guess he's not in here. How about we try Tom Frisch's cell?"

"You think Frisch—Maybe he—?"

"That's exactly what I think, Vinnie. Frisch turned the tables on Bill Todd somehow. Then while your crack guards were dunking their donuts, Frisch just waltzed out of here."

Lyons rushed past her into the corridor. Kinsella followed him through a nauseating minty cloud of Le Mâle by Jean Paul Gaultier. "Let's hope Frisch didn't kill Todd," she barked. Lyons's meaty shoulders shuddered.

They went down a metal staircase into the cell row. Lyons yelled for the guard to open up Frisch's cell. He burst inside when Kinsella was still five yards behind him. "God damn it," he bellowed.

Kinsella got to the door of the cell. Bill Todd sat on the cot in denim pants, a gray T-shirt, and orange Crocs. Lyons reeled around the cell cursing. Kinsella measured the pitch of the agent's panic. He was beyond anger, spiraling into despair.

"Let's go, Bill. You're coming with me," she said. "Agent Lyons, you want to stay in the cell? We'll just lock the door, and you can call it time served before you come up for trial on this one."

Lyons didn't argue with her. His wet eyes were pleading in his orange face. He looked like a jack-o-lantern in a dumpster the day after Halloween.

"Aw, all right," she said. "Bill, we're going to help out Agent Lyons."

Todd stopped at the doorway. "We are?"

"Tom Frisch is dead." She turned her head to the side and winked.

Todd picked up on the signal. He turned to Lyons. "Oh, man. That sucks for you, Vinnie."

"You're the one who was supposed to take him out of here." Lyons had his hands on top of his head. "You're the reason he got this opportunity to escape."

Todd shrugged. "But here I am. He wasn't in *my* custody."

Kinsella stepped past Todd toward Lyons. "Seriously, Bill, we've got to clear this up for Vinnie. Frisch was a stinking mope. It's a shame we don't have him for further interrogation. But there's no reason for an ICE agent to go to jail over that guy's death."

Lyons quivered. "What're you saying?"

"Bill's going to suck this one up for you, Vinnie."

"Screw that." Todd slapped his hand against the door.

Kinsella raised a finger in warning. "Bill, you're going to report that Tom Frisch was in your custody this morning when he was killed by a runaway truck."

"Why would I write that?"

"Would you rather explain why you were sitting in this cell like a dipwad?"

Todd's features darkened. Kinsella grinned, enjoying that she could tease him as well as torment Lyons.

"Vinnie, here's what I need from you," she said. "I want access to the security log database for Special Agent Roula Haddad. She'll know how to fix all this without some hump in internal investigations finding electronic fingerprints that might lead them to suspect things aren't right."

"Roula Haddad, okay." Lyons nodded eagerly.

"Bill, you agree?"

Todd shoved his hands into the pockets of his cheap jeans. "Sure. I'll do it."

"Thanks, man," Lyons said.

"Don't thank *me*." Todd gestured toward Kinsella.

"Yeah, thanks, Noelle."

"You're welcome."

Kinsella and Todd were back at the field office in fifteen minutes. Haddad beckoned to them urgently as they passed her cubicle.

"Did you hear from Vinnie Lyons?" Kinsella said.

"It's taken care of. Our Tom Frisch is officially dead. Bill can write the report. I've doctored the detention center entrance logs to show Bill left with Frisch shortly before the Dariens crashed."

"Thanks, Roula."

"Don't thank me yet. Thank me right now. Because I've got a lead for you."

CHAPTER 6

Beyond the window of the Delta terminal at Detroit Metro Airport, battered Dariens littered the ramp, crushed against the yellow cabs or overturned by collisions with big tour buses. Verrazzano came up the escalator from the government flight that had brought him from JFK with Jahn and Frisch. He turned toward the rental car desks.

Frisch came into the concourse behind him. He whistled at the chaos. Jahn shoved him forward. He stumbled against Verrazzano and scowled at the FBI agent.

"Now you see why we're willing to work with a traitor like you." Jahn gave Frisch another poke in the shoulder to get him moving.

The concourse was jammed with travelers, none of whom had any prospect of traveling anywhere. Commercial flights were grounded across the country. The people inside the terminal were stuck, hoping that the skies would be opened soon enough to save them a night in a Detroit hotel or on a bench in the airport. Every child appeared to be bawling and crying. Every couple bickered. Everyone was scared, and a shrill tone of panic echoed around the high, sweeping ceiling. Verrazzano's group picked their way through the crowd. Frisch edged slowly to the side of the bustle. Verrazzano took hold of his arm.

Frisch shook him off. "I've been in solitary for six months. All these people are freaking me out, is all. So give me a break and let's go around the side here."

Jahn tapped Verrazzano's shoulder. She held up the screen of her phone to show an FBI alert. "Domestic flights got shut down right after the crash. International flights just got grounded too."

"Makes sense. If they can get inside the computer in a car," Frisch said, "they can hack a plane and bring it down, right?" He spoke loudly enough that the panicked vacationers and business travelers around him glared, angered and horrified.

"Let's move," Verrazzano said.

Frisch looked up at the welcoming smile of the Mexican farmer in the logo of the Juan Valdez Café. "I haven't had a decent cup of java in six months. Get me some joe right here. You'll see a totally different guy. I've got a smile like Julia Roberts."

"We've got to see *that*. I could use a cup anyway." Verrazzano went toward the café's counter. He called to Jahn, "Watch him."

"What do you *think* she's going to do?" Frisch said. "Give me a ticket to Hawaii and send me on my way? The flights are all grounded. Just get me the coffee."

"The flights are grounded?" A man in a gray suit turned toward Frisch. "I just spoke to a desk agent over there. She said we might be able to take off with a delay of only a few hours."

Frisch shook his head. "They just don't want you to panic, man. No one's going anywhere. What part of 'terror alert' do you not understand?"

Jahn yanked at Frisch's shoulder. "Shut up."

The man in the suit didn't question Frisch's authority or knowledge. Instead, he started to spread the news about the grounding of all the flights. The murmur that circulated through the crowd rose in volume and became shrill.

Verrazzano dropped a few balled-up dollars on the counter at Juan Valdez. They had been in his pocket for days. He generally only ate at the cafeteria in the ICE field office. He didn't spend money on entertainment. He'd been unknowingly saving up to buy a caffeine jolt for the worst man in the world.

"Three coffees." He glanced up at the TV screen behind the counter. The news anchor's baritone guided viewers through footage from the Golden Gate. The span of the famous old bridge was choked with car wrecks. The crawl line at the bottom of the screen told him riots had spread to inner cities all over the country. Police had shot looters dead in Atlanta, Houston, and Miami.

The skinny Indian behind the cash register rubbed his eyes. The whites were discolored to a caramel tone. Overindulgence in the store's product must have been wrecking his kidneys. He laid Verrazzano's change on the counter and set to work pouring the coffees with shaky hands. Verrazzano collected his coins and corrected himself. The *second-worst* man in the world. Wyatt could buy his own coffee.

"Oh my God." The woman at the head of the next line gawked at the television screen above the counter. Verrazzano followed her glance. The news channel had cut away from San Francisco. Instead, it showed the traffic circle outside Buckingham Palace, where black taxis and passenger cars were tangled together. A few seconds later, the image cut to a similar scene around the Arc de Triomphe. In the time it took for the woman's coffee to arrive, the news showed destruction in Berlin, Rome, Istanbul, and Tel Aviv. Verrazzano ran his hand over his face. It was everywhere. Each wrecked car on the screen was a signal to him from Colonel Wyatt, a reminder that no one in the world would be safe until Verrazzano and his old commander had their reckoning.

He stuck his change into the side pocket of his jacket. The pocket was empty. The fake ICE ID he had used to get Frisch out of the detention center in Brooklyn had been in there. Now it was gone. He glanced over at Frisch until he was sure he had caught his eye. Then he turned away.

The woman picked up her cup and moved off slowly, dazed, cradling the coffee in both hands. She reminded Verrazzano of his sister. She had the same bump halfway down her nose. He watched her walk toward the crowd. He wished he could be with Helen now, eating her brownies and playing with his niece. He would call them as soon as he was back from . . . from wherever he ended up in the next few days.

The woman with the coffee halted beside Jahn and Frisch. She squinted at the big departures board, looking for news of her flight.

"Three coffees, sir." The Indian set a tray down on the counter with Verrazzano's order.

Verrazzano had started to turn toward the counter to pick up his tray, when Frisch's arm snapped out toward the woman with the coffee. Frisch braced his palm under the cup and jerked his hand upward. The cup flew into the air and dropped toward the crowd. The woman yelped in surprise.

The coffee cup came down on another woman's head. The scalding liquid blew across her scalp and face. She shrieked. The crowd was suddenly in motion. They were in an airport, already tense because of the clogged terminal and cancelled flights and the fear of terrorism, and now someone was screaming in agony.

Frisch elbowed Jahn sharply on the nose. He punched her in the ear, kicked her kneecap, and was gone into the roiling crowd.

Verrazzano tried to follow, but Frisch ducked low. The crowd hid him. Jahn came to her feet. Her nose gushed blood. She wiped at it with the sleeve of her jacket. "I'm okay," she said.

The woman with the scalded scalp wasn't the only one scream-ing now. The wailing children turned up the volume. Men pushed each other in the melee, guarding their families and yelling in many languages.

"We've got to stop him before he gets out of here." Jahn moved ahead. The exits were crowded with people trying to escape from whatever the panic was about.

Verrazzano cut through the crush in the opposite direction to Jahn—toward the security check. She followed him, shouting, "What the hell are you doing? Why would he go that way?"

A TSA agent stepped toward him at the metal detector. "Sir, the checkpoint is closed. Stay where you are."

Verrazzano flipped his wallet to show his ICE identification. The TSA guy blinked at it, but Verrazzano was already gone. The metal detector beeped loudly. He waved his badge again and kept going.

He charged past a Cajun burger joint and a Mediterranean grill. Verrazzano cut along the shopping concourse. He didn't see Frisch.

Jahn came up behind him. "We should be at the exits to the terminal. So he can't break for the open."

"Whatever you expect Frisch to do, he'll do the opposite."

"Well, I expected him to escape, and now he's done just that. So much for your theory of doing the opposite."

He sprinted away, past the luggage shops and food concessions. "Where the hell are you going?" Jahn came after him. At the fur-thest end of the concourse, Verrazzano halted at an unmarked white doorway. He took out his ICE ID and slipped it through the card reader beside the keypad. The lock clicked and he went inside.

A guard in a tan uniform looked up from behind a Perspex win-dow. Verrazzano flashed his card. He jerked a finger at Jahn. "She's with the Bureau." The guard's expression became less friendly. He examined Jahn's identity card. The ICE logo on his sleeve rippled as he rolled his shoulders.

"Agent Todd?" Verrazzano asked the guard. "From the New York field office?"

"Down in the motor pool." The guard directed them to a staircase.

As they leapt down the stairs, Jahn called to Verrazzano. "Agent Todd? But he's still in—"

"Frisch is good at picking pockets."

The stairs took them to a recess under the terminal where a row of dark-blue cars were parked. Another uniformed guard sat in a booth at the end of the rank, studying the sports pages. Verrazzano ran toward him. "Guy just took out a vehicle. Tall, long beard."

"He sure did." The guard set aside his newspaper.

"I need a car too."

Verrazzano signed for a set of keys and jumped into a long dark sedan. He pulled away as Jahn dropped into the passenger seat and shut the door.

"How are we going to catch him?" she said. "We can't have him pulled over. He's supposed to be in a jail cell in New York. We're never going to explain that."

Verrazzano thumbed through the screen of his cell phone, even as he took the car toward the security gate out of the terminal area and into the public roadway.

"What've you got?" Jahn asked. "Is there a tracking device in the car he took out of the ICE pool?"

He smiled at her and held up his phone. A map of Detroit on the screen showed a pulsing dot progressing northeast along the interstate.

"Frisch?" she asked.

"Sure. Don't you recognize him?"

"What if he stops and switches cars?"

"We're not tracking the car. He tried to keep the fake ICE ID when we left the detention center. I figured he'd steal it again, so I doctored it while we were on the plane. There's a microtransmitter taped to the back of the card."

"So he didn't escape. You let him go just now. You couldn't have told me? So as maybe I wouldn't get smacked in the head and have my kneecap near stomped off?"

"Your knee's okay. You ran just fine through the terminal."

"What if he ditches the ICE ID?"

Verrazzano pulled onto I-94. "The entire country is in lockdown. If Frisch wants to get around, he's going to hang onto the ID. Keep an eye on that signal for me."

A half hour later, they pulled up outside a house of brown and tan brick with a tall chimney stack and gabled windows south of Cherry Hill Street. At the curb was a beaten-up German midsize car. Verrazzano glanced through the driver's side window. The housing of the steering column dangled where Frisch had ripped it away to hot-wire the engine when he switched vehicles.

The house looked like a chunk of Henry Ford's old Fairlane estate had broken loose and floated across the Rouge River to settle in this wealthy corner of Dearborn. It was the kind of place where a thirties mogul might have set up his secretary so he could come by anytime to give her a session of energetic dictation. It was also, Verrazzano figured, home to whoever owned the Bitcoin wallet to which Colonel Wyatt had sent money from Beijing. He hadn't trusted Frisch to take them here the way they agreed. But now he'd led them to the place.

"This isn't right."

Jahn got out of the ICE sedan. "Frisch brought us here."

"I mean, it doesn't *feel* right."

He went to the path across the front lawn. He scanned the dark, leaded windows of the house. The house broadcast the absolute quiet of a hidden presence. The very bricks seemed to hold their breath. "Go around the back, Gina."

Jahn cut across the lawn and went around the corner. Verrazzano gave her time to get to the back door. Then he nudged the oak front door. It swung open.

He went through the hallway and spun into the living room with his weapon before him. He let his back brace against the wall and listened to the silence for its deepest point. That was where he'd find Frisch. Or whoever else was hiding here. The room was empty.

He returned to the hallway. Jahn was in the kitchen with her Glock ready.

Verrazzano went to the dining room door. He sensed the cold quiet of death within. He wheeled inside. A man lay on his back on the dining table, arms and legs spread. He stared straight up at the ceiling. His broad, round face and the low bridge of his nose suggested he was East Asian. His hair was bristly, as though it had been shaved not long ago and was being allowed to grow back.

Except on top. From the center of his brow to the crown of his head, his skull was visible and scarred with gouts of drying blood. Verrazzano went closer. The man had been scalped.

Jahn spoke from the doorway. "I guess those Bitcoin payments really *weren't* innocent. Did Frisch do this?"

Verrazzano leaned over the corpse. *Nothing Wyatt does is ever innocent,* he thought, *and Wyatt's behind this, not Frisch.* He followed the dead man's eyes. They stared at the ceiling. A man being scalped would've turned his eyes up in his sockets as far as he could, drawn to the source of his pain. But there was a horror that would've been even worse for the man on the table, Verrazzano realized, and his eyes were on *that.*

He went quickly out of the room and mounted the stairs. He crossed the landing to the room directly above the dead man. The room he had been looking toward when he died. It was a bedroom, undisturbed by the killer. Nothing in the house had been tossed. Whoever killed the man on the table had gotten what he wanted.

In the doorway Verrazzano listened. The dog-whistle murmur of electrical gadgets flowed toward him from the nightstands, cell phones and tablets plugged into the outlets. On the dresser, a remote audio speaker burped its barely audible low-battery signal.

In the far corner, there was an antique cherrywood closet. The quiet around it was deafening. He crossed the room smoothly, threw back the door, and pulled the rack of light floral dresses aside on their hangers. A small woman shrieked and buried herself farther back into the closet. She held her thin arms up over her head and pulled her knees into her chest, kicking out feebly at Verrazzano.

The things we can't live with don't actually kill us. So, unfortunately, we all live with things we can't live with, and each time we confront them we sense the death that dwells within us. For Verrazzano, the sight of a woman cowering before him, expecting him to kill her, took him back to that stairwell in Beirut where he had realized that the only source of fear in his world was himself.

"It's okay." He moved his gun behind his leg to put it out of the woman's sight. He touched her quivering arm. "I'm a federal agent. Ma'am, you can come out of there now." He called for Jahn.

A heavy fist shot through the clothing on the hangers. It caught Verrazzano square on the nose. He rocked back onto the bed. Tom Frisch leapt out at him, reaching for the gun in his hand. Verrazzano stretched his arm away. Frisch head-butted him full in the face and buried his teeth in the skin around his eye. Verrazzano yelled. His mouth filled with Frisch's long beard. He coughed and bit at the chin beneath it. Frisch growled and bit down harder.

Then Frisch flew away from him, tumbling to the floor. Jahn jumped across Verrazzano's prone body with the impetus of the punch she'd delivered to Frisch's head. She wrestled Frisch's arms behind him, cuffed him, and dropped her weight on her knee between his shoulder blades. When she stood up, she kicked Frisch hard in the ribs. She went to tend to Verrazzano's eye, but his urgent gesture directed her toward the closet.

She holstered her Glock and knelt before the frightened woman, talking to her softly.

Like the dead man downstairs, the woman was Asian. She looked about thirty years old and appeared not to weigh a lot more than that in pounds. Her tension and fear burst out of her with the arrival of a sympathetic woman and the realization that she was safe. She wept hard.

Jahn drew her out of her hiding place. When the woman stood, her flower-print dress bulged over a pregnant belly. Jahn glanced at Verrazzano, both agents hoping they were putting it together the wrong way. But they both sensed that the father was the man dead on the table on the ground floor. Jahn tipped her head toward the still, furious figure of Frisch on the floor. "Was it him?" she whispered.

Verrazzano shook his head. "Don't think so."

"Honey, what's your name?" Jahn helped the woman sit on the edge of the bed. She knelt in front of her.

"Mo Hui," she sobbed.

"We need your help to find out what happened here, Mo."

"Hui. Her name is Hui." Frisch wriggled angrily as he spoke. "Mo's her family name. They put the names the other way around from us."

Jahn glowered at him.

"I heard him die." The pregnant woman collapsed forward, bawling.

"Do you know who did it?" Jahn pointed at Frisch. "Was it him?"

"Sorry to disappoint you, sister." Frisch grinned.

"No, he came later," the Chinese woman said.

"I bet the guy downstairs is her husband," Frisch said. "Terrible way for a marriage to end. But maybe not the worst, eh, Verrazzano? Could be better to be dead than to have your wife say you're dead *to her.*"

Verrazzano lifted Frisch by the elbows and hauled him onto the landing. He shoved him into the bathroom and shut the door. Back in the bedroom, he went onto one knee beside Mo Hui. For a moment, he made a deliberate effort to shift his focus away from the case. He brought his mind to bear on his compassion for her and her unborn child. It was a meditation technique he used every day, and like his work at ICE, it was intended to repair the world he had done so much to damage. He knew she would hear it in his voice when he spoke. "Hui, my name is Dominic."

She sniffed at her tears. She linked her fingers across her bulging stomach. Then she nodded.

"Who did you hear?" he asked.

"My husband. Dying." Her voice was precise and demure, every word in English requiring just a little thought, translated from her native language.

"What's your husband's name?"

"Gao Rong."

"What does Rong do? What's his job?"

"He works at Darien."

The room seemed to fill with the squealing brakes and the compressing metal that had sounded on every street and highway from Los Angeles to Boston that morning, from Melbourne to Milan. Verrazzano focused hard, so that the connection to the company whose cars had gone out of control wouldn't make his questions too eager and clumsy. "What does he do at Darien?"

"Rong is a computer programmer."

"How long have you been here in Dearborn?" Verrazzano said.

"One year and a half." She looked up with sudden urgency. "He changed the date."

"What date?"

"Of the bad thing. It was the big crash. I figured it out this morning when I saw the news. We argued about it, me and Rong. He always said he couldn't let the real attack happen. He had to give a big warning. So he changed the date. He said people would figure it out and stop the rest of it."

The rest of it. A picture of something bigger than the crash of all the Darien cars formed in Verrazzano's mind. What could be bigger than the disaster that had hit the roads that morning? "When Rong did this, did it put him in danger?"

"He thought maybe it did. The trouble started when I got pregnant. He began to talk about feeling guilty. He had to let people know somehow—let them know what would happen. His mood got worse and worse. Until a month ago."

"What happened a month ago?"

"He went on a trip. He came back after a week. He was crazy. He was crying all the time. His hair was shaved. He wore a baseball cap, and he wouldn't let me look at his head until the hair grew back. That was when he said he was going to give a warning, even if—even if it meant something bad would happen to him." She covered her mouth with her hand.

"Did he tell you where he went a month ago?"

She shook her head and sobbed into her palm. "He said the trip started fine, but then it all went wrong when the big man took off his wig."

"When the big man took off his wig? Were those his words?"

"He wouldn't tell me what he meant. But that was exactly what he said."

"What did he need to warn people about?"

"Rong said if he went to the cops he would die for sure. If he gave the warning his way, maybe he would be okay and we could live here and have our child in America." She pressed her hands over her belly. "But he didn't believe it. He knew what they would do to him."

"Did you see anything?" Verrazzano dipped his head toward the ground floor. "Did you see anyone this morning? Apart from that man I put in the bathroom?"

"A man with skin like a crocodile. But red. Bumpy and split, like the scales of a crocodile."

"What could that be?" Jahn whispered.

"Did this man have a skin disease?" Verrazzano asked.

"He was sick, I think, yes," Hui said. "Rong saw him in the yard. He told me to hide. Then he went out to the man. The man's face and hands were covered with big scabs. Like the scales of a crocodile. I could see them across the yard."

Verrazzano murmured, "It's Krokodil."

"What's that?" Jahn said.

"A cheap high. Started out in Russia. You cook codeine, paint thinner, and phosphorus. Then you inject it. Soon enough your skin starts to come away in scaly lumps. You die within a year. Which means you lose some of the inhibitions most of us have about risking your life or your future."

"Could this have been a Russian that did this? Jesus, we've got China involved. Now Russia. And mass car crashes in every major city."

Verrazzano touched her arm to quiet her. He focused on Hui. "This man who came to find Rong, did you hear him say anything?"

"He said nothing. Rong tried to speak to him. I heard Rong cry out, then he screamed, and then—" She whimpered and went silent.

"When did this happen, Hui?"

"After breakfast. Eight o'clock. Maybe after that, yes, a little bit later."

"Try to remember if Rong said anything more about his feelings of guilt."

"This morning he was calm at last. He said it happened and he had done all he could. Now it was up to other people to understand the signal he sent them."

Verrazzano lifted his head in understanding. It *was* the Darien crash. "He was part of something bad. When he tried to make it right this morning, his partners came and punished him."

"I think so."

"Did he ever tell you who those partners were?"

"He got angry when I questioned him. He got angry when *anyone* questioned him."

Verrazzano was about to try another angle, then he picked up on her emphasis. "Anyone? There was someone else. Someone who talked about the bad thing he had been part of?"

"His friend Su Li."

"Tell me about Su Li. Did he work at Darien too?"

"Li lives in New Jersey. We visited him last weekend. I was in the garden with Li's family. I went inside and found Rong arguing with Li."

"About what?"

"Li said that Rong shouldn't feel guilty. He said, 'We were all thinking about our careers when we agreed to be part of this. Now you want to ruin all our careers.'"

All. More than just Li and Rong, Verrazzano thought. How many people would be involved in a plot that caused every new Darien vehicle to speed to its doom? "When he talked about 'we,' did he mean other Chinese people? Did he say who he meant?"

"I think it must have been Chinese people. He spoke of training in China. He accused Rong of failing to speak up back then, when his feelings of guilt could have been easily corrected."

"How did Rong react?"

"He slapped himself on top of the head. It was a strange gesture, but I remember it clearly for that reason. He shouted that he had something on his head that could never be corrected and it was very dangerous."

"On his head?" Verrazzano wondered if she meant that Rong's guilt weighed on him.

"He grabbed Li and rubbed his hand hard on Li's head. Li pushed him away. Rong was yelling, 'It's on your head too.'" She seemed to return to the room in Jersey where her husband had grappled with his friend. The violence and shock of that moment overcame her. Her eyes flickered and she passed out. Jahn caught her by the shoulders.

"She's got to have some rest," she said.

Verrazzano reached for Hui's chin as she came around. He looked closely into her eyes. "Hui, we are going to find the man who did this to your husband."

"He will kill you. He cannot be killed. I sensed it."

"Su Li lives in New Jersey?" Verrazzano said. "Do you know the name of the town?"

She frowned, thinking hard. "Part of it was his name. Something ending in Li. Yes, Rockleigh, it was called Rockleigh."

"That's up the Hudson on the New York state line," Jahn said. "We'd better send someone over to find the guy. Hui, do you know his exact address?"

Verrazzano checked his watch. It was just before 2 PM. "He's going to be at work at this time. Where does he work, Hui? I'll get someone to go and make sure he's safe."

"Li is a computer programmer, same as Rong," Hui said. "He makes to write on computer—"

She was exhausted and in shock. Her English was falling apart. Verrazzano repeated his question. "Do you know the name of the company where Li works?"

"He works for Theander."

A Swedish car company. Jahn glanced grimly at Verrazzano, as she laid the woman on the bed. Verrazzano went onto the landing. Jahn joined him.

"You think we're going to get a bunch of Theanders speeding out of control next?" she said.

Verrazzano thumbed the screen of his phone for Haddad's number back at the New York field office. "Maybe."

"Everyone always says they're the safest kind of car to drive. But even in a Theander, you won't be safe at a hundred miles an hour and gaining when the light turns red ahead of you."

Haddad answered the call. Verrazzano lifted his hand to quiet Jahn. "Bill and Noelle need to head for Rockleigh, New Jersey. They're looking for a Chinese male named Su Li. He's an employee at Theander, the Swedish automaker. I want you to go with them. Su Li is a computer guy. It could be Bill and Noelle will need to gather cyber intel at Li's home or office. I want you to oversee that."

"Will do."

"Get to him quick, Roula. He's an associate of someone we believe was involved in the Darien crashes. He may have information about the incidents."

"We're on our way."

"Okay, thanks." He hung up.

He turned to speak to Jahn. Hui stood in the bedroom doorway, wavering on her thin legs. "You cannot kill him," she said. "I saw him. The crocodile man wishes to die. But his fate is to live and give to other people the death he wants for himself."

"We're not going to kill him." Verrazzano put his phone in his pocket. "We will catch him, Hui. Now go lie down. We'll call some people to come over here and help you." He went down the stairs.

Jahn came with him. "She seems damned sure the guy can't be killed."

"She's right. He takes a drug that destroys you from within. He's already dead." Verrazzano crossed the hallway and fixed his eyes on the corpse in the dining room. "That's why he's so dangerous."

CHAPTER 7

At the detention center in Brooklyn, Vinnie Lyons clutched the cell phone hesitantly until it slipped in the sweat of his palm. He punched up the Silent Circle app. He swiped a connection and lifted the phone to his ear. He wiped his brow and leaned his elbow on the desk. A low Southern voice answered the call.

"Tom Frisch is dead, sir." Lyons cleared his throat, a softly desperate sound like a corpse expelling the last air from its lungs in the moments after death.

"I very much doubt that, boy." The man on the line wasn't guessing. He meant only what he said, as always. Colonel Lawton Wyatt was all about distillation. Give an order in one word. Terrorize with one blow. Kill with a single bullet.

"I just had two ICE agents come into my office and tell me that he died this morning in the big crash. They showed me the death certificate, sir."

"Give me the names of the agents."

"Noelle Kinsella and Bill Todd. Special Agents from the New York field office."

"How is Frisch supposed to have died?"

"Todd came to the detention center this morning to take Frisch over to the field office for interrogation. Somehow Frisch overpowered Todd and escaped, using his ID. He was run down by a truck over on First Avenue." Lyons fumbled the cell phone into his other hand and wiped the sweat off his palm onto his pants. "I'm not implicated, so there's no chance they'll trace anything back to you, Colonel Wyatt, sir. Kinsella and me, we did a deal. Todd's going to write a report says he had custody of Frisch when he died. To cover for me."

"That's very accommodating of them."

He hesitated. "I guess."

Wyatt spoke like a sarcastic schoolteacher out of patience with the dumbest kid in the class. "Why do you think they're being so understanding toward you, Special Agent Lyons?"

"I guess—I thought they—" Wyatt didn't have to explain. Lyons saw it now. He'd been duped, and he couldn't call Kinsella on it without admitting to a cover-up that was almost as bad as letting Frisch escape.

"Tom Frisch won't be dead until I kill him," Wyatt said. "That's the way things are with operatives on my team. I choose them because they're indestructible. They don't sit behind a desk in an office in Brooklyn." He put an effortless mountain of scorn into his voice. "They certainly do not get run down on First Avenue, Special Agent Lyons."

"So you're going to try to find Frisch?"

Wyatt ignored the question. "Who else was at your facility today from the New York field office?"

Lyons scrolled through the names of Mexicans and Guatemalans visiting their cousins as they awaited extradition hearings. Then he saw it. "Special Agent Verrazzano was here in the morning."

"Todd and Kinsella are on Verrazzano's team."

"How do you know—?" Lyons caught himself. Wyatt knew everything.

"So my guess would be that Frisch is with Verrazzano right now," Wyatt said. "The Darien crash is the biggest case around. Verrazzano will be on it."

"But that doesn't have anything to do with Frisch. He's been in here for months. In the detention center. He couldn't be part of it."

Wyatt was quiet. Lyons waited, knowing the colonel would be figuring out angles far beyond his own understanding.

"Frisch did a deal with Verrazzano," Wyatt said. "Which means he must have information strong enough to persuade Verrazzano to bust him out. How would Frisch get a hold of such information, Special Agent Lyons?"

It was the Detroit address check; Lyons knew it. Frisch had forced him to go out to Dearborn and fake an immigration interview with a young married couple. He hadn't known why Frisch would care about two sweet kids from China. But Frisch threatened to kill Lyons's family if he didn't go. It was hard to see how the prisoner could get at them. Still there was enough menace in him that the ICE agent was too terrified to risk it. For an instant, he considered telling Wyatt about his Detroit excursion. Then he felt the danger in it, nameless and barely understood. "I can't imagine what it could be, sir."

"Was Verrazzano alone?" Wyatt spoke slowly.

Lyons went back to his computer screen. He checked the credentials column beside the names on the list near to Verrazzano. "There was an FBI agent who arrived at the same time. The desk guard logged them in together. Special Agent Gina Jahn, National Security Branch, New York field office."

"Wipe them."

"You don't mean—You mean, wipe them off the *computer*, right?"

"If I meant 'kill them,' I'd ask someone else, believe me, Special Agent Lyons. Same with Todd and Kinsella. Wipe them too."

"Okay, sure." Lyons talked himself through the computer commands. "Select. Delete. Yes, I want to delete. Okay. Confirm? Right, confirm. It's done." Lyons listened to the quiet on the line. Slowly he put it together. Wyatt came to him when Verrazzano brought Frisch to the detention center. He had kept the colonel apprised of anything learned about Frisch's interrogations and even tried to get information from the guy himself, though he hadn't mentioned the Dearborn trip. Now that Frisch was gone, Wyatt didn't need Lyons anymore. Maybe the Detroit lead wasn't a danger. Maybe it was information that would buy him a little credit, keep him safe. "I performed one service for Captain Frisch. I guess you should know about it."

"What kind of service?"

"I went out to Michigan. Interviewed a Chinese guy who works for Darien as a computer engineer. I don't know why Frisch wanted to know about them."

Wyatt was silent a moment. "Them?"

"Guy's wife was pregnant. Really sweet couple. I don't know what Frisch's interest was, but I figure you should know." He waited. "Colonel, you there?"

"Mmn-hmmn." Those two syllables were loaded with contempt. Lyons sensed that the Colonel understood why Frisch had been interested in the Chinese couple. Somehow the information Lyons had given him had spoiled the colonel's plans or highlighted a mistake. The way Wyatt had said "them" gave Lyons the hint. The colonel hadn't known the programmer was married. He wondered how that might have undermined his plans. Then the colonel said, "What kind of car do you drive, Special Agent Lyons?"

"A Portsmouth Freedom."

"What's that, an SUV?"

"A small one." Lyons found himself speaking with the apologetic tone he used when his fourteen-year-old daughter criticized his choice of vehicle. She had read a book on global warming and started bitching at him to take the train to work instead of driving a gas guzzler.

"When did you get it?"

"A month ago."

"With the payment from me? For your services in the case of our old pal Frisch?"

The air whistled in Lyons nostrils. "You don't have to—I'm not going to say anything about—"

"It's a good thing you didn't buy a Darien, right, Lyons?"

He didn't join in Wyatt's soft laughter. "Yeah, I guess."

"You made a fine choice of vehicle. Stay safe. Give my regards to your family." Wyatt hung up.

Lyons put the phone down. On the desk, his car keys lay in front of a photo of his wife and kids. He had never talked to Wyatt about his family, never even mentioned that he had one. Wyatt never wasted words either. With a feeling in his stomach like the end of all life, Lyons grabbed the keys and rushed out the door.

It was a fifty-five-minute drive from the detention center on Atlantic Avenue to the Lyons home in Melville, but it took him two hours through the wrecks and the traffic jams, even with the magnetic siren stuck to the roof. He took his red SUV onto the Jackie Robinson Parkway and onto the Long Island Expressway just as it exited from Queens. He tried to dial his wife on his cell phone, but when he swiped at the screen, it refused to respond to his passcode. Wyatt had hacked the phone and locked it, he was sure. He hammered his hand on the steering wheel and bore down hard on the gas pedal. The radio was a litany of bereaved relatives and stern politicians vowing revenge on whoever was behind the Darien crash and even on some others who surely weren't. With the siren and his fist on the horn, Lyons made a new lane for himself, forcing the slow traffic to edge aside. He snapped away more than a couple of wing mirrors before the expressway let him off a half mile from his house.

He roared down the quiet suburban streets toward his split-level ranch. His chest seemed to close tight around his organs. He pulled up in front of the double garage and ran up the steps. Inside the front door, he called his wife's name. The house was silent. He went to the kitchen and checked the whiteboard scheduler on the fridge. He matched it with the time on his watch. Alison's neat block letters noted a gathering with a few other mothers at Half Hollow Park. They'd watch the kids play, and they'd talk about their husbands and how the kids were doing at school. *Wyatt would strike there*, Lyons thought. He'd kill them and he'd escape through the trees. "No, no, no, no, no," he bawled, as he ran out to his car.

He sped down the street and onto Old South Path. He was doing sixty-five down the two-lane, the sun flashing through the trees at the roadside, when the gas pedal dropped limply to the floor of the SUV. Lyons bellowed and stamped on the brake, but the car picked up speed. He went along the road, weaving around the light traffic under the afternoon sunshine. A station wagon moved into his path, a woman driving and a row of blonde toddlers in the backseat. Lyons spun the wheel to get by them. He wrenched it back to beat the grasp of the trees that seemed to reach out for him.

The SUV was doing one hundred and thirty when he passed the gate attendant's white awning at the entrance to Half Hollow Park. Just before he skidded off the twisting roadway into the trunk of a massive oak tree, Lyons thought of his daughter and her obsession with climate change. Then he whispered, "I should've taken the train."

CHAPTER 8

At Theander's US headquarters in New Jersey, Su Li's boss was a sandy-haired, bloodless geek, who would have been the nastiest math teacher at the Rockleigh high school, if the Internet had never happened. Instead he ran a floor full of diligent Asian computer programmers and wore a black shirt and a black tie and black Prada glasses with a thin pink stripe around the lens. When Kinsella and Todd showed up, he reported with disgust that Su was absent and hadn't called in sick, as if the guy might have been taking time away from the office to eat babies.

The agents raced for Su's home, a quarter mile away, with Haddad in the back seat to handle any computer issues they came up against. At a stop sign, a big Ford hit the back of their car with moderate force. Kinsella and Todd leapt out of their car, holding their weapons at the driver. He was a burly, middle-aged guy in a white T-shirt and red baseball cap. He raised his hands and stared at the agents with terror. They got him out of the car. Kinsella braced him against the rear door.

"The car went out of control, officers," he moaned. "Way all them Dariens did."

Todd came around from the passenger side. He held up a cell phone on the dial screen. It showed an area code and three digits entered. "He was halfway through dialing. Had his eyes on the phone instead of the road."

"I swear it was the car."

"Don't push your luck." Kinsella went back to the ICE car. "Come on, Bill. We don't have time for this."

Todd made a quick assessment of the damage to their vehicle. He tossed the cell phone to the man. It slipped through his sweaty palms, and the screen shattered. "Drive safely, buddy."

Two blocks farther on, they reached Su's house. It was a big colonial just across the state line into New York. In the drive sat an old Theander station wagon.

"He's got a nice house and a good job, but he's not driving a new car?" Kinsella said. "Guess he knows something we don't know about new vehicles going to crash?"

"Everybody knows something we don't know." Todd passed the station wagon and headed for the front door.

Kinsella drew her Glock from her holster. Haddad gave her a frown. Kinsella pouted. "You think I'm going to scare him? If this turns out to be a guy who's prepared to help us with our inquiries, I'll put the gun away and make nice." She flipped her long, dry auburn hair across her shoulders. She went up the steps. Todd also had his pistol out in front of him with stiff arms.

Through the door, loud music vibrated with a two-step beat. "Su Li's a country fan?" Kinsella thumped the door.

"He's not going to hear you knocking. Music's too loud," Haddad said.

Kinsella went around the side of the house. She put her face close to the screens on the bay window. Inside, the room was sparsely furnished: a couple of sofas and a wall-mounted flat-screen. At first she thought the maple floor was spread with rugs. Then she saw it was two people flat on their backs. She sprinted to the front of the house.

"Kick it in," she shouted.

Before Todd could move, Haddad raised her leg and brought the heel of her boot down just below the door handle. It shattered and sprung open. The burglar alarm wailed.

Kinsella went in first, her pistol held straight out before her. Her heart was loud enough to overwhelm the noise of the alarm and the country song blaring through the speakers of a Danish hi-fi system in the far corner of the living room.

She swung around, gesturing for Todd and Haddad to check the other rooms. She went to the living room and knelt beside the two people on the floor. A Chinese man and woman, side by side. Both dead, throats slashed, each with a single sharp strike. The man had been scalped.

Kinsella turned away. She had seen corpses in much worse condition, but the scalping was a psychotic gesture that disturbed her.

Haddad came into the living room. They heard Todd upstairs. His footsteps relaxed, the lightness and poise of a search replaced by slow, heavy treads. No one up there. Haddad holstered her weapon.

Kinsella tucked her long hair behind her ear. She opened the picture of Su Li's New York State driver's license on her cell phone and compared it with the stricken face of the corpse. "It's him."

"I guess that's Missus Su?"

Kinsella wiped the back of her wrist across her mouth. "I guess." She forced herself to take her focus away from the gore. She needed to look for clues in the details of the room. She shut her eyes. When she opened them, she frowned at the hi-fi on the coffee table. It repeated the same couple of seconds of music over and again. Johnny Cash at high volume. Haddad went to turn it off.

"Don't touch it." Kinsella shouted.

"Come on, I can barely hear you—"

"Wait." Kinsella went toward the hi-fi. It played a single line: *"I know you hate me, and you got the right to kill me now, and I wouldn't blame you if you do—"*

"It's a loop," she said.

Todd came out of the hallway and into the room with the two scalped bodies. "Why would they be listening to a loop?"

"They wouldn't be *listening* to a loop. The killer put it on."

"To cover the sound of their screams? Why not just put on the whole song? Why loop that line?"

Kinsella found a pink iPod shuffle at the side of the hi-fi connected by a white wire to the USB port. "I don't think they screamed. They went quickly and cleanly. The one that died second had a moment to cry out, but I'd bet they were too scared to open their mouths."

"So what's the loop for?"

"Maybe it's a message. Something in the song. These words are being highlighted for some reason."

Haddad shrugged and cocked her head, searching for something significant in the music. "Do you know the song? It's country, right?"

"You don't know who Johnny Cash was?" Todd said.

"Give me a break, Bill. I was born in Lebanon, and I grew up in Jersey."

"Didn't you ever get farther south than Philadelphia?"

Haddad's cheeks colored. She was as American as you could be, given that her first years had been spent in a Middle Eastern war zone. But these gaps in her cultural knowledge still embarrassed her.

"It's okay, hon," Kinsella said. "It's music for rednecks like Bill. This one's about a boy named Sue. Maybe it's someone's idea of a joke on Mister Su here."

"We've got to make a connection," Todd said. "To get us to the next step in the chain."

"To another Chinese programmer?"

"At another auto company. It started with Darien. You've got to think that this killing means the crash has the potential to extend to Theander vehicles too."

"We have to figure out which auto company is next. Roula, go check out Mister Su's computer. There's a desktop in the room across the hall. Bill, call this in to the local police department and FBI. I'm going to call Dom and let him know what we've got."

Kinsella stepped out of the front door as her phone connected to Verrazzano. "Dom, it's Noelle. Su Li and his wife are dead. Roula's checking out his computer right now to see if it gives us a lead to any more Chinese programmers." She put a finger in her other ear. "What's that? I can't hear you." She pulled the door shut behind her. "What'd you say, Dom?"

Verrazzano's voice came down the line. "What's that music?"

"It's Johnny Cash. Real loud, a loop of a line from 'A Boy Named Sue.' It was playing when we got to Su Li's place. Like the killer put it on to send a message or something."

Verrazzano's voice was quieter when he spoke again. Kinsella wasn't sure if he said, "I heard you," or "I heard it." *What was* it, she wondered? Verrazzano said, "Let me hear the loop."

She opened the door and held her cell phone up while the loop played through. "Did you get it?"

"I got it."

"You know what it's about? I mean, why is it playing?"

"It's a message. You're right about that."

"A message for who, though?"

"For me."

Kinsella listened to the words of the loop again. "Unless your daddy came in here and killed Mister and Missus Su, I don't get it, Dom."

"Not my daddy. Someone like my daddy. I'll explain later."

Haddad opened the front door. "Noelle, come check this out." She went back down the hallway and into the computer room.

"Roula's got something, Dom. Stay with me." Kinsella entered the house and followed Haddad. "What've you got?"

Haddad sat at the laptop on the desk. Todd paced behind her in a room that was otherwise entirely empty. "Mister Su was using

Vuvuzela. It's an anonymous messaging system developed at Harvard last year."

"Vuvu-what?" Kinsella asked.

"At the soccer World Cup a few years ago in Africa, the crowds blew on these long plastic horns. They made a god-awful noise that filled the stadiums and everyone hated them. This message system took the same name because it's designed to create a big, confusing mass of noise. It makes any single message almost indistinguishable."

"Su sent a message on this system?"

"Here it is." Haddad called up a screen with a few brief Chinese sentences.

Kinsella leaned over and read, "Gao Rong is dead. Soon I will be dead. You must contact Turbo and the others."

Haddad blinked in surprise. "You speak Chinese?"

"My Korean's better." Kinsella smiled. She liked to shock people with her knowledge of Asian languages, the result of assignments two decades ago as an immigration investigator on the Chinatown squad. She pointed at the address line. "It's to a guy named Du An." Then she spoke into the phone. "You heard that, Dom? Roula, can we figure out where this guy is?"

"That's where the noise comes in. Vuvuzela sends the message through three different routers. At each router, it sends out the message to a bunch of fake addresses, along with the actual address. So you can't pick out the real address."

"Where are the addresses?"

Haddad called up a list of server locations that scrolled over her screen. "This list tells us where the computers are, basically, for all the messages—the fake ones and the real one."

"How many are there?"

"One hundred sixty-five."

"But only one of them is the real address of the guy Su wanted to contact?"

"Yeah, the address of this Du An."

"Christ, how in the hell are we—?"

Verrazzano broke into Kinsella's thoughts. "Put the list in a file and send it to my phone."

Kinsella put her mobile on speakerphone. "Send the addresses to Dom."

Haddad tapped at her keyboard. "They're on their way. But the addresses are all over the place. Look, there's about"—she counted quietly as she glanced down the screen—"about one hundred in the US. They're in big cities, Chicago, Seattle, and small towns I never heard of too. Same thing with the foreign addresses. That's how the program works. Confusing information from a wide range of locations, so you can't detect a pattern."

"We're looking for a place with a big auto industry." Verrazzano's voice came through the speakerphone. "I'm reading over the list now."

Haddad and Kinsella scanned the addresses too. Todd squinted over their shoulders.

"Motor companies. I don't see an address in Detroit," Haddad said.

"There," Verrazzano called. "Near the end of the list. Rüsselsheim."

"Where?" Haddad said. "Where's that?"

Verrazzano's voice came down the line, terse and already seeming to be on the move to his next destination. "I spent some time near Frankfurt on an operation a while back. Rüsselsheim is just outside that city."

"So what is it? A little German village or something?"

"Not a village. A town of about fifty, sixty thousand. There's only one industry in Rüsselsheim."

"A car factory, I'll bet," Kinsella said.

"It's where Mister Jansen and Mister Trapp made their first car. Now the company has a big plant there. We need to find out if there's a Du An working there."

Haddad went to work on her keyboard. "I'm checking with one of my guys at German Immigration."

"Let me know as soon as you get anything," Verrazzano said. "When you've done that, I want you to try to track a hitman who's a known user of Krokodil, the Russian street drug."

"The killer in Detroit was a Russian?" Kinsella asked.

"A user of a Russian drug. Maybe a guy who'd been in Russia recently enough to have become addicted to Krokodil and not died yet. It puts you in the ground pretty quick. Within a year or so. Check it out for me, Roula." He hung up.

As Haddad wrote her message to Germany, Kinsella went into the living room. She shut off the music. The suburban quiet enveloped her. She stared down at Su Li and his wife. *A message for me*, Verrazzano had said of the music. From someone who was "like" his daddy. She shuddered. She couldn't tell if it was the silence of the midday neighborhood that chilled her or the fact that somehow this was all personal.

CHAPTER 9

Jahn drove into the rental car lot in the northeast corner of Detroit Metro Airport to pick up the government jet for their flight out of town. Verrazzano saw her looking across at him in the passenger seat, trying to catch his eye. Frisch napped in the back.

"My husband was military too," Jahn said.

"Uh-huh." He didn't want to talk just then. He wanted to figure out the connections to Wyatt and trace a map in his head of what he knew now and what he would need to know to make everyone safe. Then he thought of the scars on Jahn's cheek. The wounds that became scars had no doubt left her with the memory of that powerless moment. The hardest thing to face in life, whether you were a small child beaten by an angry parent or a Special Forces operative tied to a chair in a basement, was the realization that you were defenseless. He wanted to ask how it had happened. Instead, he said, "What branch did he serve in?"

"He started out in infantry. But he went into Special Forces. Same as you and Captain America back there." She jerked her thumb at the backseat. Frisch snored and grumbled. "I understand the price you pay."

His openness ebbed away. Everybody always told him they understood. The only one who didn't had been his wife when he tried to explain himself. He remembered Melanie's slow headshake of incomprehension, her features twisted with disgust. "What price is that?"

"The price you pay for other people's mistakes."

"Who said anything about mistakes?"

She took the car through the barrier into the drop-off zone. "Well, you know, everyone makes mistakes."

"There's a difference between the consequences of an accounting error and a failure in the Special Forces."

She licked her lips nervously. She must have heard the resentment in his voice. "Based on what Frisch said, you were involved in something more than an accounting error."

"Based on what Frisch said?"

"I mean, you haven't told me what you—"

"You want to know about me?"

"I just thought I—"

"You want to know about my mistakes?"

"No. Yes. Why are you—?"

"I killed a woman in front of her kid because my commanding officer told me to do it. No, that's not enough. The truth—I did it because I believed she had information that could be a threat to me, and so I silenced her."

The car rocked slowly on its soft suspension as Jahn rolled over a speed bump and halted behind a blue Honda. She spoke quietly. "You couldn't live that down." It wasn't a question.

He shook his head. He couldn't tell her the true scope of what he had done. Before he murdered Maryam Ghattas, there was the death of the prime minister. An assassination that killed off a peace deal the man had been about to strike with Israel. That had been Verrazzano's real mistake. Maryam Ghattas was the cleanup afterward.

"I'm sorry." Jahn shook her head. "What the hell do I know? I mean I—"

"The thing is," he said, "the worst thing I ever did was also the best-conceived, most perfectly executed operation I carried out. I was absolutely the best operative there was. And I used my skills to kill someone who could have made a difference in people's lives. A positive difference to millions of people."

She shut off the engine. "The place was screwed up. Whatever you did, there'd still be trouble there."

He ran their conversation back through his head. He hadn't mentioned Lebanon or the Middle East. He turned to her slowly. "What place?"

"The place you did the operation."

"*I* didn't tell you where it was."

"Do you have to? I figure, where do you go to do assassinations? Not Topeka, Kansas, right? It was in some screwed-up place, surely." She watched him with a strange desperation on her face.

He considered that look for a moment. Then he saw that it was her knowledge of her husband's work that informed it. "You said your husband *was* military."

"My husband *was*, period. He was on an operation and he went missing. Two years ago. He's presumed dead."

"Do *you* think he's dead?"

"I hope he's dead. The alternative is that for two years he's been—" Her voice quavered and cut off. She cleared her throat and took the keys from the ignition. "I'm going to drop these off."

She got out of the car and crossed the parking lot to the rental office. He turned away. *I hope he's dead.* He had heard spouses and parents say that about missing soldiers. It was never true. They didn't mean it. Torture and suffering could come to an end, and there could be a reunion and maybe even psychological healing. People held onto that chance until they were as gone as the loved one they mourned.

Frisch coughed and snorted and came awake. "What's next, hombre?"

"You go back to jail, that's what's next."

"That's a damned shame. Where are you going?"

"Germany."

"They make a lot of cars over there. You found another car company?"

Verrazzano nodded.

"Down south?" Frisch said. "Where they make the Wolfwagen?"

Verrazzano shook his head. "You shouldn't waste brain cells on this. You should be working on your defense for the UN attack."

"What about our deal? Where's the ticket to Caracas you promised me?"

"Sue me."

Another car company in Germany, Verrazzano thought. Another computer programmer. He had to find out whether there was another day of destruction coming. He had to stop it before it happened. Maybe once he'd done that, he could find out who was truly behind the whole thing. He thought of the music at the scene of the Su couple's murder. Even if Johnny Cash hadn't been his old commander's favorite singer, Verrazzano would have known it was meant for him. He had gravel in his guts and spit in his eye.

"Wyatt's waiting for me," he said.

"I figured he would be." Frisch rolled his shoulders. "Don't worry, Sergeant Major. I'm going to be there with you, and I'm ready for the son of a bitch."

"Forget it. When I bring him in, I'll see to it that you get adjoining cells."

"Sergeant Major, I'm not going back to a jail cell, and you and I both know there's no prison could hold Colonel Wyatt."

A text came over Verrazzano's phone from Haddad. He read it. German Immigration confirmed a Chinese national named Du An worked at Jansen Trapp in Rüsselsheim. He wrote back, telling her to set up a government plane to fly him and Jahn from New York to Frankfurt.

"What're you going to do when he finds us?" Frisch said.

Us. Verrazzano ignored that. Instead, he pictured the moment. Imagined Wyatt's face, a few years older than when he saw him last, new tensions marking his face. "I'm going to find *him* first."

Frisch lifted a finger and wagged it at Verrazzano. "You're going to kill him. You're after revenge, Sergeant Major. That's my boy."

Verrazzano's cell phone hummed in his pocket. He took it out and swiped the screen. A text message, from a scrambled address. It read: "Dinner at Odin's table for you soon, son." The muscles in his arm trembled as he held the phone. It was from Wyatt. That was the line the colonel used before every mission. It meant that death in action was not to be feared, because it would be followed by a feast at the side of the Viking gods in the resting place of the heroes, Valhalla. Right now, the message signaled that Wyatt knew Verrazzano was on the case.

Some swift motion in the corner of his eye caught Verrazzano's attention. He looked across the parking lot to the rental office forty yards away. Jahn was against the wall, face first. A man twisted her arm high in a half nelson. With his other hand, he held a pistol to her head.

Verrazzano leapt from the car and ran. Jahn's eyes were wide, staring over her shoulder toward the man who threatened her.

"Step away from her," Verrazzano called out. He drew his H&K and leveled it as he sprinted. "Put the gun down."

The man swiveled toward the ICE agent. His skin was red and scaly. The Krokodil man who had killed the Chinese engineer. The gunman spoke emphatically into Jahn's ear, as he watched Verrazzano approach. Verrazzano read his lips: "You understand? You understand me?"

Jahn twitched her head to signal that she understood.

The Krokodil man stepped back and hammered Jahn's neck with the butt of his pistol. He fired two rounds at Verrazzano and dodged behind the rental office.

Verrazzano reached Jahn. She was out cold, spread across the low, dry bushes outside the office. He ran around the building. As he came into the alley between the office and the chain link fence by the runway, a Toyota sedan sped around the corner with the Krokodil at the wheel. Verrazzano jumped out of the way and dropped into a crouch. He squeezed off four shots, but the Toyota squealed to the right and was gone toward the gate.

He came quickly back to Jahn. She blinked hard as he lifted her. "I'll be back for you," Verrazzano said. Jahn groaned.

Verrazzano was running for his car, when it started away through the parking lot. Frisch weaved it between the parked vehicles and headed for the gate. Verrazzano waved for the security guard to drop the barrier, but Frisch was out of the compound before the guard saw him. He went fast down the access road toward the highway, the same direction as the Krokodil. Verrazzano watched the two cars disappear in the heat shimmer as the security guard came out of the gate hut.

Verrazzano rushed into the rental office. The staff of four were behind their counters in their green blazers. They lifted their hands in surrender. "Keys, give me a set of keys right now," Verrazzano shouted.

"He took them." A bronzed woman with hair dyed to a deep black pointed through the window toward the gate. "The guy with the ugly skin."

"All of them?" Verrazzano leaned over the counter. There had to be a set of keys among the rental contracts and credit card machines.

"All that was out here," the woman said. "The rest are in an electric lock box in the back office, and he pulled the cord out of the wall. It won't open until that's fixed."

Verrazzano ran into the parking lot. He scanned the roadway in case a client was returning a car that he might commandeer. The blacktop was empty. He was stuck.

The gate guard jogged heavily toward him, calling into his walkie-talkie. He glanced at Verrazzano's ICE ID. Jahn wavered to her feet and showed her FBI card.

"Who are those guys?" The guard gestured over his shoulder in the direction the Krokodil and Frisch had fled.

"Fugitives. You need to track these cars." Verrazzano reeled off the plate number he had committed to memory on the Krokodil's car as it sped away from him, then he called out the registration of the car Jahn had rented.

"Fugitives from ICE or FBI?" the guard asked. "I mean, it might be important. I don't know."

Verrazzano squinted hard toward the highway. "Fugitives from me. That's what's important."

Jahn stumbled. He reached for her and held her head so he could check her for a concussion, examining her pupils for dilation. She tried to turn away from his gaze.

"We have to get after them," she mumbled.

"What did the Krokodil say to you? When he had you with a gun to your head?"

She rubbed her eyes. "I don't remember. When he hit me on the head, I guess I—I just don't remember now. Come on, let's get going."

"We don't have a vehicle. The Krokodil took all the keys."

"All of them. But we have to—"

"We need to stay focused on tracking the crash software through these Chinese guys and stopping any further incidents. We're going to leave Frisch and the Krokodil for the FBI Detroit field office to track."

"They're going to have a lot of work right now, with the Darien crash. They might not be able to find resources for Frisch and the Krokodil."

Verrazzano watched an airport security cruiser roll through the gate of the rental company's parking lot and turn toward them. "They're going to have to try."

Jahn called the Detroit field office. After she hung up, they waited impatiently for an agent to arrive.

"Thanks," she muttered. "I mean, he could have killed me just now."

If the Krokodil had wanted to kill her, she would be dead. Verrazzano knew that. He wondered why she was still alive. "He could have. That's correct."

"You don't sound like you'd be too upset, if he had."

"It's a hypothetical. I'm more concerned with the people who are dead and the others who soon will be."

She scratched at her lower lip and stared toward the approach road, watching for a black FBI sedan. "You live out on the Island?"

"No, I don't." Home was a tiny basement room Kinsella let him have for nothing in her row house in Astoria, Queens. He visited it once a week, when he needed to stare at a familiar, blank wall.

"Why were you out on the Island this morning, then? When the crash happened, and you came upon that guy, Anthony—"

"Gibson."

"Right."

"I was taking my niece to school."

"You have a niece?" Jahn raised her hands. "Sorry, I just didn't see you as a guy who had a niece. I guess I didn't think of you as— well, you know, human."

"Today has been full of surprises for you. My sister is a single mother. She spends a lot of time looking after my dad. So I stay over a couple nights a week to help her out with her daughter."

"What does your wife think of that?"

"Wife? I'm not *that* human."

A black Chevrolet rolled along the approach road. "That'll be Agent Hemming. I've worked with him before. He's our best chance if the Detroit field office is going to get Frisch and the Krokodil."

Verrazzano shook his head. "We'll see Frisch in Germany."

"You told him we were going to Germany?"

"That's on me."

"Did you tell him *where* in Germany?"

"Makes no difference. Frisch will find us. The Krokodil too, I bet. Same as they'll find a way out of the US. Frisch has in mind to kill someone."

"Who?"

He waved his hand to signal that he'd tell her later. "The only way for him to track his target is to shadow us."

PART 2

CHAPTER 10

They drove him around the teeming warren of Beirut's southern slums for a half hour so that he wouldn't know where he was. Wyatt didn't care. He knew where he was going.

The cinder-block apartment houses cut out the sun, towering over the narrow streets, dropping his vision into darkness behind his Persol shades. Then light burst through where a building lay in ruins, destroyed by an Israeli raid a decade before. Suddenly it illuminated jostling traffic and bustling women swathed in abayas and children moving in erratic, excited packs. On each wall was a poster of the martyrs or of Sheikh Hassan, the dead and the soon to be dead, Hezbollah's pantheon of the gone. *They're living it up in* Jannah *with Allah and Muhammad and the dark-eyed* houris. *Enjoy it while you can, guys,* Wyatt thought. *Nothing lasts, not even heaven.*

The two-inch-long metal cylinder taped to the back of his testicles grew warm. It was like wearing a shot glass full of the worst thing the world had ever seen. He wasn't scared, only a little constricted by its position. He shifted his weight to make it less uncomfortable.

The burly gunman beside Wyatt in the backseat sweated heavily through his black T-shirt. He held a Makarov pistol across his stomach, training it on the American. He rubbed at the perspiration beading in his beard, nervous and losing focus. The man in the passenger seat twisted toward Wyatt, a Kalashnikov aimed at the colonel's face. The windows of the old Mercedes sedan were rolled down. Dust and heat wafted through them from the unpaved streets. Wyatt ignored the guns twitching at him. No wonder the poor bastards were sweating so hard: they knew who he was.

The driver turned on his tape deck. The sound of an imam reciting the one hundred and third sura of The Koran blasted through the car, high and nasal and hanging onto the vowels. "By the mysteries of the dimensions of time, truly man is lost," he recited. *There are more reasons than that,* Wyatt thought. The gunman in the passenger seat reached for the tape deck and turned down the volume. The driver gave him an accusing look.

"It's too loud," the man with the Kalashnikov shouted.

The driver waved his hand angrily. "Don't yell at me."

They swung into a side street and dropped down a slope, cutting into a short access and then making a sharp turn into an underground garage. Wyatt noticed that the street outside the building was empty. The locals knew that Hezbollah wanted to see who was coming and they kept the road clear for the surveillance cameras on each corner. Three gunmen with the build of Turkish wrestlers rolled the heavy iron door closed behind the car.

Inside the parking lot, the darkness was absolute. Wyatt let them drag him out of the car. With each step, the short metal cylinder nipped at his testicles. Everything worth accomplishing demanded a price in pain, and Wyatt had endured suffering much more horrible than a brief discomfort in his nuts.

His eyes adjusted as they climbed the stairs, picking out the uneven surface of the gray, unfinished steps. They took him into a room decorated with embroidered images of the golden Dome of the Rock in Jerusalem and verses of the Koran. The sun crept through the shutters and the thin curtains and lit the opaque yellow of the walls. One of the wrestler-types gestured for him to sit on a thin mattress in the corner. He lowered himself down. Then the gunman kicked Wyatt in the head.

As Wyatt lifted himself back into a sitting position, he savored the impact. When he boxed or fought a karate bout, he savored being hit as much as he enjoyed delivering a blow. He sucked in the other man's aggression and added it to his own considerable store. That's why he had let the Hezbollah guy kick him. He had seen it coming. He could have avoided it and snapped the guy's ankle. But that wasn't where he was at. Not yet.

"Who told you the American was here?" Another man spoke, not the bully boy, a slighter figure emerging through the doorway. He wore a burgundy suit and a collarless shirt done up to the top button in the Iranian style. He was strong, but fat in the middle. Wyatt sized him up. This was one of the group's thinkers, a policy guy. Kidnapping, of course, was a policy matter in Beirut. The man moved toward Wyatt and frowned down upon him. "Speak. Who told you the American was here?"

"The hell do you care?" Wyatt rubbed his head, pretending the kick had truly hurt him. "You want what I've got, and I want the American. It's a trade."

"This is the Middle East, Colonel Wyatt. We must bargain a long time before we strike a deal."

"I don't have a lot of time."

"Which is why I prefer to take a lot of time to make our bargain. To increase the pressure on you, no?"

The wrestler swung the butt of his AK-47 at Wyatt's head. The colonel moved just enough to be sure that it didn't take his eye out. He let it connect with the hard part of his brow and dropped back onto the mattress with a groan.

Three sets of footsteps, heavy in boots, came over the floor toward him. The gunmen pinned him. One of them patted Wyatt down carefully. As Wyatt foresaw, the searcher didn't dwell on his genitals and the metal cylinder stayed where it was. Then a hood went over his head, a pillowcase of cheap nylon. Even before the water spilled over him, Wyatt prepared to die, and to die again and then again after that.

It was waterboarding without the board, the way American troops first did it in the Philippines to insurgents there a century ago. Wyatt suffocated, emptying his mind, knowing that there was nothing in the world that mattered except his mission. To accomplish that mission, he had to allow himself to believe that it too was insignificant. Only when he was detached from all existence could he allow these men to murder him over and over and yet remain alive. Each time they lifted the pillowcase off his head, the man in the burgundy suit bellowed, "Who told you? Who told you we had the American?"

He gave the same answer over and again. "You want the sarin. I've got it for you. Give me the American."

He made it sound like a simple trade, but it wouldn't look that way to the man in the burgundy suit. Wyatt knew Hezbollah didn't have the American that he wanted. The Islamic State had him. If the man in the suit was smart and suspicious—and Wyatt gave him an A-plus on both counts—he'd realize that whoever told Wyatt that Hezbollah had the American also wanted to get Wyatt's stock of sarin. That person might want the nerve gas for the sake of Hezbollah, to kill the Sunni Muslims of the Islamic State. But if that person had failed to mention his contact with Wyatt and his possible acquisition of the world's deadliest substance, then the Hezbollah chiefs would no doubt conclude the man intended to use the sarin for his own purposes, maybe even to take over the group.

"Who told you we have the American?"

They knew Wyatt was tough. He couldn't appear to break too easily. He had to convince them that they had destroyed him. The

pillowcase went on and off four times and his body was shuddering almost beyond his powers of endurance when he finally told
them. "Abu Aisha," he murmured.

The goons holding him went still. The man in the burgundy
suit glanced around at them. This was the most dangerous moment
any one of them had ever experienced. Wyatt was counting on
that. Abu Aisha was the head of Hezbollah's military wing in Beirut, the only man with a network powerful enough to threaten the
dominance of Sheikh Hassan and the other religious leaders.

The man in the suit jerked his neck to signal another torture.
Wyatt wondered this time if he was, indeed, dying. He had been
close before, in Vietnam, in Haiti, in Afghanistan. He reminded
himself that the closest death had actually come to him was in
Woodley Park, Washington, about five hundred yards from the
vice president's mansion on Observatory Circle. He found that
fact humorous, given all the crazy-ass places he had been and the
full set of bad guys who had tried to rub him out. He would
have laughed at the thought, if he hadn't been suffocating. The
memory of that moment in northwest DC drove him to survive,
because the thing that wouldn't let him die was, in the end, always
his thirst for revenge, and the man who tortured him in Woodley Park was either going to die before him or because of him—
once Wyatt had completed the operation that man demanded of
him. Until then, nothing would scare him and absolutely nothing
could kill him. If these Hezbollah men could've forced Wyatt to
swallow a hydrogen bomb, he'd have crapped out a mushroom
cloud and carried on.

"Who told you we had the American?" the suit man bellowed.

"Abu Aisha." Wyatt struggled to hold onto consciousness.
This was the moment, the turning point.

Calculation flickered over the interrogator's features. "When
are you going to give him the sarin?"

Smart and suspicious, Wyatt thought. But a sucker anyhow. "I already—" He coughed and choked, as he laid the trap for Abu Aisha. "I already gave it to him."

The man in the suit came out of his crouch. He went toward the door. "I'll be back," he said to his thugs. He gestured toward Wyatt. "Don't kill him. Break him to pieces."

Before the door was shut, the four men were kicking Wyatt and hammering him with the butts of their rifles. As he went into unconsciousness, he thought: *this is working out just fine.*

When he came around, the sun was very bright. One of the windows was open, and a shutter had been raised a few inches. It was enough to blind him briefly. He was propped against the wall. With a moment's surprise, he realized that he was standing up, held by a gunman on either side. He tested his legs, letting his weight go from foot to foot. They weren't broken. *Amateurs*, he thought.

From out of the glaring sunlight, a man walked forward. He wore a black T-shirt and a black hunting vest. His beard was slick, and his receding hair was black and cut very short. One eye was closed and sunken, the lids fused together over the missing eyeball. Abu Aisha, the man every intelligence service in the Western world—including a few that weren't incompetent—wanted to kill. A hero of Shia Islam, feted in Tehran, reviled by the Sunnis of the Islamic State. The plotter of terror attacks in two dozen countries from Israel to Argentina and in cities from Paris to Bombay. Wyatt saw how much Abu Aisha wanted to strike him. The fact that he didn't was, perhaps, a measure of the superficially top-notch job the thugs had done on him. There was nowhere left to punch that looked as if it could hurt any worse.

The man in the burgundy suit shut the window and dropped the shutter. The air had been cleansed of the stink of the beating. Now Abu Aisha wanted privacy, in case Wyatt said anything dangerous. Anything more dangerous than he had already said.

"You screwed up the sarin deal, Colonel Wyatt." Abu Aisha's voice was hoarse and low. "The American ICE agent took it from Damascus six months ago. From under your nose. When you were supposed to deliver it to us."

"Not all of it." Wyatt wriggled a little against the hold of the gunmen on either side of him. Not to escape. Only enough to free his arm from the elbow down. To reach behind himself.

"Where do you keep the rest?" Abu Aisha didn't look directly at the man in the burgundy suit, but his eyes flickered that way, as though he were performing for his benefit, trying to clear himself of suspicion, to be sure the man would report his innocence to the supreme council and on to Tehran.

"Where?" Wyatt slipped his hand slowly into the back of his pants and reached down for the cylinder between his legs. He had a story to play out, so he made his eyes confused and sent them from Abu Aisha to the man in the burgundy suit and back again. "You know that already."

"You are lying."

That was always a big win. Get the man who's under suspicion by his own people to call you a liar. Those are usually his last words. Wyatt saw no reason to make an exception in Abu Aisha's case. He ripped the cylinder out of his pants and hammered the pin at its base against the wall. He jerked free of the two gunmen on each side and grabbed Abu Aisha, spinning him around to face the man in the suit and the other two gunmen. He held the cylinder beside Abu Aisha's head. As he did so he stopped his breath and started a countdown at sixty.

The gunmen stumbled away. They lifted their weapons. The man in the suit called for them to hold their fire. He had made a mistake about Abu Aisha, bringing him here to face an accuser who had now turned on them. He didn't want to be held responsible for the hero's death too.

"Wyatt, what do you want?" Abu Aisha tried to turn toward the cylinder.

The gunmen frowned at the small object in Wyatt's fingers. It must have appeared to be some kind of tiny grenade, perhaps. They hesitated. The man in the suit called out, "Wyatt, you will not leave here alive."

Forty-five. Wyatt clenched his arm across Abu Aisha's chest and pinned him close. The Hezbollah man's struggles were for nothing.

Abu Aisha coughed hard and wheezed. Then he went still. *He's getting the idea now*, Wyatt thought.

"Shoot him, quickly," Abu Aisha said. His words came choking and desperate.

"Abu Aisha, we cannot—"

"It's sarin. Quickly, kill him."

Thirty. Wyatt's pulse hammered, but he didn't breathe.

The gunmen took a few seconds. Then they got it. They leveled their weapons and moved to the side to try to get a clear shot. Wyatt dragged Abu Aisha to the corner. They couldn't shoot him without putting a bullet in their military chief. Then the man in the burgundy suit was coughing and so were the gunmen. They collapsed to their knees.

Fifteen. Abu Aisha was heavy in Wyatt's arms, ready to drop.

The room filled with the stink of the sudden diarrhea in the gunmen's cargo pants. The man in the suit vomited and lay on his side. The thug nearest the door fired off a few rounds as he fell, but they hit the wall six feet above Wyatt's head.

Zero. Wyatt dropped Abu Aisha. He took a knife from the belt of one of the gunmen and quickly slashed the carotid artery of each man to be sure of their deaths. He hurried to the window and opened it, breathing for the first time in over a minute. The hot breeze ballooned the light curtain. *Halfway there*, he thought.

He knelt beside Abu Aisha. With the knife, he sawed through the dead man's neck. He stamped on the vertebrae to shatter them and cut through the spinal cord. He tugged Abu Aisha's black T-shirt over his shoulders to wrap the head. He took a PC9 pistol from the belt of one of the corpses and strapped a Kalashnikov over his shoulder. He put a spare magazine into the pocket on the thigh of his pants. With the pistol out in front of him and the severed head at his side, he went into the stairwell.

Two of the men who had guarded him on the car ride were coming up the stairs. He double-tapped each of them, bullets to the head and chest. At the foot of the stairs, he took out the driver of the car. He moved into the garage and killed another two by the door. He rolled the heavy gate back and ran for the Mercedes. He set Abu Aisha's head on the passenger seat and started the ignition.

The Koran blasted from the tape deck just as the engine caught. Wyatt let it play as he drove up the slope through the slums. "I will punish them with terrible agony," the imam recited on the tape, "in this world and the Hereafter. Nor will they have anyone to help them."

Wyatt let the traffic take him north and west, toward the Palestinian refugee camp of Bourj al-Barajneh. The effect of the waterboarding and the beating pulsed through him. He tensed every muscle, clamped his teeth together, and wiped the sweat from his eyes. He was nearly there.

He turned off the Coastal Highway and weaved through the lazy pedestrians in the alleys of the slum that was still called a refugee camp by the UN, even though it had been there since 1948. Wyatt was sensitive to the presence of death, and Bourj al-Barajneh had been the scene of massacres and sieges during the Lebanese Civil War. There were souls around him now long gone from this life who smiled grimly in welcome, anticipating that his arrival in the camp was no more than a staging point and that he would soon join them in the other world. He cursed them and coughed. He wondered if he had managed to keep the sarin out of his lungs.

At the open storefront of a falafel restaurant, he turned into a side alley. The scent of frying chickpeas on the air made him nauseous. He rolled his neck and shoulders. "Jesus, soldier, get it together," he muttered to himself. "You're Colonel Lawton Wyatt. You're not going let a team of half-assed dune coons put the scare on you. You're not about to die. You've got a job to do."

He rolled the car to a halt at the end of the alley and ducked into a stairwell. He struggled up to the second floor with the Kalashnikov on his shoulder and Abu Aisha's head in the T-shirt dripping blood on the cheap tiles of the steps. He rapped on a pink metal door. It opened slightly. A man who bore an unsurprising resemblance to the Hezbollah guys Wyatt had just killed stared out at him. "Who are you?" he said.

"I'm done answering questions today, buddy." Wyatt pushed inside and shouted, "Touma, I've got what you want. Marwan Touma, come out here, damn it."

The man at the door checked the stairwell and bolted the door. He didn't challenge Wyatt again.

A short, stocky man with a neat black mustache and thin hair flapped out of the bathroom in a long white jalabiya and a pair of cheap sandals. "*Ahlan wa-sahlan, ya Pasha* Wyatt," Touma said. "Welcome, my bad, bad brother." He took hold of Wyatt's shoulders. "Truly we are brothers. Many people have tried to kill me and failed. Look at the state of you. Evidently you have also disappointed a would-be murderer today. We are the same, you and I. We cannot be destroyed."

"Can't say the same thing for some people." Wyatt dropped the T-shirt to the floor. The head hit the tiles with a dull thud.

Touma bent over and rolled back the fabric of the T-shirt. He examined the face of the dead Hezbollah military chief. He squeezed Abu Aisha's cheek gently between his thumb and forefinger, an uncle congratulating a small child on its cuteness. He took a cell phone from his pocket and dialed. "Sit down, Wyatt. This will only take a few moments."

Touma was an arms dealer. He usually based himself in Damascus, where Wyatt had first done business with him. He used Beirut as a base when things were too hot across the border in Syria and because it was easier to find women to sleep with there. He survived because he was close to everyone, including the Islamic State. In the Middle East, Palestinians like Touma had to have good relations with every kind of sect and splinter group because no one loved them and everyone needed a very good reason not to just go out and slaughter them.

He spoke quickly into the cell phone. He glanced up at Wyatt and smiled. But in his eyes, Wyatt noticed an underdog resentment that reminded him of black kids during his childhood in Tennessee. Touma hung up. "A few minutes."

"They're waiting nearby?" Wyatt went to the window and peered down at the alley. Two small boys were tossing an injured kitten in the air.

Footsteps sounded on the staircase, coming down the next flight. "*Very* nearby." Touma grinned.

Wyatt stretched his arms over his head, working against the stiffness of the bruises from his beating at the Hezbollah hideout. He was in a refugee camp where there was no law, in a country where there was very little law, in a region where the only real law was the kind that was administered with maximum cruelty. He was about to do a deal with people who put men in cages and burned them alive. He moaned pleasurably as he brought his arms down. Now he was really enjoying himself.

The guard opened the door. Two gunmen stepped through. They had covered their faces with kaffiyehs, wrapped across their chins and noses, their eyes rheumy with the hot wind off the Mediterranean and the dirt of the Beirut alleys. Each held a Kalashnikov on Wyatt. The taller one spoke to Wyatt with the flat accent of northern England. "Why are you carrying an AK-47?"

Wyatt grinned. "When in Rome." He rolled Abu Aisha's head across the floor with a flick of his foot. "There's your guy. Where's my guy?"

The gunman called out in Arabic. "Bring him in."

A third man appeared in the doorway, his features covered in the same fashion as his companions. He shoved a stumbling, bent prisoner into the room. Where the man's hands and feet were manacled, his skin was abraded and infected, with suppurating open sores. A stench of excrement and urine and old, old sweat and dirty wounds filled the space. Touma scuttled to the window and opened it.

Wyatt crooked his finger and beckoned. The first gunman thrust the butt of his rifle into the prisoner's back and sent him spinning across the room. Wyatt caught him with a hand on his shoulder. He leaned over him. "We're going home, buddy," he whispered.

The man stared up at Wyatt like a beaten dog. Wyatt knew him to be in his midforties. But his hair was either ripped away in chunks or gone white, his beard was gray, and his face was as blue as an old lady's varicose veins, it had been so long since he saw the sunlight. His neck bore a thick scab from ear to ear. Someone had played at beheading him, probably just to mess with him, Wyatt figured.

The first gunman lifted Abu Aisha's head. "Hey, mate," he called out to his former hostage. He waved the severed head. "This Shia bastard lost his noggin so you could keep yours."

The prisoner cowered. Wyatt squinted at the gunmen, trying to read them, attending to every motion. The humor with which the English jihadi swung the severed head at his laughing comrades could go sour fast.

"Time for you to take that thing and go now," Wyatt said.

The gunman let his laugh trail off. He tossed the head toward Wyatt. "Why don't you say good-bye?"

Wyatt caught the head. He never did anything that didn't contribute to the completion of his mission. He wasn't about to start bantering with a cheeky lad from Bradford who had decided that England's morals weren't up to the standards of the Prophet, blessings be upon Him, and that torturing American Special Forces operatives would be his contribution to setting the world on the right path.

Touma was quickly at the side of the Islamic State man, simpering and offering elaborate Arabic formulas of thanks. Two of the jihadis seemed ready to leave. But the English guy found something in Wyatt that spurred him to confrontation, some power that made him doubt his eventual victory over the West, perhaps.

"You people make me sick, mate." He pointed accusingly at Wyatt. "What are you doing in the Middle East, anyhow? You don't belong here."

"I plan on leaving right away." Wyatt balanced Abu Aisha's head in his right hand. With his left, he touched the hostage's shoulder. "Let's go, buddy."

The gunman leveled his Kalashnikov. "Hang about. I've done and gone and changed me mind, in't I."

"I hope your Arabic grammar is better than your English." Wyatt tossed Abu Aisha's severed head into the air. It looped across the room.

The gunman glanced up at the head. Wyatt fired the Kalashnikov with one hand. It took out the gunman with a quick burst to the chest. He steadied the barrel with his other hand and shot down the other two before they even lifted their weapons.

Touma put his hands to his head. "Wyatt, screw your sister's cunt, you son of a whore. That fool was just playing around. He was posturing. He wasn't going to shoot you."

"I always did hate a show-off." Wyatt hooked his arm around the hostage and went into the stairwell.

"How the hell am I going to get out of this, Wyatt?" Touma yelled.

"You're a dealmaker, Marwan. You've still got the head of the Hezbollah military chief in Beirut there. I bet these aren't the only Islamic State guys you know who'd look mighty kindly on the guy who killed Abu Aisha. Meanwhile, Hezbollah will want revenge, and you've got the bodies of the three guys who killed their boss right here. Leastways you can sell it to them that way. I think I gave you a pretty neat gift. You love to play both sides against the middle, don't you? Knock yourself out."

"Screw you, Wyatt."

"You're welcome, partner." Wyatt went down the stairs to the Mercedes with the hostage. Before he sat him in the passenger seat, he shot off the manacles. With each report from Wyatt's pistol, the man shuddered and whimpered.

Wyatt reversed the Mercedes down the alley and out into the main street of the camp. He pulled onto the highway toward the airport. "We're going to stop and get you cleaned up, buddy. Then we're going to fly out of this dump."

"They—They—" The man doubled over and wept.

Wyatt knew the need in hostages to tell a rescuer what they had endured. He didn't want to hear it. He didn't need to imagine. He'd been on the receiving end more than a couple of times. Anyhow, this guy had to pull himself together quickly. "No need to explain, buddy. You're with me now."

"Who are you?" He still sounded scared.

"I'm Colonel Lawton Wyatt, and I was a Delta Force operative just like you, son."

He took out his cell phone and swiped to a preprogrammed number. He dialed and held it so the man in the passenger seat could see who he had called. Tears filled the guy's terrified eyes. He took the phone shakily from Wyatt and held it to his ear. "What do I say?"

Wyatt steered with his left hand through the weaving madness of the Beirut airport highway. With his right hand, he reached the pistol from his waistband and thrust it against the passenger's head. "You say whatever I tell you to say. You got me?"

The man nodded. The curt voice of a woman sounded from the phone. The man's jaw shivered, and he was unable to speak. The voice came again, asking for a response. Wyatt shoved the pistol against the man's temple, harder.

"It's me," the man said. The woman's voice on the line went silent. Through his tears, the man said, "Gina, I'm alive. Gina, baby, I'm alive."

CHAPTER 11

The German policeman yawned and blinked at the luminous hands of the clock over the window. He stretched back in his chair. "Aren't you hungry?" he asked.

Du An watched him from the corner of the dark office. *White men never stop eating*, he thought. He shook his head and turned back to the window. The parking lot outside Hall Six was empty, except for his black Jansen Trapp Insignia and the policeman's cruiser. The production line had closed two hours ago. The workers had gone home. He picked up the desk phone.

"Who're you calling?" The policeman was tired. Since 8 AM, he had been watching Du An do nothing much of anything except sweat. But the policeman was a German, and he had his job to do.

"The security gate." Du An dialed.

"When the American agents arrive, the security gate will call *us*. They will send them straight over here. Don't worry." The policeman stood and adjusted his pants around his belly. "I'm hungry, even if you aren't." He checked his watch. "The cafeteria is closed, right?"

"There's a vending machine at the end of the corridor."

The policeman belched slightly. He shifted the holster to make it comfortable on his bulky hips and went out.

The security office at the front gate of the Jansen Trapp factory picked up Du An's call. "Hi, this is Heinz again," he said. "Yes, Chinese Heinz."

He would have thought An was an easy enough name for these Europeans to remember, but they only stared at him when he spoke it. So like most Chinese, he took a Western name. In Germany he was Heinz.

"Okay, well, you'll call me as soon as they arrive, right? I'm waiting." He hung up. He touched the flat of his hand to the top of his head. The short hair, growing back from the close shave he had given it a month earlier, prickled against his palm. He brought his hand down in front of his face. He would have sworn he could see little welts on his palm, as though the hair was poisoned. He would have shaved it all away again. But that was most certainly not allowed.

Something crashed down beyond the office door. Du An jerked away from his desk, shooting on his rolling chair toward the dark corner. He heard the pop of a tab being pulled on a soda can and realized the thunderous sound was only the policeman getting a drink at the vending machine.

The air wheezed in his throat. He hadn't drawn a relaxed inhalation since Feng Yi picked him for the project. But the last couple of days had been worse. When the warning message arrived from Su Li in New Jersey, his asthma started to crush his chest as if it knew time was running out for it to inflict pain on him. Someone was coming for them. The killing started with Gao in Detroit. That hadn't surprised him. After all, Gao had defied them. He had changed the execution date. Du had known it as soon as he heard the squealing tires and the crushing impacts and the sirens on the streets of Rüsselsheim. It was the Dariens, he had thought. The German chancellor broke out of a summit meeting with the French president to talk of terrorism, and skinheads sprayed swastikas on the mosque near Du's home and burned down the local Turkish kebab restaurant. But Du had known that Gao had issued his warning to the world, and killed thousands of people in doing so.

There has to be a better way. Those were the last words Du had spoken to Gao over a Skype connection to Detroit. His attempt to persuade the guilt-ridden fool to wait until they could figure out a way to stop it. To stop *themselves.* All the engineers had agreed that they would defy any order to activate the plan, but Gao was impatient. Perhaps he didn't trust Su Li to go up against Beijing, or he figured Jin Ju wouldn't risk her family. Then there was Turbo, who was completely unreliable. *Gao trusted me though,* Du thought. *Didn't he?* Yet Gao had brandished an ultrasound photo of his unborn child in front of the webcam. "If I knew that this baby was evil, I would kill my wife and the baby. Without hesitation," he had bellowed. Du hadn't doubted him. General Feng made each of them crazy in their own way. Gao had simply cracked worse. Or first.

He wondered if one of the others had made a mistake, let the secret of their opposition to the crash plan slip out. Maybe that was why someone was coming after them, rubbing them out one by one, before they could betray the whole project. But General Feng needed all of them in place, inside the car companies and able to manipulate their computer networks, or the plan wouldn't work. Unless the general had figured out a better way to make it happen.

Du had found a better way to stop it, at least, as he had promised poor Gao. Rather, a better way had found *him.* Thanks to the American agents, he had hope now for the first time in months. The German police had come to him in the Jansen Trapp factory just after he arrived for another day at his computer. They told him the Americans had traced Su's message to him. The Germans would watch over him here until the Americans arrived to question him. The cops refused to let him leave the factory. They wouldn't even take him to the police station. The Americans had insisted that he was in danger and that he should be kept secure wherever they found him. Even a few minutes on the road would be enough—that was the message the German police received from the US agents. Du didn't ask them "enough for what." Gao was dead, and he assumed Su was gone too. A few minutes outside the Jansen Trapp compound would be his last few minutes on earth.

He listened for the policeman's footsteps. The big man was still down the corridor by the vending machines. Du picked up his phone and dialed a number in Cologne. "Turbo, it's Du," he said. "The Americans contacted me. Gao's warning worked. It got their attention. I'm going to make them protect us."

The man on the other end of the line spoke fast and loudly. Du barely listened. Turbo seemed high, even when he wasn't. He sounded as though he had mainlined panic and fear. "I will kill whoever comes for me," he yelled. He made a machine-gun noise. "Say hello to my little friend. I'm going to kill you, Al Pacino." Then he wept, calling out the names of the dead engineers.

Du heard footsteps in the hall. The policeman was coming back. "Turbo, if the Americans don't get to me in time, you must be the one to warn our last comrade. Do you hear me, Turbo? Go to Saskia. She will help you." He set the phone down softly.

He glanced up at his whiteboard. Saskia Hütz's phone number was there, hidden in plain sight among all his equations and meetings scrawled across the wall. Turbo could hide out at Saskia's environmental watchdog agency in Cologne. It was a short drive from the Wolfwagen subsidiary in Holland where Turbo worked. Saskia didn't know what they were up to, but she was glad to have inside sources at the auto companies. They fed her leaks on the carbon dioxide emissions that she devoted her life to stemming. In return they knew they had an underground bolt-hole when they needed it. Du stood quickly and rubbed Saskia's name away. He cleared the entire whiteboard. Just in case.

In case the Americans didn't get to him first.

The phone trilled. The sudden noise in the silence made Du jump. He wasn't used to the quiet. Throughout the day, the production line buzzed and rumbled beneath him. He snatched the handset to his ear. "This is Heinz." He listened. "Thank you. Yes, I am waiting for them."

He went to the window. The moonlight glimmered on the rippling surface of the wide Main, flowing to the Rhine. The Americans had arrived to protect him. He smiled with relief. They could put him in an orange jumpsuit and waterboard him for all he cared. They weren't about to kill him. He would tell them everything, and they would stop it all from happening.

The front gate was a three-minute drive, unless they took a wrong turn between the identical green-roofed factory buildings. His mouth was dry. Someone moved in the parking lot. He stared at the motion, squinting and blinking. It was just a cat. He puffed out his cheeks in relief.

He went to the door and opened it. He leaned into the corridor to alert the policeman to the arrival of the Americans.

At the end of the corridor, a man was bent over the prone body of the German cop, his back to Du. He straightened up at the sound of the door moving on its hinges.

Du ran to the other end of the corridor and scrambled out onto the gantry overlooking the factory floor.

The killer's footsteps approached behind him.

Du backed away, tripping to the far corner of the platform.

The man came out onto the gantry. He raised his head and smiled cruelly. His skin was ridged and scaled like a crocodile's hide. Du An opened his mouth to scream.

CHAPTER 12

The security guard glided the shuttle to a halt in the parking lot outside the Jansen Trapp factory. The complex was enormous. It seemed to take an age to get from the gate to the building where Du An waited for them. The driver had the radio on a German news station. It rounded up the news on the crash. The House majority leader in DC wanted the president to act against the terrorists with a strike against areas of Syria controlled by Islamic State. As if there were only one terrorist group in the world. The White House response was that the terrorist plot was still under investigation and it was too early to act. But Verrazzano knew that the politicians wouldn't be able to wait long, and when they pushed the button, it would be guys like him who would end up either dead or with a conscience bad enough to blight the rest of their lives.

He stepped out of the bus beside a parked police car and a lonely sedan he assumed must belong to Du. Dull orange lights glimmered over the lot. The factory and the offices built along the edge of its roof were dark. On the tarmac, Jahn stretched and groaned. Verrazzano felt a sudden chill in the summer air off the river.

From inside the factory, there was a loud buzz and three electronic warning bleats. Then the quiet night gave itself up to the rattling thunder of machinery. "What's that?" Jahn said.

The security guard frowned. "The production line has been turned on. That is not right. It was shut down already."

"It's a cover for something," Jahn said. "Something noisy. Like a killing."

"The Krokodil is here." Verrazzano charged toward the door. He drew his H&K. Jahn cursed and followed.

The entrance to the factory was dark and the door was locked. Gunfire sounded above, three single shots. The security guard fumbled at the keypad.

"Open the goddamned door," Jahn shouted.

The guard got the right number into the keypad and stepped back to let the Americans through.

Verrazzano opened the door. The handle was grubby from contact with the oil-stained hands of thousands of workers. In the massive, dark hall he glimpsed the movement of the robotic arms and the crane gantry up by the roof.

The security guard activated the lights. They flickered a moment and then lit up the confusion of the assembly line. Immediately above them, unpainted car bodies glided past on the roof-mounted crane. Across the shiny gray floor of antislip epoxy, the crane dipped the sections down into the paint pools.

"Turn off the production line," Verrazzano told the security guard.

The guard stared at the button board mounted on the wall and waved his arms to show that he was confounded by it.

Jahn's cell phone trilled. She glanced at the screen and rejected the call. "Du An?" she called out. "Do you hear me, Du An?"

Feet stumbled on the observation gantry above them. A Chinese man stood outside the offices. It was the spot where a boss would survey his workers. But there was no command in the Chinese man's features. His face glinted with sweat.

"Du An, I'm a US agent," Verrazzano called. "We're here to help you."

"He's here." Du An climbed onto the railing over the factory floor. "I can't let him have me."

Jahn's phone rang again. She muttered a curse and rejected the call once more.

"Where, Mister Du? Where is he?" Verrazzano walked carefully toward the metal steps that led to the office platform. "I'm coming up to you now, Mister Du. Everything's going to be okay."

Du was poised, ready to jump. "Whatever happens, he mustn't get me alive. I'm a dead man. There's nothing you can do about it. You can't help me, and you can't help the rest of them."

"The rest of who?" Verrazzano was halfway up the steps.

"The Happy Five we called ourselves. Now there's only three. Soon—" He pointed at his chest. "Soon just two."

"Two computer engineers?"

Du looked along the platform, searching for the killer. Verrazzano reached the platform. "He doesn't need us alive," Du said. "It's easier for him this way."

"Easier for who, Mister Du?"

Jahn's phone sounded once again. This time she accepted the call. "Maybe it's something," she muttered. She put the phone to her ear.

"Who's *he*?" Verrazzano spoke quietly. Du was spooked already, scared enough to climb up where he could throw himself to his death before the man with the crocodile skin might reach him. "Why are they trying to kill you?"

"We were supposed to do the job for him. But something has gone wrong. Someone else got involved. I don't know why."

"What were you supposed to do?"

"Now they're silencing us. One by one. You have to find the others. Save them."

Jahn hung up, shaking her head. She walked quickly to the stairs and started coming up behind Verrazzano.

"I'm going to find them, Mister Du," Verrazzano said. "Tell me who your friends are and where, and I promise I will get to them first. But what were you supposed to do?"

The overhead crane clanked and jarred. Du frowned at it. Then he looked back to Verrazzano. "Every car sold in the last year. Every one of them will accelerate. Hundreds of thousands of people will die. Unless you find my friends."

Jahn mounted the stairs. She came level with Verrazzano. "We've got to get into cover. Mister Du, come with me now."

"It's okay." Verrazzano glanced toward her. Jahn's impatience could spook the engineer enough to make him jump. "I've got this."

"You're taking too long. We've got to move. Mister Du, come on now."

Du seemed to notice Jahn for the first time. He backed away. "Who are you?"

"Gina, go wait down below," Verrazzano said.

Jahn shoved past him. "Du An, come with me right now."

Du got down from his suicide perch on the railing and stumbled away from her to the end of the platform. He looked about him for an escape.

"Gina, do not approach," Verrazzano called.

She turned on him. "You don't know what you're doing. Did you not hear what he just said? This thing is huge. We have to get this guy into—"

Verrazzano saw a flash of raddled skin under the steel body of a sedan passing along the elevated robotic line under the ceiling. He bellowed at Jahn, "Down."

A man in gray camouflage dropped out of the swinging car body, holding on by his knees like an acrobat on a trapeze. His face was a mass of peeling, scabbing crusts and welts. The Krokodil addict. He thrust down and, with two slices of his knife, he cut through the Chinese man's throat and, as the crane carried him away, sheared off his scalp.

Verrazzano pushed by Jahn to get off a shot, but the crane had taken the Krokodil around a bend in the assembly line. The assassin lifted himself back inside the car body.

Verrazzano took a quick look at Du and touched his neck for a pulse. The man was dead. Verrazzano climbed onto the top rail of the office platform and jumped for an auto body on the roof crane. He caught hold of the metal strut along the bottom of the door. The car swung out over the factory floor, a forty-foot drop.

"Go shut it off," he called.

Jahn stumbled down the steps toward the security guard. She shot a couple of rounds into the control panel on the wall.

All the machinery across the factory halted. The crane track stopped. Verrazzano hauled himself up into the car body. Three cars ahead of him, a sky light was opened to ventilate the space. *Maybe the Krokodil intended to leap up and go out that way.* "Gina, head out to the parking lot in case the guy goes out there."

Jahn sprinted through the door.

Verrazzano crawled onto the hood of the car body. The Krokodil was inside the skeleton of a car just ahead of him, out of sight around a turn in the robotic line. The bodywork swayed as Verrazzano propelled himself forward, leaping to the back of the next car.

He clambered through the car to the hood. He repeated his jump to the next car along. He dropped through the space where the chassis would fill the bodywork when the car was completed. He clasped the seat anchors, but his right hand slid away.

He held on with his left, suspended high over the quiet floor. The metal cut into his fingers. He reached up and strained to hold on with both hands. Then he swung forward.

Dangling from the front of the car, he stared at the next auto body. The one where the Krokodil hid. He levered himself back and forth, building momentum. He flung his body forward and caught the rear of the next car. Two quick forward movements and he was beneath the car.

He yanked his pistol from his holster and twisted to cover the inside of the car. It was empty. The Krokodil should've been in there. Where had he gone?

He glanced around. Away to his right, a second walkway connected the office corridor with a lunch area above the factory floor. Verrazzano grimaced against the fatigue in his arms. He holstered his gun and levered himself over to the walkway. He jumped onto it, barely spanning the gap, lying flat in relief.

A few inches from his face, a smear of blood on the metal seemed to have been spread hastily with a bristly brush. Verrazzano knew it was the hair on the strip of Du An's scalp that the killer had taken. He had gone this way, still holding the bloody skin in his hand.

Verrazzano lifted his H&K in front of him and went carefully into the office corridor. At his feet, a tubby man lay dead. He wore blue pants with a yellow stripe down the side. His torso was bare, his throat slit. The cop who had been guarding Du An. Verrazzano frowned, then he ran into the nearest office and scanned the parking lot.

The police car was gone. The killer had taken the policeman's shirt to disguise himself and driven away in his car. Someone lay on the ground in the shadows where the police car had been parked. It had to be Jahn. The chill in Verrazzano's stomach was stronger than he'd have expected. She wasn't moving.

He rushed back to the walkway and leaned over the factory floor. The security guard was on his walkie-talkie, shaking his head and staring at the shot-up control panel. Verrazzano called to him in German. "Are you in touch with the gate guards?"

The guard nodded.

"Tell them to shut down all exits. They're looking for a police car."

"A police car?"

"They must not approach the man in the car. But they mustn't let him leave the compound."

The guard mumbled into his walkie-talkie. Then he shrugged. "The policeman has gone. My colleague just let him out."

"Get your colleague to call the police and put an alert out. They have to stop that car."

He ran down the stairs and passed the guard, into the night. He was beside Jahn just as she made her first movement, rolling onto her back. He lifted her into a sitting position. She rubbed her head. "Knocked out by the same guy twice in twenty-four hours," she muttered.

"Ring my bell once, shame on you," Verrazzano said. "Ring my bell twice, it's the last damned time you get close enough."

"I feel like death."

"I'm pretty sure you're alive."

She turned her head to vomit. She wiped her mouth with the back of her hand.

"Dead people can't throw up, right?" He took her into the factory. In the office, Verrazzano flipped on the lights. The German police might arrest the Krokodil, but he thought it more probable that they'd find the stolen cop car abandoned over in the fields by the riverbank. Du An said there were two more computer engineers. Two more who'd be dead within days.

He scanned the room. People spent half their lives in their workspace. They marked it with their thinking. He scanned the room for clues about whatever might have been in Du An's head while he waited for his American rescuers to show up—or for his killer. He ran his finger along the calendar on the office wall. It showed a dreamy picture of a young Chinese actress. Which date was the one set for the next disaster? He stared at the month of July that was just starting, wondering if one of the little squares on the glossy paper would soon be spread with blood.

His finger came away dusty from the calendar. He coughed. The room was coated in dirt. The corridor outside was clean and the factory floor was well-kept. The key to the door was in the keyhole. Perhaps the cleaners didn't come in here because Du An locked it whenever he wasn't around.

He pushed a few files around on the desk. Papers in Chinese and German, brochures for Jansen Trapp cars, notebooks with lines of computer code scribbled across the pages, Post-its with Chinese characters drawn on them. He shook his head. He couldn't figure out what to do next.

He let his mind clear. This was where he had stood out from other soldiers back in basic training, and where he was different from other ICE agents too. His Special Ops mind would help him. Wyatt had trained him never to get blocked, never to experience the frustration that takes up the very brain space you need to get unblocked. Wyatt used to say something else too: "If you can't figure out which way to go next, it's because you're already there."

Verrazzano turned around slowly, not looking for anything. Just seeing.

He stopped at the whiteboard. He watched it, waiting for it to speak to him. And it did. It told him it wasn't dirty. Everything else in the room was under a thick coat of dust, but the whiteboard had recently been wiped clean.

Du An knew Verrazzano was coming. But he must also have suspected the Krokodil was looking for him. Maybe there had been something on the whiteboard that could have led the killer to the other computer engineers. So Du An had wiped it away.

Verrazzano went close to the whiteboard. It had been wiped hastily with a regular fiber eraser. It hadn't been cleaned with a wet cloth. There were traces of the writing still on the metal. He went over it section by section. Notes on coding. Departmental phone extensions. Diagrams and graphs sketched in black, blue, and green. Then he saw some letters, down in the bottom corner. They had been written in red above a phone number. They were barely legible.

He took a sheet of paper from the desk and a pen. He wrote the number, guessing at a couple of the digits that hadn't adhered to the whiteboard as well as the others. Then he wrote down the letters. They spelled a woman's name. Saskia.

He picked up the desk phone and rang the number. A woman answered. "*Hallo, Hütz hier.*"

"Saskia Hütz?" Verrazzano asked.

"*Ja.*" Her answer was hesitant, as though her very name could put her in danger.

He spoke in German. "I'm Special Agent Dominic Verrazzano, United States Immigration and Customs Enforcement."

"Do you have Du An?" She was relieved now. "You got there in time."

She spoke to him in English, but he continued in German. Even the best non-native speaker of English may stammer or think too hard about what they have to say. The only disturbance to the woman's natural rhythm that Verrazzano wanted to hear was the one that might signal she was lying or keeping something from him. "Du An is dead." He waited. She didn't react. He gambled. "Can you help me find the others?"

He heard a sudden blast of Chinese rock music down the line. Urgently the woman said, "Turn that off. It is late. Markus is asleep." Someone laughed manically near her and the music cut out.

Then Saskia came back onto the phone. "At Cologne main station, there is a Lavazza coffee bar underneath the platforms. Be there at six AM." She hung up.

Verrazzano's cell phone buzzed in his pocket. An e-mail from Haddad in New York. He opened it. It contained a photo of a tanned kid in desert camo. The kid watched the camera with a simplicity that somehow was at odds with the evidence of his clothing, the fatigues that proved he was on his way to kill people or to be killed by them.

The phone rang. Verrazzano picked up. "Who's this kid, Roula?"

Haddad's voice was flat. She was reading from a file. "Shane David Getmanov. Born 1985, Lexington, Kentucky. Russian father, mother from Harlan, Kentucky. Infantry training. Ranger qualified. Four tours in Iraq. Decorated. Discharged for repeated drug abuse. Told psychs the illegal drugs killed his PTSD."

Getmanov sounded like Wyatt's kind of guy. Highly trained. Damaged. Seeking a new purpose.

"Last drug-related AWOL—the one that broke the camel's back—Getmanov went to his uncle in Moscow and was arrested by Marine guards at the US embassy shooting up on the steps," Haddad said. "No further record of his whereabouts."

Verrazzano heard the tension in her voice. "Except?"

"The officer who recommended a discharge for Getmanov, his eight-year-old was on the way home from school when someone ran up to him and jammed a syringe into his arm. Injected the kid full of Krokodil. The only thing the kid remembered about the assailant was that—"

"His skin looked like a red crocodile."

"That's right."

Verrazzano went down the stairs to the factory floor with the cell phone in his hand. Jahn sat on a metal bench by a water cooler with a cup in her hand. Her nerves seemed to throb outside her skin.

"Thanks, Roula," he said. Jahn spilled her water in surprise at the sound of his voice. "See if you can find anything else on Getmanov." He hung up his cell phone and crossed the plasticized flooring to Jahn.

"How about some coffee to settle you?" he said. "Apparently there's a good café in Cologne."

CHAPTER 13

When Maj kissed the skin of his cheek, Shane Getmanov felt it burn, as if the diseased surface of his body had peeled off, dropped away from him, and left his true self exposed to her. She was the only one who ever saw it. Except for Wyatt.

He reached his arms around her to hug her to him. Then he remembered how his torso looked, and he couldn't do it to her. Couldn't press her clean, pure body against the filth that spewed out of his every pore. She seemed to sense his self-disgust, because she plunged forward and was on top of him, her breasts against the scabs and sores that covered his chest and belly. He braced his hands against her shoulders to move her away. "No, Shane," she whispered. "It's who you are. It's okay."

"It's not. Not who I am. It's filth." Krokodil. The cheap concoction of morphine and red phosphorus chipped from the heads of matches. Attacking the skin, building abscesses around the point of injection, leaving patches of rotted flesh that resembled the scales of the predator that gave it that name. It destroyed the blood vessels, the bone and muscle. It wrecked the spirit. The drug had been around almost a century, first prescribed by doctors who hurriedly discarded it as a treatment as soon as they observed the side effects. But when the Russian government cracked down on heroin in 2003, it was resurrected, cooked for the streets and sold to the most hopeless of junkies. Like him.

"Shane, it's the drug. It's not you. I can see *you*." Her face in front of his. How could she bear to look?

Under his lower rib, his liver buzzed with the thousand tiny impacts of the poison in its shattered lobes. Stress squeezed around his heart. In one moment, he experienced all over again the trauma of his military service in Iraq and the horror of the murders he committed now for Wyatt. The shuddering fear merged with the abhorrence that underlay his Krokodil highs, and—*admit it*—the love that he betrayed with his every waking thought. His love for Maj.

Her long, straight blonde hair fell over him, covered his face. For an instant, its perfume overwhelmed the rotten stink of his flesh. He cursed the path that had brought him to her at the clinic in Stockholm after he fled Petersburg. If he had met her somehow without the intervention of the drug, he could only imagine the man he might now be. A man with a beautiful, intelligent Swedish girlfriend who cared for him, loved him. A man with a future. A man who possibly could learn how to love.

But it hadn't happened that way. She worked at the rehab clinic, tended him, and fell for him because she found a crack in the absolute concrete silence behind which he hid all his pain. She even left her job and followed him when Wyatt called him away. She stuck with him when she found the hidden syringes and vials. Now as she kissed his neck and delicately tickled his waist, it dawned on him that she was so pure as to be almost unnatural. No, that was the word for *him*. His body, his mind, his life defined it. She was absolutely natural. So why did she want to be with him? She detested all other contraventions of nature's true order, even the international conglomerates whose control over the world economy she protested in the streets whenever prime ministers and presidents got together at summits and trade talks.

"Didn't nothing—" He coughed and stammered. "Didn't nothing bad ever happen to you?"

She smiled down at him. "Of course it did."

"Then why—why are you like this? I mean, how come you're—? I don't know the word for it."

She laughed. "You mean, why am I happy?"

He couldn't help it. He laughed too. "I guess, yeah, that's exactly what I'm saying. I figure I'd be happy if nothing bad had ever happened."

"Instead you take that drug *because* of the bad things that happened to you."

"It's eating me alive. Same as the bad memories."

She ran her finger along his jaw. "The only difference between you and me is that I don't hate myself. So stop hating yourself. Give yourself some love."

"I can't do that."

She kissed his lips lightly. "Then let me give it to you, and perhaps you'll start loving yourself without realizing it."

"The difference between you and me is that I'm going to die."

"If you keep taking Krokodil, yes, you will be dead within a matter of months."

"So? Don't that seem like a pretty basic difference?"

"Until the day that you die, you are alive. That's basic. That's the way I live. You should try it, silly man."

Sobs shook through him stronger than anything he had ever felt. *Until the day that you die, you are alive.* She gathered him to her.

"I'm dead," he moaned. "I'm already dead."

"You're not. Look at me—"

"No, I don't want to. I want to be dead. I deserve it."

As if it were happening right now, he saw himself scalping the Chinese, counting them off, knowing how many more there must be. All of it was to keep himself alive. All of it made him feel more dead than ever.

"The world needs a man like you to change it for the better." She touched her palm to his raddled cheek. "The world is ruled by men who dominate entire continents with their corporations. They control our thoughts with their online networks. But you are beyond their control, because you know how to defy everything. Even death. You only need to be cured of your addiction, and you will be the most powerful man on earth."

"I just got to do this last job for Wyatt."

"Then after that, you will use your power for good?"

"You and me, together, we're going to change the world. The globalization thing, right? We'll take it on."

He wanted to believe it. But Wyatt never let anyone go. If the colonel kept him alive, it would be as a tool for dispensing death. Until he himself was dead.

His cell phone buzzed on the mattress. Maj picked it up and read the text. Getmanov tried to measure her reaction. He knew what was coming. Wyatt had given him enough of a hint. It was a deal only a killer or a junkie could accept. Once you poison yourself the first time, you know that you would extinguish a universe if it meant you might continue murdering yourself with the drugs. And Getmanov was both a killer and a junkie.

She turned to him, puzzled, and showed him the phone. "What does this mean? Shane, what does he want from me?"

"He wants you to make someone think you're going to screw him, so that *he'll* do what Wyatt wants."

"Screw?" She spoke the word with wonder and curiosity.

His laughter was sinister, and she recoiled in fear. She'd better get used to being scared. She ought to have let him die. If she wanted him alive, she'd have to trip the light frightful with him from time to time.

She reread the text message. "He says I have to go to Vienna."

"My army psych told me about Vienna. That's where Simon Freud is from."

"Sigmund Freud."

"The psych told me that Freud wrote something like this: Wars happen because being civilized is too much stress for human beings. Every couple of years we have to go totally wing nut and fight a war. It scares us into being kind of peaceful again, until a couple of years later the same thing happens—we just can't take it, and so we fight another war."

"But you can't ignore the fact that wars are fought for corporate interests. That isn't because of a great cultural psychosis. It's because some fat, white man in New York wants to boost his profits, so he calls another fat, white man in Washington, and they arrange to fight a war."

"What I think is that all men want to be killers. See, when you're a soldier, every guy you meet pretends like you and he are the same. You can hear it in the way they use military jargon, and they get this tone of voice that's just too casual. Like they know *everything*. Bottom line: the guy believes he's less of a man than you because he was never in a war. When I meet a guy like that, I just want to blow him away because I know that he's envying me for the exact thing that's making me crazy. The thing that makes me want to die. That's why I mainline this Russian shit, and it's what I feel every day—please God let me die real soon."

She gazed at him, and this time her pity angered him. "So Maj, what you're going to do in Vienna is, you're going to keep me alive because you want me alive. You want to use me for something that you think is important to the future of the world? To fight globalization? What the hell, I'll go along with that. But you're going to Vienna for your own sake, baby. Don't make it like you're going for me. I'd rather be dead."

She crossed her arms over her breasts.

He crawled toward her, his eyes narrowed and his lip caught between his teeth. He was ready to make love to her now. She seemed not to notice his excitement. She picked up the phone and read the rest of the message from Wyatt. "He wants *you* to go to Cologne."

The message meant that the next victim was ready. Wyatt had found another one of the Chinese guys. The caustic sensation in his liver started again. His sexual excitement died.

"He writes something else. What does this mean?" She stared at the screen of the phone. "'The past is all ahead of you.'"

He means I'm never going to get away from him, the Krokodil thought. He stood up. The skin of his knees tugged around the joints like a severe sunburn. Those were new scabs. He'd be lucky to last long enough to nail the fifth Chinese engineer. He grinned, bitterly. Lucky, indeed.

CHAPTER 14

Todd and Kinsella sifted through digests of the accident reports, the news of the dead and injured from the Darien crashes coming in from all over Europe, the Americas, the Middle East, the Pacific. They looked for a pattern or a connection beyond what they already knew—that everything had gone down at the same moment and had affected every Darien car purchased in the last year. Kinsella sat back and watched Todd stare at the printouts on his desk. The concentration on his face made him look youthful, a college kid cramming for a test. She pushed her hair out of her face. The bangles on her wrist tinkled. He glanced up at her.

"We've got to get out there and do something," he said. "These reports are making me nuts."

"Me too. But . . . do what?"

Todd sighed.

From the next cubicle, Roula Haddad called out to them. "You guys need cheering up. Just this minute, I happen to have found the very thing."

They were out of their chairs and into her small office space in an instant. They crowded either side of her, leaning over her desk eagerly, staring at the dozen browsers and apps open on her two screens.

"I tracked the Bitcoin transfer," Haddad said. "The one from China to the dead computer engineer in Detroit."

"How'd you do that? Bitcoin's anonymous, no?" Kinsella said.

"Up to a point. Once you get a break in the anonymity, you can work away at it until it starts to crumble. That's what I've been doing all night."

"So where did it take you?"

"The dead engineer's wife, Mo Hui, told me her husband's Bitcoin address. She looked it up on his phone for me. It's just a string of numbers." Haddad called up a file of digits and brief notes on her screen, and pointed at a row of figures.

"That takes us into the Bitcoin system?" Todd folded his arms. He wasn't great with numbers. When he was groping intellectually, he did the very opposite with his body.

"It gets us in. But it doesn't get us far, unless we get lucky."

"Please tell me we got lucky." Kinsella put her elbow on Todd's shoulder and leaned against him. She felt confident. Roula Haddad was always lucky. She was also smarter than anyone Kinsella ever worked with, at least when it came to the mysterious realms of the digital world.

"Not at first. I identified the transaction from China. But it was made with an onion router. So I couldn't track it to the Internet service provider."

"From the ISP, you would've got address and bank details."

"That's right. But I had the Bitcoin address of the China guy. So I took it to the exchange."

"The Bitcoin exchange?"

"Not *the* Bitcoin exchange. There's a bunch of different ones. This is where Bitcoin turns out not to be as anonymous as criminals and privacy freaks believe. The Bitcoins are issued by an exchange, and they're subsequently traded through exchanges too. That's the weakness in the system, if you're a criminal or a paranoid guy who thinks the government's going to come whisk you away in silent black helicopters."

"What does the exchange tell us?"

"Like all the Bitcoin exchanges, the exchange that this transaction went through is subject to international banking laws, including money laundering regulations. They're also evangelists for Bitcoin. They want people to feel safe using the currency, and it bugs them that it has a reputation for criminal activity. So the moment I called them and gave them my tough-guy voice, they threw up their hands."

"Can we hear the tough-guy voice?" Todd said.

"I don't want to scare you."

"I can take it. What, do you model the voice on some bad dude you've arrested at ICE?"

"Bill, I grew up in Lebanon. We learned the tough-guy voice before we learned how to cross the road and write cursive." She scrolled down her screen to a pasted e-mail from the Bitcoin exchange.

Kinsella read it aloud. "The source of the funding is a bank account in Luxembourg?"

Haddad moved her cursor to the next paragraph. "Here it is. Bainc Príobháideach."

"Is that Gaelic?"

"Congratulations to the Irish lady with the red hair."

Kinsella growled.

"Apparently you pronounce it more or less like the word 'private,'" Haddad said. "Which is what it means. Private Bank."

"But it's based in Luxembourg?"

"A lot of financial services companies have at least an address there. Luxembourg doesn't ask too many questions, and it has a very, very easy corporate tax regime. The bank uses Irish Gaelic for its name because it makes it different from any other Luxembourg bank, I guess, so no one gets confused—and because it's run by an Irish guy."

"You called him up?"

"Mister Dermot McCarthy was very polite at first. Then a little nasty."

"I assume you said something that *turned* him nasty. The tough-guy voice?"

"IRS is conducting tax evasion investigations into one hundred and twenty United States citizens with accounts at Bainc Príobháideach. The probe is at a very early stage. I contacted one of our counterparts at IRS and asked him to give me a stick to beat Mister McCarthy with."

"Talk or we fast-track the investigations of his American account holders?"

"Bingo. But I offered him a carrot too. When IRS heard the connection to our investigation of the Darien mess, they okayed me to make an offer to McCarthy. If he gives up the details behind the Bitcoin account, we give him six months' grace. Time he can use to protect his American account holders and shuffle their cash off to his bank's subsidiary in the Bahamas."

"So he doesn't lose the clients, who in turn love him forever for beating the Feds. Did he go along with it?"

"As enthusiastically as if I had offered him a trade-in for his new Darien sedan."

"Who's the account holder linked to our Bitcoin transfer?"

"It's a guy named Nabil Allaf. It's a pretty common Arab name, and I don't have any further trace on it. I'm also not yet certain that it's a real identity. McCarthy says he opened the account remotely. He's never met Allaf."

"Do we have documentation from the bank?"

"McCarthy is sending it."

Todd shook his head. "We can't trust him to be open with us. Bankers are bigger scum than dope dealers. We've got to go there and lean on him."

"To Luxembourg?" Kinsella said.

"You can work your Irish charm on him."

"Christ on a bike, Bill. I pride myself on being the only charm-less Irish person in the world."

"Even better. You won't fall for his blarney."

"Don't use that word. No more Irish stuff."

"We're going, though?"

Kinsella showed her crooked teeth. "We're going to Luxembourg."

CHAPTER 15

Behind the straggling early commuters, the bulbous dome of St. Mariä Himmelfahrt squatted at the top of its square, cream-colored steeple and Cologne's massive Gothic cathedral reached up into the gray sky. Jahn craned her neck and peered at the flying buttresses and the prickling stonework of the spires. "We're surrounded by God," she whispered.

Verrazzano ignored her and strode faster toward the main railway station. No heavenly power was about to swing down from those medieval towers to drive out evil. That was his job.

They entered the station and went down the steps to the broad tunnel that accessed all the trains. Under platform four, a young woman dealt out espresso beneath the canopy of the Lavazza store. Verrazzano greeted the woman in Italian and ordered an espresso. Jahn frowned at the menu above the counter. "Americano."

The Italian barista slipped an extra couple of tiny square chocolate mints into the saucer of Verrazzano's coffee and smiled, rewards for speaking Italian and ordering his coffee made the right way. She set Jahn's coffee on the counter with the dismissiveness of any Italian who's asked to dribble way too much water through a perfectly good shot of espresso. Verrazzano took his cup, sank it in one gulp, and set it down. "*Bravo*," the barista said.

Jahn's phone buzzed. She took it from her pocket and read a text message. "It's from Hemming at FBI Detroit. No luck finding

Frisch. He's going to keep trying, but the Detroit field office is stretched pretty thin with all the fallout from the crash. He has to go interview a bunch of executives at Darien today." She put the phone away.

Verrazzano glanced about him. Someone was watching, he sensed it.

"What is it?" Jahn sipped her coffee. Then she picked up on his alertness and rattled the cup into her saucer. "Is it Frisch? Is he here?"

"I don't know."

"You said he'd get to Germany. The Detroit office couldn't track him down. It's him, isn't it?"

Verrazzano felt a hand against his elbow. He looked down. An eight-year-old boy watched him with a pale, blank face. He wore a black hoodie and sweat pants. Without a word, he turned and ran, ungainly and stiff, through the commuters dodging for the steps to the platforms.

"Let's go, Gina." Verrazzano set off, tracking the boy by the red lights that glowed in the heels of his sneakers with every step.

They came out of the tunnel at the rear of the station. The eight-year-old ran past an impromptu shrine to the victims of the big crash, candles and flowers and smiling photos of the dead attached to a Darien van that had run up onto the curb and smashed into a lamppost. The kid jumped into an orange Mini Cooper. The car sped away east, dodging between the traffic and the roadblocks created by wrecked Dariens that were still to be removed. Verrazzano dashed for a taxi and jumped into the passenger seat beside the driver, a trim, young Turk with tired eyes and his hair done in a fauxhawk. Jahn climbed in the back.

"Go this way," Verrazzano told the driver.

The Turk rolled his skinny shoulders under his tight T-shirt and swung across the traffic.

The Mini led them down a broad tree-lined avenue of plain sixties architecture. It moved carefully. Verrazzano figured the driver of the little car was probably the eight-year-old's parent—worried enough about being recognized to send the child to signal Verrazzano but not sufficiently reckless to crash the car with their son on board. In any case, the roads in the city had seemed unnaturally calm and silent as he drove in from Frankfurt that morning. Drivers were still in shock from the Darien crash, piloting their cars delicately and with an awkward awareness of death, like people whispering at a funeral. He laid his hand on the taxi driver's forearm. "Stay back a bit," he said.

The driver frowned lazily and shifted down to third.

Verrazzano watched the sideview mirror. A man on a motor scooter weaved along the street behind them. He wore a white helmet with the visor pulled down and a brown bomber jacket.

"What did you see?" Jahn said.

"Don't turn around. Someone is onto us."

Jahn keep her eyes to the front. "If the Mini is taking us to where we want to go, we can't stay there long. Whoever's on our tail might intervene."

The orange car turned onto a narrower street of Internet cafés, Indian restaurants, and Turkish bakeries. A quick cut into a side street, and the car was out of sight. Verrazzano tapped at the driver's elbow urgently. The taxi pulled around the corner.

The Mini was nosed up to the curb beside a row of green plastic trash cans. Verrazzano got out of the car in a hurry. The scooter hadn't made the turn into the side street behind him. He passed the orange car. It was empty. Across the sidewalk was a boarded-up storefront. Posters for DJ nights at the local clubs covered the planking. A door sawed from the wood creaked open.

Verrazzano pushed the door in the storefront boards and went inside. He crept through the darkness, carefully and decisively.

Jahn stayed a couple of paces behind him. Verrazzano used his peripheral vision, where the rods around the edge of his eye were less sensitive to changes in light than the color receptors in the central cones. The room was a profoundly messy office, maybe a reception room for a bigger office beyond the back wall. Papers were stacked all over the three desks, on chairs, on top of filing cabinets. On the walls, posters showed lonely polar bears on shrinking ice floes, Indian children starving, ugly fat cats in mammoth SUVs. In the half-light, he saw the open door in the back of the room. He went silently through the door. The room was darker still. He made his eyes wide.

A desk light flicked on, directed at his face. He dropped his glance to the floor. Behind him Jahn covered her eyes with her hand.

"Put your guns on the ground." A woman's voice, German accented. The woman who had told him over the phone to come to Cologne.

Verrazzano drew his H&K and set it on the floor.

"You too," the woman said.

Verrazzano gestured for Jahn to put her pistol down. Reluctantly she bent and set it beside his H&K.

The woman whispered, and the boy scuttled through the dark to pick up the guns. He held them flat in his hands and disappeared beyond the spot lamp. The woman reached out and took the H&K. "Sit down. On that chair beside you." She held the gun on Verrazzano.

He stumbled against a bent-chrome chair and lowered himself onto the worn fabric of the seat. "I'm going to show you my ID." He waited a moment, then took out his wallet. He held up his ICE picture card.

A striplight in the ceiling flickered into action. The room went ice blue. It was as cluttered as the reception office. Aung San Suu Kyi and Bono looked inspiring and compassionate in posters above the desk. Beside them, George W. Bush wore a pair of cartoon devil's horns and a stiff breeze lifted Donald Trump's hair to give away the secret of his double comb-over.

The woman was less than five feet from Verrazzano even though she kept her back against the far wall. She was about fifty, her hair gray and layered short all over her head. She wore a dirty green parka, though the room was warm. She blinked her eyes hard. Verrazzano wondered if the tic was permanent or only a result of the stress of having two law enforcement officers in front of her and, he believed, knowledge of a series of deaths. She raised Verrazzano's H&K toward him. "Why do you want to see Turbo?"

Verrazzano glanced about him. On the desk was a pile of letters, ready to be folded into envelopes. The letterhead was a cartoon of a kid filling his lungs and swift marks suggesting the air he sucked in. The cartoon boy leaned back happily against the words *Luft und Leben*—Air and Life. Verrazzano figured that was the name of the organization that kept its offices in these rooms under the railway embankment. The top letter asked for help, a fund raiser. It was signed Saskia Hütz. Probably the woman in front of him, and hopefully the Saskia whose number the dead Chinese engineer had erased from his whiteboard at the factory in Rüsselsheim. The walls showcased still more misery and injustice from around the world. The photos were stark and hard to bear. *If Saskia only knew the true depths of that injustice, she'd rip this shit right off the walls in frustration*, Verrazzano thought. *But God bless her for caring.*

"What's Turbo's real name?" he said.

"Wang Fu."

A Chinese name. The next engineer. "Where does he work?"

"The Wolfwagen subsidiary just across the border in Holland."

"What's his connection to you?"

"I am opposed to high carbon-dioxide emissions by cars. The car companies try to convince people that they are environmentalists, that they are green, that they will not destroy the environment. I develop sources inside the car companies so that I can find out what they are really doing."

"Turbo is one of your sources."

"He was. Now he is scared. He came to me to hide."

"We believe Turbo can help us stop a very serious event that may be about to happen. An event that could kill a lot of people. We also believe Turbo can help us figure out who's responsible for something that already killed a lot of people."

He expected more questions. Instead, the woman said, "Yes, he can."

Verrazzano waited. "Where is he?"

"Maybe he doesn't want to help you."

"But you do."

"Do I?"

"A lot of kids just like your boy could be hurt if we don't stop this." Verrazzano gestured to the walls of the room, the posters of starving children and dried up riverbeds. "Clearly you care about people's lives."

She lowered the gun and came forward, crouching, filled with anger. "Maybe I think everyone in the West should get a wake-up call. Maybe they need a very, very loud noise for that. Maybe a lot of cars—"

Jahn flashed out her hand and snatched the pistol from the woman. The woman shrieked. Jahn jumped toward the door and raised the gun.

"What the hell are you doing, Gina?" Verrazzano said.

Jahn snarled at him. For an instant, Verrazzano couldn't tell if she aimed to shoot him or the German woman. The little boy sniveled.

"Gina, you're out of line." He stood in front of her.

Jahn's teeth showed in the bright spot lamp, on edge. She growled as she relaxed her arms and lowered the gun.

"Go watch the street." Verrazzano took his pistol from her. "I'll take care of this."

Jahn picked up her weapon from the desk. She turned to the German woman. "Special Agent Gina Jahn. Federal Bureau of Investigations."

"I know all about the FBI."

The defiance in the German woman's voice seemed to needle Jahn. "I bet the FBI knows all about you too. What's your name?"

"Saskia Hütz."

"That your boy?"

"His name is Markus."

"He's a cool little customer. Where's this guy Turbo?"

"I'm almost right up your ass." A Chinese man in a brown bomber jacket came through the door behind Jahn. He held a white motorbike helmet. The man who followed them from the station on his scooter. "Don't worry. I said 'almost.' Turbo only likes black guys."

He was tall and skinny. His cheeks were dark with a slick black beard and punctuated with white eruptions of acne.

"Be serious, Turbo," Hütz said. "And do not speak that way in front of Markus."

"He doesn't speak English, Saskia."

"I'm not referring to your words. He will understand your tone and your behavior."

Turbo's laugh sounded like someone had stamped on a cat. He held his hand out for a high five. Markus nipped forward and laid it on him with a shy smile. "That's my little man," Turbo said in German. He turned to Verrazzano. "Are we ready to save the world? Let's go, GI Joe."

"We are ready." Verrazzano tried to pick out the Chinese man's eyes in the shadows cast across his face by the ceiling light. Turbo was so shrill, Verrazzano wondered if the guy was high.

Maybe the stress of whatever he was involved in had sent him over the edge.

Turbo struck a pose, legs braced, fists pumping at imaginary enemies. "Before you can save the world, you've got to make sure you have Turbo in your pocket, Davy Crockett."

"How do we do that?"

"Get me the hell out of Dodge. Turbo knows what Turbo shouldn't know." He made his voice childish. "Bad guys want to kill Turbo and take his scalp. Turbo's almost a dead 'un, General Patton."

Jahn moved forward. "Why do they want your scalp?"

"It's a hell of a head of hair, Kemosabe."

"Gina, we have to secure this location," Verrazzano said. "Go out and keep watch. In a few minutes, we're going to leave with—with Mister Turbo."

"The guy is disturbed," Jahn said. "I should be in here with you. What's with all these weird Americana references?"

"Hot damn, Harriet Tubman," Turbo said, "you're an American hero. America is Turbo's thing. I know more about America than Charlie Chan." The man danced and made pistol-shooting fingers at Verrazzano. The little boy giggled.

"Gina, I want to be sure there's no one waiting for us out there." Verrazzano went close to Jahn. "Come on. We've got to move. Go make certain the road is clear."

Jahn went through the front office to the street.

Turbo slunk across the room to Saskia Hütz. "You saved me, baby. You brought the cavalry. General Custer's going to take Turbo to safety."

Hütz grinned. "Better not call him General Custer. You know what happened to him."

"General Lee?"

"Not much better."

"Turbo knows how to recognize a real man." He came to his feet, jogging in place before Verrazzano. "Because I'm totally gay, JFK."

Verrazzano lifted his hands, a calming gesture. "I need information now. Start by telling me your name."

Turbo made a kung-fu kick in the air. "Wang Fu. Spelled F-U. But the real me is Turbo. Because I'm turbocharged. I force air into my combustion chamber and it makes me run at twice my natural level, Evel Knievel."

"Got it. You're one of the Happy Five?"

Turbo raised his eyebrows at the name the Chinese engineers had given themselves. "Oh-ho, somebody talked."

"Du An told me about the Happy Five. I was with him in Rüsselsheim right before he died."

Turbo faltered, the manic expression on his face momentarily disintegrating. Then he was back, eyes wide and fired up. "The Happy Five is no more. Three are dead. Now it's just the Scared Enough to Poo Two."

"I can protect you, Turbo. Who's the last member of the Happy Five?"

"It's just me and Ju."

"Me and you?"

"Ju. It's her name, Billy Graham. How did Du An get whacked and waxed?"

"A man leaned out of a crane, cut his throat, and scalped him."

Turbo touched his fingertips to the top of his head. "Feng Yi told us not to worry."

"Who's Feng Yi?"

"He said, 'It's all in your heads. But if you screw it up, it'll be *on* your heads anyway.'"

The German woman caught at Turbo's wrist. "I've done what I can for you, Turbo. I hid you here. But this man is your best hope now. Be as serious as you can."

"Turbo's in big doo-doo."

"I tried to help Du An, but I was too late. Don't you dare mess this up."

Turbo stepped back and shrugged himself free of her. He rolled his neck and muttered resentfully in Chinese. Then he took a pace toward Verrazzano. "Saskia's right. She tried to help Du An. He was a good guy. Just like Gao and Su over in the US of A. Du An warned Frau Hütz, and she got me into hiding before they came for me."

"Who're *they*?"

"The real monsters with the fangs so long, King Kong." He was shuffling quickly on his feet again. "All I ever wanted to do was break into American corporate computer networks or hack the Pentagon. I was good at *that*—sitting in the military intelligence tower in Beijing, drilling through all these systems that were supposed to be secure, laughing my skinny ass off about how easy it was to get around the security systems. Then the Big Pig put me on the team. The Happy Five. He trained us, brainwashed us. Did other stuff to us that you wouldn't understand."

"Try me."

"He made me into a piece of computer code. That's all I am now. My soul is so weary, Timothy Leary."

Verrazzano had interrogated drugged-up street mopes. But this interview was all over the place, throwing up too many questions he needed to answer. "Do you have a chip implanted in your head?"

"This isn't a sci-fi shtick, Philip K. Dick. This is really real reality."

"Then who is *he*? Who's the Big Pig?"

Turbo shook his head. "You make me safe, and if nothing goes wrong, Neil Armstrong, Turbo tells you the whole story."

"We don't have much time."

"You've got more time than Turbo does if you don't look after him right."

The German woman put her hand on Turbo's shoulder and spoke to Verrazzano. "I have a friend who lives in the forest south of Bonn. She will let us hide out there, if you can get us out of Cologne. It's about an hour's drive."

Verrazzano stroked at his chin. "I'll send Agent Jahn to get our vehicle, and we'll leave as soon as she's back."

"You're so awesome and handsome, Charlie Manson." Turbo raised his hand for a high five.

Verrazzano didn't respond to the gesture. "I need you to talk now, Turbo."

"He just agreed to tell you everything," Hütz said.

"I want to be sure I'm protecting a guy who's worth keeping safe."

"You're making Turbo angry." The man blinked frantically. "You want to be told, Lee Harvey Oswald? Okay, the Party put our team together."

"The Chinese Communist Party?"

"Yeah, which is also known as 'the government.' We wrote a program that would make a car go out of control on certain dates. The boss man sent us to work at different car companies in Europe and America."

"Who's the boss man?"

"I already told you. It's Feng Yi, Muhammed Ali. We were undercover more than a year after he sent us out. In that time, all the cars produced by those companies were infected with the virus."

Verrazzano's guts chilled. "How many cars would that be? Every car produced by five companies?"

"More than that. Every car company owns a bunch of other companies. Say you put something in the computer at Wolfwagen, it gets written directly into the software on all the company's sub-sidiaries. In the Czech Republic, Spain, and the rest of Germany."

"How do I stop it?"

"You don't leave me alone, Al Capone. Make me safe. That's how you stop it."

"You know the code? How to deactivate it?"

"I know how to *activate* it."

"Tell me. Maybe we could reverse the code and—"

"Actually it's me and the other Happy Five guys. We all know. All of us together."

"But three of them are dead. Does that mean the code can't be activated?"

Turbo faltered again. "I—I don't understand it. It's only going to work with all of us."

"So why are they killing you? Is the killer trying to *stop* the cars going out of control?"

Turbo sank into the chair by the door. "The big swine in the Party wanted to use the threat of chaos and death on the roads at the trade negotiations."

The trade talks were happening now in Vienna. Verrazzano imagined a scenario—someone else had uncovered the Chinese plan, and the killings of the engineers were intended to stop the cars crashing. Something about that didn't sound right. "The first crash with all the Dariens was meant to be a warning. By Gao Rong in Detroit. Was it a warning to the parties at the trade talks? If so, it could actually make the Chinese threat more real, more powerful."

Turbo howled a few words in Chinese, angrily, cursing. Verrazzano couldn't pick out anything except the name of Feng Yi. "The Big Pig had to get someone outside the Party who he could use to activate the code. He hooked up with some nasty American wacko."

That had to be Wyatt. "What was the American's name?"

"Whichever way I turn, I'm screwed like hot booty, Bill Cosby." He lowered his head and rocked back and forth.

The German woman got in Verrazzano's face. "You're thinking someone else decided to snuff out these computer guys so the Chinese wouldn't be able to use them to activate the code?" she said.

"It's possible, isn't it?"

"So you're also thinking you should just let them rub out Turbo and the other programmer? In fact, maybe you should give them a hand right now."

Verrazzano glanced at the woman's kid.

"Oh, of course, you won't do it in front of the little boy." Hütz's voice was loaded with contempt. "But you'll murder Turbo as soon as my son is out of the room. You disgust me, you government people. I won't let you do it. If you don't protect Turbo, I will go to every investigative journalist in Germany with this story. I have been recording this meeting."

Turbo seemed to catch the hardness in Verrazzano's face. It brought him out of his reverie. He jumped up from the chair. "He'll kill you too, Saskia."

"I'm not going to kill you." Verrazzano watched the boy reach for his mother's hand. That hadn't stopped him before. In the stairwell of the building in Beirut. He had assassinated Maryam Ghattas in front of her own child. On the orders of Colonel Wyatt. A Lebanese human-rights campaigner who, Wyatt told him, was working for Syrian intelligence and had helped kill American agents. A woman who was about to implicate him in the killing of the country's prime minister. "I'm not going to . . ." His whisper trailed off.

"I'm not scared," Hütz said.

"Everybody's scared."

The woman lowered her voice. "Tell your colleague to get the car."

"We have to stop at a pharmacy on the way." Turbo rubbed at his stringy hair.

"A pharmacy? What do you need?" Verrazzano asked. The guy *was* drugged up, after all. Maybe he was on prescription medication.

"You'll see." Turbo gave a crafty smile and mimed the twirling of a big mustache. "I've got a hell of a surprise for you, Nancy Drew. But you have to let me buy a couple of things at the pharmacy when we're on the way out of town. I need them to show you what I've got."

"Fine."

From out on the street, Jahn shouted words Verrazzano couldn't pick out. He rushed through the front office. As he reached to pull back the board door, bullets ripped through it. It swung open. Verrazzano stepped onto the sidewalk.

To his right, a man in a black pea coat and jeans ran in a crouch in the lee of the buildings. He ducked into an alley.

Jahn was on the far sidewalk. She held her pistol, trained toward the alley, looking for a shot at the man in the pea coat. She gave it up and sprinted across the empty street. "That's the guy," she shouted. "In the alley. It's him."

The Krokodil. They jogged to the alley where the man had run. It was short and ended in a ten-foot wall. Verrazzano braced himself across the narrow space, back against one side and feet climbing the other. He wiggled his shoulders to raise himself up. Beyond the wall, a slope of untended grass and a light sprinkling of trash rose to the train track at the top of the embankment. He kneeled on the top of the bricks and leaned out, scanning along the bank.

He jumped back down to Jahn. "I don't see him."

From the street back down the alley, they heard a woman scream. "No, don't do it. No, Turbo."

Jahn took off. Verrazzano hurried after her. In the doorway of Hütz's office, the German woman stood with her son, holding him tightly to her side. She lifted her eyes to Verrazzano, and he understood that she thought he would kill her now to erase the story she might tell the investigative journalists. There was also another dimension to her fear that he recognized immediately. Like the Ghattas woman in Beirut, not afraid for herself, but terrified that he would kill her in front of her child.

"It's okay, Saskia," Verrazzano said. "We're going to get you out of here. Everybody's okay."

The boy pressed his face into his mother's belly. She kissed the crown of his head. "Turbo's gone. He got scared. He ran out of the door. You didn't see him?"

"Which way did he go?"

"I couldn't tell. I saw him go out. Then—"

Verrazzano looked along the street. Turbo might have gone past the end of the alley while he was climbing the wall with Jahn beneath him. But Turbo could just as easily have fled the other way, under the railway bridge. And the Krokodil could have him already.

"Gina, you go that way toward the main street. I'll take this direction. Find Turbo."

Jahn ran fast down the block.

Verrazzano came close to Saskia Hütz. He gave her the pistol from his hand. "Stay in your office. Turn off the lights and stay inside. If anyone comes in and doesn't identify themselves, shoot them without asking questions."

"You don't have a weapon," she said. "You're going after a killer without a weapon?"

"I'm going after Turbo. The only way he can hurt me is with famous American names and bad rhymes."

He sprinted under the railway bridge, trying the doors of all the workshops and storerooms in the arches under the track. They were locked. Around a sharp corner, the street ran into a dead end at the tall gates of a haulage company. He tried to climb the gates, but he couldn't get over. The yellow iron struts were too tall and slippery with the damp air. Turbo hadn't gone that way.

A red-and-silver commuter train sped by on the rails above him. The overhead electrical line spat sparks from the trolley pole that connected it to the train. Amid the crackle and hiss from the catenary, Verrazzano heard another noise. Gunfire. The sound was distant enough that he knew it wasn't from the vicinity of Hütz's office. The woman and her kid were safe for now.

He sprinted toward the main street through the Ehrenfeld district. A siren started a long way down Venloer Strasse. Someone else had heard the gunshots and called them in. He didn't want to explain himself to a German cop. But he wanted to fail even less, so he put aside those distractions.

At the corner, he dodged through the traffic and crossed into another side road. Turbo would've gone for a quiet street—amateurs who ran always did. A professional assassin would've disappeared down the busy main drag, matching his pace to the other pedestrians, making himself invisible. Verrazzano passed a laundromat where a few glum immigrant women stared at their spinning clothes. The lights inside the FedEx office next door fluoresced on the purple and orange of the company logo. In the middle of the street, Jahn wheeled about, holding her pistol at her side, staring up at the windows of the five-story buildings around her. She ejected the magazine from the pistol and slipped in another.

"You lost him?" Verrazzano came up beside her.

"I'm sorry, Dom." She pointed into a small indoor parking lot that ran along the side of the street. A thin man clad in black lay flat on the ground between a parked Mercedes and a hydrant in the corner.

Verrazzano knelt beside Turbo. The man had two bullets in his chest and one through his brow. Blood pooled beneath his head, dripping from the bare skull where he had been scalped.

The siren was loud now. Verrazzano left Turbo and dragged at Jahn's sleeve. "Come on, let's get out of here."

They crossed Venloer Strasse and headed into Hütz's street. "Why did you need to reload?" Verrazzano asked.

Her face registered an instant of shock. Then she said, "I fired off those rounds at the Krokodil, the ones that went through the door of Hütz's office. I don't like walking around without a full deck when the Krokodil's nearby. So I switched magazines."

"Did you see him? The killer?"

"I heard the shots. But I didn't see him. When I came around the corner, Turbo was already dead and scalped."

They went back to Hütz's office. The woman and child were still in the corner. Verrazzano's face told her what had happened. She covered her mouth with her hand and hugged the boy to her.

Verrazzano retrieved his H&K from Hütz's hand and holstered it. Turbo was gone, and that was a problem for his operation. But Hütz was safe. The child was alive. That was something. He stepped out into the street. When he killed Maryam Ghattas, he had driven down to the Corniche and stared through his tears at the deep blue of the Mediterranean. The light was gray in Cologne, but he sensed all the shame he had felt back then, and his eyes were wet. The wind through the railway arches chilled him. He wiped his knuckle across his eyes.

He tried to figure how the Krokodil got around him. The last he saw him, the Krokodil had gone down the alley. Going south. Verrazzano had followed Turbo right away. The Krokodil hadn't had time to make the loop ahead of him, unless he was some kind of superhuman. The Krokodil was one of Wyatt's boys. He wasn't super, but neither was he human.

Still it troubled Verrazzano. How did the Krokodil weave through these streets to kill Turbo without being spotted? And how did he know to come to Cologne? He wondered if the assassin had seen Hütz's phone number on the whiteboard in the office at the Jansen Trapp factory too. He had assumed Du An rubbed off the German woman's name to protect her. But maybe the killer erased it so Verrazzano wouldn't see it and wouldn't follow the lead. He tried to remember if Hütz's full name had been on the whiteboard. He was sure it had been only her first name. Could the Krokodil have known of her connection to the Chinese programmers? If not, the killer had made a big bet on the chance that she was linked. Either that, or someone had told him about it.

The Krokodil was gone. Turbo was dead. There was just one more Chinese programmer out there, and she would die soon. That programmer was the only one who knew how to stop the attack that Wyatt was about to launch all over Europe and America. But Special Agent Dominic Verrazzano was clueless and stymied on a side street in a German city in the dark. He swayed with exhaustion. He was beyond the fatigue that manifests itself in the lactic-acid grip on the hamstrings during a long run or the burn in shoulders struggling to lift more weight. It was the desperate weariness of a soul surveying the landscape of malevolence and disorder in which it exists and hankering for the freedom of the grave.

Jahn came to his side. "What next?"

It took him a moment, but he brought himself back to action. "Get Hütz and the boy. We're taking them with us."

CHAPTER 16

Verrazzano reached the Audi amid a sudden burst of heavy rain over the Rhine. The downpour pitted the great river like the skin of the Krokodil. For an instant, he gazed at the wide water and thought that he could no more stop its motion toward the North Sea than he could end the assassin's killing spree. Then he shook his head and unlocked the convertible. Restaurants lined the embankment up to the Hohenzollern Bridge, where the trains rumbled out of the main station across to the giant conference hall on the eastern bank. The rain had cleared the sidewalk and the steps up to the cathedral. He slipped into the driver's seat and pressed the ignition button.

The storm drummed on the soft top. He put the car in reverse and turned in his seat to look out the rear window. The right back seat dropped forward. A Glock 19 came out of the space where the seat had been. Then the Krokodil eased his torso out of the trunk and held the weapon on Verrazzano. "The scalp," he croaked. "Hand it over."

Verrazzano frowned. The Krokodil didn't have Turbo's scalp? So who did? "I'm not the guy running around two continents leaving dead people with bad haircuts."

The Krokodil kept the Glock steady and aimed at the ICE agent. The orange streetlamps came on despite the early hour, lighting up the rain on the side window to speckle shadow over the Krokodil's face. He eased through from the trunk. The car filled with a ripe scent. The Krokodil grunted as he unfolded one leg across the back seat. His eyes glinted with the concentration of a chess master. Verrazzano held still.

"Wyatt promised you something?" Verrazzano said. "What's he going to do? Buy you a warehouse full of that drug that's eating you alive?"

"You can't make me angry enough to make a mistake," the Krokodil growled. "There's no room in me for no more than I already got." He brought his other leg through from the trunk.

"He's going to cure you. Is that it?" Verrazzano shook his head. "Don't believe anything he says."

"The hell do you know?" The Krokodil sat upright behind Verrazzano. "Just drive."

"How'd you start shooting up? To shut everything away. All the horror. Right? You were in Iraq, Afghanistan. That's where Wyatt found you."

The Krokodil jerked his Glock into Verrazzano's neck.

"You're not going to kill me," Verrazzano said. "You're going to keep me alive because you think I know where Turbo's scalp is. Anyhow you couldn't kill me if you tried."

The breath came hot and filthy over Verrazzano's shoulder, clouded with anger and hate. "You want to bet?"

"Wyatt screwed me over too. He told me I was working for the government. Special Ops. Special targets. Big policy stuff. Secret orders from the Oval Office itself. What'd he tell you?"

"To go kill a bunch of Chinamen."

"I guess he refined his methods since he worked with me. Wyatt stands to make a lot of money, right? What'd he promise you? Are you ready to do something that could cost tens of thousands of lives for that—whatever it was? Are you ready to die for that?"

"I am dying to be dead, man. I don't care what for." He pressed the Glock harder into Verrazzano's neck. "Where's the scalp?"

"The scalp of the guy you killed today?"

"The Chinese guy. Where's his scalp?"

"Why're you asking me?"

"I got you beat, old man. I'm asking you because maybe you want to save your life."

"Calling me 'old' doesn't encourage me to make you happy."

"You don't got the scalp?"

"I repeat: I do not know where Turbo's scalp is."

"If you don't got the scalp, then you don't got nothing. Except no time to live." He twitched at the barrel of the Glock to indicate that Verrazzano should turn the car. "Drive. We're going back to that German woman's office."

"I'm not taking you there." Verrazzano put the car into drive and rolled forward.

"I told you, I want the scalp."

"It's not at the office."

"Drive."

"Okay." Verrazzano made half a turn. He pointed the car toward the river and stamped on the accelerator. The Audi jumped the curb and skidded across the sodden grass and mud.

The Krokodil reached over, grabbing at the hand brake.

Verrazzano clamped his grip down on the Krokodil's wrist. He kept his foot on the pedal. The car slewed over the pedestrian walkway and hammered through the light metal handrail.

The rumbling of the wheels on the cobbles cut out. For an instant, they were in the air and it was silent, then the nose plunged into the Rhine and the mass of water arrested their speed. The river surrounded them. The convertible roof creaked.

Verrazzano grabbed the Krokodil's head and pulled it forward. He shoved the man's shoulder low to divert the pistol. "Why do you need the scalps?"

The Krokodil writhed and bellowed. Verrazzano knew he didn't have long before the roof gave way. The pressure of the water would crush them, hold them down, and drown them under the synthetic fabric. The Krokodil would know that too, but he wasn't giving up.

"Why does Wyatt want the scalps?" Verrazzano said.

"He doesn't. It's just me."

"Wyatt only wants the Chinese dead?"

"The scalps is just my thing."

"Then why didn't you scalp Su's wife in New York?"

Even while they wrestled, there was enough hesitation in the Krokodil's answer for Verrazzano to know that he was lying. The scalps were the key. "She's just a bitch. I want *men's* scalps," the Krokodil said. "Like a warrior."

The car struck a rock and tipped on its side, settling on the riverbed. The shift in the angle of the vehicle freed the Krokodil from Verrazzano's body weight. He rolled on top of Verrazzano, butting his jaw. The darkness of the river lit up with a flash of pain.

Verrazzano blinked hard. He saw a heavy knife in the Krokodil's hand. It swung at him, then cut into the roof of the car. Icy water spat through the gash. The Krokodil made another chop and shoved himself through. Verrazzano grabbed at the man's legs, but the Krokodil kicked him away and was out in the river.

The car filled completely, just as Verrazzano filled his lungs. Bullets from the Krokodil's pistol ripped the dark water around him. He struggled through the tear in the convertible roof, which was crushed down about him now. He let himself rise to the surface.

He came up, staring around for the Krokodil. He picked him up at a narrow set of steps ten yards along the embankment. Verrazzano went back underwater to stay out of sight and swam for the steps as the rain came down harder.

A train threw sparks from its overhead cable and rolled out of the main station in the direction of the railway bridge. The

Krokodil climbed the grass bank at the side of the bridge's first pillar. He looked back.

Verrazzano reached the top of the steps and jogged toward him along the embankment. "I can help you," he shouted.

The Krokodil may have heard him, through the rain and the approach of the train. Verrazzano couldn't be certain. He reached the bottom of the slope and called again. The Krokodil showed no surprise to see Verrazzano still alive, but he watched him long enough for the ICE agent to know that the assassin had believed him to be dead. Then the Krokodil swung over the barrier and rolled onto the tracks.

Verrazzano scrambled up the muddy grass. It was him up there, a boy like him who had given what no one should ever be expected to sacrifice. Given it to the military, to the country, and received nothing in return. That's why the Krokodil had been prey to the only person who showed him kindness and respect, a colonel who turned out to be the worst abuser of a man's trust you could find. Verrazzano shouted for the Krokodil to come to him. He seemed to experience all the secret terrors that had afflicted the Krokodil, compounded with his own memories of battlefield horror. He slipped on the mud, dragging himself to the side of the rails.

The train came slowly, accelerating only enough to get across the river to the next stop at the conference center on the other side.

Verrazzano staggered to the edge of the bridge. The Krokodil lay on the crossties, his eyes closed against the heavy rain. Verrazzano lifted himself over the handrail. "I can help you."

The train was less than ten yards away. The Krokodil raised his arms and held them flat to the rails above his head. He turned his face to Verrazzano and opened his eyes. He registered the compassion on the ICE agent's face, and he smiled. He moved his mouth, exaggeratedly. Verrazzano read the word on his lips: "Gotcha."

The locomotive passed over the Krokodil. Verrazzano recoiled from the crushing weight of the rail cars as they squealed by him. When the last one passed, the Krokodil was gone. Verrazzano figured he had reached up and grabbed the slow-moving train by the axle like a thirties hobo, hauling himself away from the wheels and onto the coupler.

He watched the train reach the conference center station. A moment later, it was gone again.

CHAPTER 17

The offices of Bainc Príobháideach overlooked the picturesque gorge that wound through the middle of Luxembourg City. The Alzette meandered past the old breweries, converted now to restaurants, five hundred feet below. Beyond the high span of the *Pont Rouge*, the towers of the European Court of Justice and the other institutions of the European Union climbed out of the forest of Kirchberg. In the reception area, Kinsella gazed at the skyline through a wide picture window. She perched on an ultra-modern couch that looked as though it had been designed by a toddler with a very thick crayon. Above her, a sketch of a medieval cathedral seemed lonely in the center of the wall. She twisted to examine the signature. *Jesus, it's a Warhol*, she thought. *There sure is plenty of money in private banking.* Then she whispered, "Dirty money."

"There's no other kind, darling. After all, laundering it to make it clean is a crime." A tall man in a silvery gray suit crossed the reception with his hands held out before him, going in early for the shake. "Dermot McCarthy. This is my shop. They told me two of you were coming. But there's only you? Well, you must be Special Agent Kinsella." He had a rising and falling Irish accent that seemed designed to remind you that his native country was a land of peaks and glens.

"Is it that obvious that I'm Irish?" Kinsella accepted his hand.

"It's obvious that you're the one of the two named Noelle. Where's your colleague, William?"

Waiting outside in case you try to run. "Sightseeing."

He led her down a silent corridor and into a big office. The furniture might have been rescued from a palace in some fallen Central European empire. He settled behind the gilt desk, crossed his leg, and steepled his fingers. His eyes were comfy in the hammocks of gray skin slung beneath them. He gestured to the chair across the desk.

Kinsella sat. A tumbler of whisky was ready for her. Beside the glass lay a red binder.

"I'd have just as soon sent you the material by Federal Express." McCarthy tipped his head toward the binder. "It's all in there."

"The dirty money?" Kinsella reached for the binder and opened it.

"Well, you have to allow me to keep a few secrets. Dirty money's like a dirty mind. We are all in possession, but some of us prefer to maintain a little mystery."

Kinsella scanned the first of the two dozen sheets of paper in the binder. She came across the identity page of a passport. "This is Nabil Allaf?"

"The account holder's passport details and a copy of his passport. The rest of it is mostly documents that are required of us by Luxembourg banking laws. You won't find much of interest there. Toward the end is a record of transactions. Beyond that, we haven't had much contact with Mister Allaf. People don't come to a private bank in Luxembourg to chat and swap photos of their kids."

The passport page showed a Syrian travel document in Arabic, French, and English. The photo was of a blank-faced man in his early fifties with pale skin and a trim goatee overlaying a fleshy jaw. "He gives his occupation as 'government employee,'" Kinsella said. "The Syrian government?"

"I believe that's correct, but now that you mention it, I can't be sure. Nonetheless, his place of residence is Damascus, and when there was an actual government there to employ people, it was, indeed, the Syrian government. In the current situation—well, I couldn't say exactly who or what is the operative administration there."

She flipped to the last page. "Didn't you wonder why a Syrian government employee would be depositing amounts greater than two hundred thousand dollars every month for—for six months."

The teeth McCarthy flashed were the brown of old ivory. "Noelle, darlin', I agreed to give you this information as part of an arrangement that your colleague Special Agent Haddad made between me and the United States tax authorities. It's already more than I actually *have* to do to help you. So I'll ask you to be patient with an old private banker—with the emphasis on 'private.' I'm breaking the habit of a lifetime here."

"So you just don't ask questions. That it?"

"You develop a sense of people in this trade." McCarthy pursed his lips against his steepled fingers. "I've had men come in here carrying sacks of dollars and reeking of the cocaine cartels. I've turned them away. Even when they threatened me with physical violence. I don't seek trouble, you see. But unless there's something about them that sets my antennas jumping, I provide them with my bank's services."

"Did Nabil Allaf not set your antennas jumping?"

"Nothing about the initial deposit made me suspicious."

"Except that it was a Syrian government employee who deposited—" She glanced at the papers. "Two hundred and forty-two thousand dollars. Do you know how much a Syrian government employee makes?"

"I don't know what kind of employee he was. As I'm sure you're aware, governments don't just pay people to issue driver's licenses and sweep the streets. Maybe he had a more lucrative role."

"Didn't you ask him?"

"As I mentioned, I didn't meet your man."

"So you didn't have an opportunity to use your antennas?"

The Irishman smiled thinly and was quiet.

"How did the guy open the account? Over the phone?" Kinsella read through the pages of forms filled out by Allaf. The handwriting was fluid and extroverted, leaning to the right in old-fashioned copperplate.

"The account was opened over the phone. You're correct there."

Kinsella raised her eyes. She had heard the overly deliberate phrasing that meant McCarthy was trying to be cagey. "Someone else opened the account? Not Allaf himself?"

McCarthy lowered his hands to his lap and licked his lips. If he'd signed up a new account based on a phone call from someone who didn't even pretend to be the account holder, the ICE agent would need to dig deeper. The Irishman didn't appreciate that. He looked at her with the face of a child disappointed to have forgotten to lie. "It was not the account holder himself who opened the account."

"Who was it?"

"An assistant to Mister Allaf."

"Name?"

"I don't recall, I'm afraid."

"Another Syrian?"

"Perhaps." He glanced toward a photo in a frame across his desk. It showed McCarthy with a young man who wore a Rutgers University T-shirt and baseball cap. He had the same nose and eyes as the banker. Kinsella figured it was his son.

She laid the binder on the desk. "Look at that handwriting," she said.

"What of it?"

"That's the hand of a native English speaker. It's completely fluent." Then she let her head angle a little to the left as she glared at McCarthy. "You made a deal with my colleague Special Agent Haddad. But you didn't make a deal with me. I'm just about ready to rip up that deal."

"You're going a little far, aren't you?"

"You're not going far enough. The person who set up the account for Allaf was Syrian?"

McCarthy decided to give up something more. Kinsella saw it in the businesslike way he answered her. "No. The accent. The vocabulary."

"What accent?"

"American."

"American like me, or American like John Wayne?"

"It's a while since I saw his movies—"

Kinsella jabbed a finger at the handwriting on the form. "From the voice, I assume you could also tell us something about the age of the person. This isn't a young guy's handwriting."

"Not John Wayne's accent, but not yours either," McCarthy said. "You're from the New York area, right? I'd say the accent was Southern. Fairly formal. Male. Deep voiced. As you've observed from the handwriting, if indeed it was the man on the phone who filled in those forms, he was an older man. I'd say older than me. Perhaps even in his sixties."

Kinsella took back the binder. She flipped to the last page and turned it around to show McCarthy. "These are transfers made in the last year. They're mostly to Asia, by the looks of it. But these here"—she jabbed with her freckled index finger—"are to the United States. Here, here, and here. To an account at EWYK. What's EWYK?"

McCarthy's eyes flickered toward the photo of the kid in the Rutgers gear. His sing-song accent was suddenly flat and tense. "It's a private securities trading company."

"Where?"

"They're in New York."

"The money transferred to this firm in New York City—what's it for?"

"To make a trade. An equity trade, most likely."

"On the stock exchange?"

"Not necessarily. EWYK are involved in private equity placements too."

"You're going to help me find out."

"If I called, they wouldn't tell me anything."

"You want one of my New York agents to go to them? Ask them questions? Tell them we got most of the story from our friend McCarthy at Bainc Príobháideach, but we just need to confirm a couple details with them?"

"Don't do that." He lifted his hand from the desk to his throat. He left the outline of his palm in sweat on the desk blotter. "They're not good people."

"They're stock brokers. How scary can they be?"

"EWYK stands for Eat What You Kill. That could be boastful, macho shite. But they have a reputation for being nastier than the average Wall Street hooligan."

"Did you send some instructions to EWYK along with the money? Did Allaf give *you* any special instructions to pass on?"

McCarthy dropped his head. "He's *certainly* a scary bastard."

"Allaf?"

"I told you, I never talked to Allaf."

"The man on the phone?"

"You have to protect me."

"*You* have to help us get to him. That's the only protection you get. When we take him out of circulation, you're safe."

The Irishman's tanned skin paled. Kinsella moved forward on her seat. They were coming to it. "The day he sent me instructions to wire the money and the trading instructions to New York,"

McCarthy said, "that same day he told me over the phone to go to my office window and watch the bus stop."

Kinsella stood and crossed the room. From the window, she looked over the entrance of an underground parking lot. On the street, a group of commuters waited under the canopy of the bus stop in the light rain. "And?"

"I didn't see who did it." McCarthy put his hands over his face. "My secretary went under a bus. One moment, she was waiting at the stop. Then her arms flew up as she fell forward. She was dead by the time I got down there."

"Her death was a warning?"

"Bloody Christ, she was a mother of three. Couldn't they have thought of an easier way to put the wind up me?"

Kinsella watched the street. She felt heat prickling at her scalp. Was it just the story McCarthy told? Or was she being observed from out there? She turned to him. "What were the trading instructions?"

His hands were back on the table, focusing, putting aside his secretary's death. "The instructions were to make a short sale."

"A trade that profits when the stock goes down? What stock?"

"More than one. There was a list." McCarthy trembled and his voice wavered. He knew he was about to take this whole thing up a notch.

Kinsella felt it. She figured out why. "Was Darien on the list?"

"Darien was on the list. You're right there. Then Theander. Jansen Trapp, Morota. And Wolfwagen."

"Add up those companies and all the different brands they control, you've got enough new cars to tie up every road in Europe and North America."

Kinsella saw that McCarthy had put two and two together when the Darien cars crashed a day ago. He didn't know where this was going, but he was alert enough to figure out that it might involve a repeat on a grander scale. "Call the brokers," she said.

McCarthy twisted his mouth. He picked up the phone and hit the speed dial. Kinsella came to the desk and leaned over it. It rang once before someone picked up.

"Michael, hey, it's Dermot McCarthy at Bainc Príobháideach in Luxembourg." He listened to a few curt words down the line. Then he recited a string of numbers, covering his mouth and the handset with his palm. He pulled away his hand and licked his lips before he spoke to the man on the other end of the phone. "Michael, I'm going to have to ask you to listen to me very well just now. Will you do that for me? I know the market's open, but if you don't pay attention and help me out, you and I will be finished with trading and quite possibly might be facing considerable legal difficulties. Do you understand? I'm going to put you on speakerphone." McCarthy pressed a button and set down the handset. The background clamor of a Wall Street trading room filtered through the speaker on the phone. "I'm here with an agent from the Immigration and Customs Enforcement, Michael."

Someone called out a trade close to the other end of the line. But the man stayed quiet.

"Agent Kinsella, we're on the line with Michael Herrera at EWYK. He's the equity products trading manager. Are you there, Michael?"

"What do you want?" Herrera's voice was pure concentration, as though his entire personality had been reduced like a sauce over heat to the essence that allowed him to do business.

"Well, now, we have a bit of a situation, and all," McCarthy stammered.

"What do you want?" The intonation was absolutely identical the second time Herrera spoke.

Kinsella kept her eyes on McCarthy. "This is Special Agent Noelle Kinsella. Mister Herrera, I'm an agent in the New York field office. I can have agents come to your premises in New York, or you can help us on the phone."

"What part of 'what do you want' do you guys not understand?"

The smartest people were the ones who knew how to give up what a government agent needed, without rolling over completely. Just keep the Feds from coming through the door—that was the smart guy's rule. Because when an agent arrived on your premises, you couldn't tell who'd open their mouth when they shouldn't or what the government might stumble upon.

"We are tracking an account at Bainc Príobháideach here in Luxembourg that is connected to the Darien crash. That account was used to transfer financing to EWYK."

"McCarthy, send me the account number and the transfer details by e-mail," Herrera said.

McCarthy figured he might be off the hook. His accent took on its charming, Irish breeziness once more. "I'll be happy to—"

"Do it now."

McCarthy spun toward the sleek laptop on the corner of his desk. "Okay, I'm just—ah, I'm not a computer guy, you know?" He fumbled with his index finger on the mouse and pecked at the keys with one hand. "Well, now you should have it."

An instant, then Herrera was tapping on a keyboard. "I'm looking at the account. Account in the name of Allaf, first name Nabil. Resident of Luxembourg, collateral certified with Bainc Príobháideach."

Kinsella glanced at McCarthy. "Resident of Luxembourg?"

McCarthy shook his head. "It's a service we—Sometimes our clients need to—You know?"

A tax scam. "Continue, Mister Herrera."

"The account was set up last year. There were a lot of initial trades. Then it went fairly quiet. In March we set up a series of positions on the instructions of Mister McCarthy."

"Short positions?"

"Short sales of car stocks. I'm sending you the list now."

"You're being very helpful. We appreciate it." Kinsella let the meaning of her words sink in. She probably needn't have bothered. Herrera was telling all this with the expectation that she'd look no closer at EWYK's overseas clients once she was back in New York. "What happened to the short sale of Darien?"

"We closed it out yesterday."

"When the Darien cars crashed, Darien stock went down. You bought the stocks at the low price to cover the shares you had sold earlier at a higher price. The difference—the drop in price—was profit."

"That's correct."

She turned McCarthy's laptop toward her. The list of car companies sold short with Allaf's account appeared on the screen. "What was the profit?"

"Darien shares dropped in one day from twelve bucks to two bucks. The account held a short position of a half million shares. The trade cleared five million profit."

"Didn't anyone in the market notice you close out the position? Didn't anyone question that?"

"Are you kidding? They couldn't get Darien out the door fast enough, and we were buying."

"What did you do with the proceeds of the trade?"

"We transferred it under instructions from Bainc Príobháideach."

"The money came back into the account?"

Herrera was quiet a moment. "You need to discuss that with Mister McCarthy."

Kinsella frowned at McCarthy. The Irishman's shoulders shrank into chest, and his torso sunk down toward his waistband. He tried to smile. Kinsella had seen dead bodies with more gaiety in their faces.

"There might be another account, see," McCarthy said. "Well, I say 'might be.' Yes, there is another account, in fact."

"Another account?" She saw the light on the phone go out. Herrera had hung up. "Held by Nabil Allaf?"

McCarthy shook his head. His face blanched to the color of his gray sideburns.

"Who's the account holder?" Kinsella said.

McCarthy shook his head again.

Kinsella grabbed the photo of the young man from the desk. "This is your son? He's studying at Rutgers?"

McCarthy murmured something that sounded like "yes," though his lips were pressed tight.

Kinsella waved the photo in front of his face. "I can make his student visa go away and have him on a plane out of the United States in six hours. You got me? I don't know what future you have in mind for your boy, but a deportation from the US doesn't look good on the background check for any job, does it?"

She slammed the framed photo onto the desktop right before McCarthy. "Talk to me."

"The account." McCarthy worked hard to get some spit into his mouth. He croaked, "It's held by a gentleman named Lawton Wyatt."

"Who's Wyatt?"

"He's the man who—" McCarthy shook his head remorsefully.

"Damn it, who's Lawton Wyatt?"

"The man who set up the first account. The man with the Southern accent."

Kinsella clicked her tongue. McCarthy had been a bad boy. "When did he open the account?"

"About a half hour after the Darien crashes."

The first Chinese engineer to die, Gao Rong, worked at Darien. The third one to die told Verrazzano that Gao had made the Dariens crash earlier than they were supposed to. This Lawton Wyatt had moved quickly to take the profit from his short sale of Darien stock. He'd have expected to have more time before the crash happened, but Gao's move blindsided him. Perhaps using his own name was an error caused by haste. Kinsella had to push McCarthy. "Is the money still in the account? The Wyatt account?"

"Some of it."

"The rest?"

"I was instructed to use it to purchase Bitcoins." He choked on the last word before he managed to get it out.

"For what?"

"To send them to another Bitcoin user."

"Give me the Bitcoin account ID."

CHAPTER 18

The pianist played another damned waltz. Wyatt had been in Vienna three hours, and he had already heard almost the entire output of Johann Strauss, the nineteenth-century king of the three-step. The waiter set down another coffee for the colonel and a plate with Feng Yi's second slice of Sachertorte. Feng leaned over the plate and sniffed the rich chocolate. He forked up a big mouthful and sat back, face toward the ceiling in ecstasy. He ran his palms over the bench seat's expensive velvet upholstery. When he brought his gaze down to Wyatt, the pleasure disappeared from his features. "You're a downer, Colonel," he said, chewing with his mouth open.

"If you want a buddy to share conversation and indulgent desserts, you'd best try one of them chubby State Department dweebs."

"Mostly those guys are all worked out. Pumped. The kind that are at the gym before six in the morning. Type A, you call it, right? But there are one or two sad fatties, you're right."

Wyatt drank the rest of his mélange and set the cup down. The Austrian coffee was bitter and thin. Like him. *At least it won't kill you*, he thought. That's where it differed from him. He folded his hands on his knee and waited.

Feng sighed. Down to business. "I am not convinced that you have done as you are required, Colonel Wyatt." He took another bite of cake. "You set everything up very well. But I asked you to make sure that we could stop things at short notice. Have you done this?"

The pianist finished the waltz. In the quiet that followed, the chants of the antiglobalization protesters came through from the street outside. When Wyatt entered the hotel, a famous Indian writer had been bawling into a megaphone for the edification of a crowd of about two hundred European kids in camouflage jackets and kaffiyeh scarves. The Indian was opposed to a big dam back home that screwed over some peasant villages. The Euro kids were mad about that. Wyatt said to Feng, "I made sure the operation could be aborted at will."

Feng glanced out of the window, into the street at the protesters thrusting their placards and banners into the air. He seemed to be looking for someone. "No, no. I mean, have you stopped it?"

Wyatt wasn't about to pull back from the edge. He had been ordered to look over into the abyss, and then he had been told to jump. Told by someone to whom he owed a greater allegiance than this Chinese cyberwarfare mope with a mouthful of chocolate cake. Dick Bruce wanted this operation to go ahead, and Wyatt was almost scared of Bruce. Scared, at least, of the power he wielded and his absolute unconcern for the welfare of any living being except himself. "I am in the process of rescinding the orders to the operatives."

Feng translated that slowly, making sure he wasn't reversing the meaning of the complicated English phrasing. "Is that a yes?"

"To what question?"

Feng threw down his tiny fork. "You think I am a joker, Colonel?"

Wyatt stared. "What do you care what I think?"

"I care how you respond to me and my orders, and I'm also noting the fact that you chose not to answer the question about

170

whether I am a joker." Feng had another hard stare out of the window toward the protesters. He wiped his mouth and stood up. "Come with me."

Wyatt followed Feng to the lobby. They went out past a crowd of security men with their earpieces and shades, the Americans and Europeans and Chinese bodyguards spread in tangents that never met. Spotlights illuminated the State Opera House for a performance of Beethoven's *Fidelio*. The Austrian police watched the Indian author give the crowd what it wanted. Feng took Wyatt's elbow and led him along Kärntner Strasse toward the Ring.

Some of the antiglobalization punks had broken away from the protest and headed for the U-Bahn. Feng and Wyatt went down the steps to the subway with them. They entered a long tunnel that cut under the old ring road and led to the Karlsplatz station. The tunnel was crowded, and the musty air smelled vaguely of marijuana. Feng gestured toward a young couple who had evidently left the protest not long before. The man's head was shaven, and he wore a desert camouflage jacket and a long, pointed ginger goatee. He was in his midtwenties, a few years older than his girlfriend, whose blonde hair was also shaved, except for a long wisp that came out of the crown of her head. She wore a shapeless green hoodie and a kilt, and her ear was circled by enough rings to hang all the curtains in a suburban family home. At her side, she held a placard made for the protest. It showed a montage of old, jowly, male faces clipped out of magazines and glued onto the wasted, black bodies of poor Africans. In the English of someone writing in a second language, the slogan read, "Imagine to live with $1 every day only. Fatfarm Nazis." Wyatt recognized the faces. Dick Bruce was on the extreme left. That, he thought, showed how little those punks knew.

Feng elbowed Wyatt's arm and winked. He took out his cell phone and scuttled to the side of the two protesters. He spoke in a voice loud enough for Wyatt to hear and in a faintly ridiculous caricature of a Chinese accent: "Hey, guys, hey. I like the placard."

The two protesters stared at Feng's blue suit and red tie with hostility. He wasn't put off. He followed them through the ticket turnstile, sliding around the barrier without paying.

"You have to buy a ticket," the girl said in Austrian-accented English.

Wyatt smiled. Just because you have a pin through your tongue doesn't mean you've quit the middle class and all its rules of good behavior.

Feng laughed and got between the two people. He led them to the end of the train platform. "Can you take a picture of me with your placard? I think it's a cool protest, man."

The girl held the placard up, examining it. "Yeah, Bernd worked hard on it. It was his idea."

"Then get a picture of me and Bernd with your cool poster, baby."

Feng handed her his phone. She didn't like being called baby, but she raised the phone to take a shot anyway. Feng got in close to the placard with Bernd on the other side. She took the snap.

"Now with you. What's your name?"

"Silvia."

"Silvia what?"

"Weiss."

"Beautiful name, Silvia Weiss. What is the name of your father?"

"My father? Gerhard. Why do you want—?"

"I'm Randy. That's not my real name. All North Koreans take a Western name when they travel. Our own names are too difficult for Westerners to say."

Wyatt waited behind the barrier, wondering what this was all about. The train rattled along the tunnel, nearing the station. The commuters and protesters leaned forward to watch its approach.

"You're from North Korea?" Her voice was awed and yet suspicious as she posed for the photo.

"Workers' paradise." Feng took his phone back. He shook hands with Bernd and held onto his pale wrist. "You guys are the best. You give me hope for the West."

The train burst out of the tunnel into the station no more than ten yards from Feng and the two Austrians. Feng yanked hard on Bernd's hand and swung the young man out onto the track. The train screeched into him, the brakes squealing louder even than the girl. Feng punched her hard in the face. She fell to the ground.

Feng skipped through the turnstile and went past Wyatt. "Clean it up," he said. He went along the tunnel, back toward the Hotel Sacher.

On the platform people screamed. Some gathered around the prone girl. She lifted herself onto her elbows, leaking blood from her nose. Bystanders stared about them, looking for the perpetrator, wondering if they had been deceived in what they thought they had seen. A pair of policemen hurried along the platform. One of them knelt beside the girl.

Wyatt's cell phone buzzed. He took it out of his pocket and glanced at the screen. A text from Feng. He opened it up. It was the picture of the young Austrian man and Feng with the faces obscured by the kind of dumb filters high schoolers slapped onto photos in Snapchat. The Austrian guy had a Mickey Mouse face. Feng had a halo. On the placard the features of Dick Bruce were replaced with the head of the devil. Wyatt spun toward the tunnel. Feng knew. Knew that Wyatt was working for the US commerce secretary. What else did he know? He had pasted the devil over Bruce's face. Wyatt thought, *I guess he knows almost all there is to know.*

CHAPTER 19

Saskia Hütz made coffee in a battered steel *macchinetta* on the gas stove. Verrazzano washed out the cups and stood them in the drying rack. He was eager to settle Hütz and her son here in her friend's cabin and head on to his next lead—Roula Haddad had texted that she'd have him on the move within minutes. It was hard to wait even that long. In the quiet kitchen, he was troubled by the extent of the threats he faced. Wyatt, Tom Frisch, even Turbo's boss, Feng Yi, they were all out there. At the root of his misgivings, however, was something or someone hidden that he could only sense right now, an unnamed peril. Tension made a tight band across his brow. The coffeepot boiled.

"Maybe caffeine will help?" Saskia Hütz pointed at Verrazzano's knitted forehead and gestured with a coffee cup. "My father called it thinking juice."

"I sure do need to think fast."

"My friend hasn't used this place for a few months." Hütz poured two cups. "Everything is a little dusty and dirty. I must apologize."

"We appreciate having a place to bring you and your son. Somewhere safe."

"It's hard to imagine we will ever be safe again."

"You don't have to imagine it. I'll make it happen."

His phone buzzed. Another text from Haddad in New York. It read: "Feng Yi at trade talks in Vienna." The Chinese cyber chief. The one Turbo said plotted the big car crash. The man who employed Wyatt to get it done and couldn't control him when China decided not to go ahead.

Hütz set down Verrazzano's coffee before him. She glanced through the kitchen door to the living room. Jahn was on the couch thumbing through cell phone messages. "Why do you do this?" Hütz sat across the table from him.

Verrazzano slipped his phone into his shirt pocket and let his eyes drop to the surface of the black coffee in his cup. His fingers played through the intro to an old Mose Allison tune, "The Seventh Son," soothing him with the silent music each motion signaled to his brain.

"Are you a seventh son?" Hütz gave him a saucy twist of her lips. "I'm a piano player too. I can read your fingers. It also happens to be one of my favorite songs. Can you 'heal the sick, raise the dead'?"

"That's just the words of the song. When I'm around, the sick feel sicker and the dead stay dead."

Her laugh reminded him of the low notes of the song, way down in the left hand, where Mose made them felt, rather than heard. "Who taught you to play?"

"My mom."

"And you try to tell me that you're not thinking about your family? Men are so easy to see through. I'm lucky I have a son. I will always know what he's thinking, even before he does. Women are harder to figure out. Tell me about your mother."

He shook his head. "I have a lot to do right now. A lot to think about."

"You need to rest, give your brain a few moments to recharge. If you won't sleep, you can at least talk about something good."

"What makes you think talking about my mom is good?"

"You use the music to find some calm. That's obvious. She is a source of happiness to you."

"Was."

"But she still is where you find your happiness. No?"

He blinked slowly. He pictured her, Donna Verrazzano, singing the old jazz standards she loved, as her teenaged son accompanied her on the piano. Then he imagined her face in the headlights of the BMW that killed her on her way home from her night shift in the cancer ward. "She still is."

"But not the rest of your family?"

"I'm pretty close with my sister. My brother's dead."

"You don't mention your father."

Robert Verrazzano wasn't much of a father after Donna's death. He couldn't help his eldest son with his drug habit or keep his daughter from moving out to live with her boyfriend when she was sixteen. He'd been sullen and drunk, and he'd sold the piano his youngest boy Dominic played so well, wanting the last two people in the house to sit in silence with the ghost of the woman they both loved more than life. "My father and I didn't get along," Verrazzano said.

"That's a big problem. I think about it often with my little boy. He was born with donated sperm. He will never know his father. I must make sure that this doesn't fill him with rage and that he doesn't spend his life looking for a father figure and choosing the wrong one for lack of a true model when he was young."

Verrazzano laughed quietly.

"You're laughing because you think I talk too formally? It's just that it's a foreign language," Hütz said. "It's hard for me to sound natural in English. But it's true all the same."

He shook his head and laughed a little louder. "It's not that, at all. We go through life thinking we're all so unique. No one could possibly understand us. Then someone you've known for about four hours lays it out there for you, and they're right on the money."

"On the money? What does that mean?"

"I'm laughing because you've seen right through me."

"I'm flattered. Father figures. That has been your issue, then."

"My issue, yeah." He sensed a complete lack of need from Hütz. Like most men, he found need irresistibly attractive, but Hütz didn't prompt the desire to protect and care for a woman that was often so strong in him. Then he thought of Jahn. It was an involuntary switch in his attention, and he saw that the moments of confusion he had felt around the FBI agent were fed by a sexual attraction.

"You are going to have to kill your father figure."

He looked up at Hütz sharply. His phone buzzed in his pocket.

"In a psychological sense," she added.

He brought the phone to his ear. "Hi, Roula."

"Are you alone? Can you talk?"

The urgency in Haddad's voice brought Verrazzano to his feet. He went into the living room. Jahn glanced up at him from her phone. Verrazzano went over to the window. A wood fire crackled in the hearth. "What've you got?"

"A lead on the money trail that might just take us to the last Chinese engineer."

"Great. Let's hear it."

"Noelle followed the Luxembourg lead. The private banker there was more than a little crooked. The Luxembourg account is held in the name of a Syrian government official named Nabil Allaf. The account was used to set up a bunch of short positions in auto stocks. In fact, the stocks of almost every major car company."

"Does that include Darien?"

"It does, and after the Darien crash, the position was closed out with a five-million-dollar profit."

"Did that money go back to the Luxembourg account?"

"It went to the same private bank in Luxembourg. But to a different account. In the name of a US national. Lawton Wyatt."

Verrazzano stared out into the stormy night.

"You hear me?"

"Go on," he murmured.

"I'll try to check out what we have on Wyatt. Maybe the bad guys didn't expect the Darien crash. They set up this second account in a hurry, and they didn't have a plan to launder the profits right away. The only movement has been a payment that went out yesterday to a Bitcoin address."

Something moved in the bushes beyond the lawn. Verrazzano watched, but he saw nothing. "A Bitcoin address. Did you track it?"

"Noelle got details from the banker in Luxembourg, so I've been able to narrow it down. The account holder has received Bitcoins from other sources in the last year. Each time they convert the Bitcoin to actual cash at the same place."

"Because you can't spend the Bitcoins."

"Right, they're just ones and zeroes on your phone, until you actually go to a dealer who's willing to give you cash for them."

"Who's the account holder?"

"It's a woman named Jin Ju. Known as Julie."

Ju. The name Turbo had mentioned. The last surviving Chinese engineer. It was the right lead. "What do we know about her?"

"Married to a Czech guy. She's a computer engineer. Lives in Prague."

"It's her. The last engineer. Get the Czech police to pick her up."

"I already sent them. They found her husband at home. He doesn't know where she is, and he was apparently not happy to find that the police consider her some kind of criminal. He won't tell them anything else."

"We're talking about his wife's life here."

"He's an old Communist. I gather he doesn't trust the police now that the Czech Republic has gone full-on capitalist."

"Like he hasn't had long enough to get over that? Then we have to follow the money. The place where Jin Ju converts the Bitcoin—what's the address?"

"It's a small loan company in a central neighborhood of Prague."

"Send it to my phone. I'll go there right away."

"That's it? You're going to stake the place out until someone goes in who looks like a lady Chinese computer engineer?"

He smiled at the slight note of derision in her voice. "It's a pretty cunning plan, right?"

She sighed. "I guess it's all we've got."

Jahn turned toward the window and caught his eye. She dropped her glance back to her phone.

"What's Noelle and Bill's next step?" he said.

"Bill's going to shadow the Irish banker in Luxembourg. See if he can pick anything else up," Haddad said. "Noelle is backing him up."

"Good. Keep me posted on the banker. I'm going to head for Prague."

"You got it."

He hung up. Jahn put away her phone too. "Prague?"

"Quite the European tour, isn't it?"

She stood and walked toward him. "Yeah, it's real romantic."

They shared a quiet smile. He thought of the need he sensed in her. He wanted to protect her, to tend to someone he could see had been wounded.

"What happened, Gina?" he whispered.

She flinched and touched her fingers to her scarred cheek.

"I don't mean your face," he said. "I mean, why are you scared?"

"Who says I am?"

"I've got a sense for it. Scary guys often do."

She was still, her features oscillating between calculation and vulnerability. Then she said, "I don't want you to end up like my husband."

"I'm not going to die."

She opened her mouth to speak, then caught herself. She changed the shape of the word that was forming on her lips. "Sometimes I think love is what you feel toward something you'd die for. Chris loved Delta Force, and I think he loved me. But if he was going to die, we both knew it'd be for Delta Force. He disappeared in Syria. His commanding officer told me there were reports he'd been transported to Lebanon. Held by the Islamic State or Hezbollah. Either way, gone forever."

"Is that official?"

She pushed her hair away from her face. The light from the wood fire danced across the scars on her cheek. "Let's go to Prague. It's a long drive. We can talk in the car."

"I'm going to Prague alone. I want you to go to Vienna." He saw the protest on her face and so he made his voice hard. "Feng Yi is there. Turbo said he was in charge of this whole thing. I need you to get a hold of him."

"No way. I'm staying with you."

"I have to head for Prague right now. You wait here until our ICE guys arrive from Berlin. They'll make sure Saskia and the kid are safe. As soon as that's squared away, go to Vienna. Roula Haddad will give you Feng Yi's location."

"Dominic, that's not—"

"That's not negotiable. It's how it has to be." He picked up on some energy twitching through her, something that seemed to take all her strength to repress, glowing within her, radioactive. He started to turn away from her.

"It was my first husband." Her words came out softly, but with enough force to stop him. "A sweet guy, when he didn't drink. He cut up my face with a bottle. Then he went out, drove his car into a tree, and died. If he hadn't have done that, I'd still be married to him. I just couldn't get away from him, no matter what he did or said. After that I never thought anyone would look at me, let alone love me."

She touched the scars. "When Chris came along, I used to talk about getting plastic surgery, but he told me, 'There's no one like you, Gina. Don't ever change.' I'll always love that man. I'll do anything for him. That's the only thing that *has* to be."

Verrazzano would have told her about Melanie right then. Told her he was waiting for his wife even though the life he had lead with Wyatt made him repulsive to her. But an impulse arose in some recess of his brain where pain and anger went to stew, and it kept his lips tight and his jaw tensed. "I still need you to go to Vienna."

"I know." She turned to the window.

"Find Feng Yi. Watch him, and be ready. We might need to put him out of action."

She was motionless and silent.

Verrazzano went out into the kitchen. "Saskia, I'm going to be on my way. Agent Jahn will wait with you until further protection arrives."

"Stay safe, Dominic."

"That's *your* job. If I intended to stay safe, I'd—"

She cocked her head, quizzically.

He stopped short and started again, "I guess I just wouldn't know how."

He went out of the back door and across the soft grass toward the edge of the lawn where it fringed the forest. The car was in the drive. Jahn watched him from the window of the living room. He waved. She went to the fireplace and sat down with her back to him.

He opened the driver's side door of the car. His phone vibrated. He thumbed through the passcode and opened the message. Haddad sent him the address of the loan office in Prague where Julie Jin cashed in her Bitcoins. He put the phone in his pocket and shifted his weight to slide into the front seat of the car.

He heard a single footstep on the gravel behind him, then an arm no less yielding than an iron bar swung around his neck and clamped tight. The bicep of his attacker pressed against the artery on the right of his neck, the forearm cut off the flow of blood down the other side. A sleeper hold. Verrazzano tried to throw the assailant. He lifted his feet onto the car's doorframe and kicked back. Both men went down on the gravel, but the sleeper hold wouldn't break.

Verrazzano's head was a single pulse of trapped blood and tension. In the blurry second before he passed out, a voice whispered for him to go quietly. "Dinner at Odin's table for you tonight, bubba." It was Wyatt's catchphrase, but the voice belonged to Tom Frisch.

CHAPTER 20

Outside the big double doors of the police station on Goethe-gasse, Wyatt gathered himself. He was angry. He knew he had to let that go. Feng Yi had teased him by killing the punk in the U-Bahn, to show that he commanded him and could put him at unnecessary risk. *Point taken, asshole*, he thought. He brought his focus back to the mission. Before he entered the ornate building, once the home of a noble family in the time of the Austro-Hungarian Empire, Wyatt made himself look just a little flustered—he was supposed to be a distraught father, but he was also acting Austrian. He went under the high coffered ceiling, came to the desk sergeant, and gave a slight bow from the neck. "*Grüss Gott.*"

The sergeant returned the greeting. Wyatt went on in the Austrian-accented German he had perfected when he was under-cover across the border in the Balkans during the nineties. "My daughter is here at the station. There was an incident of some kind at the Karlsplatz station. May I see her?"

The sergeant's face registered shock at the mention of the death under the subway train's wheels. "Your name, sir?"

"Weiss, Gerhard. My daughter is Silvia Weiss."

"Come with me, sir."

Wyatt followed the sergeant's bulky back down a corridor that had once been frequented by Mozart and Beethoven on their way to entertain princes, dukes, and other bloodthirsty crooks. It was quieter than any police station he had ever visited. Wyatt was grateful that there was no waltz playing. They reached an elaborately carved door. The sergeant showed Wyatt inside. A policewoman with black hair tied back at her neck sat across a table from the blonde girl Wyatt had seen at the subway station. Silvia Weiss held the policewoman's hand. Her eyes were on the tabletop, glazed and staring.

Wyatt went to her side. "Silvia, darling." He hugged her to him. He whispered in her ear, "They are going to kill you too because you were at the protest. I believe in your cause. You must trust me." Her face was stiff with terror. He touched her cheek softly. "I am going to look after you."

The policewoman stood and smiled. "I will leave you now. If there is anything at all that you need, come to the desk."

The police officers shut the door behind them.

Wyatt took his chair to the door and jammed it against the handle to stop anyone entering. He returned to the girl and knelt before her. "Did you tell them anything, Silvia?"

She shook her head.

"They killed Bernd because of the antiglobalization demonstration."

"But it's just a protest." Her words came out slowly, shocked and terrified.

"You don't know how far these people will go. Their power is immense, and they have no mercy. I want to protect you, so I have to know what you have told them."

"I told them a man pushed Bernd under the train."

"Did you describe him?"

She was suddenly eager. "I told them his name was Randy from North Korea." She misread Wyatt's frown. "Was that a mistake?"

"It's fine." At any given moment, Wyatt's basic mood was about 80 percent hate. He woke each day hating, before he even knew whom or what he had to hate that day. But he found an extra measure of hostility toward Feng Yi for the pointless killing at the subway station and the act he now forced on Wyatt. "You're absolutely sure you told them nothing else?"

"I don't *know* anything else."

Wyatt wished he knew as little about the world as this trusting young woman. He lifted her to her feet. "Are we going?" she said.

From low by his waist, he brought his hand quickly upward, pivoting at his hips to add force. He slammed the heel of his palm into the underside of her chin. Her head snapped back. Her neck broke. He wrenched her jaw side to side, sawing through the spinal column with the shattered vertebrae to be certain she was dead.

He laid her on the couch under a blanket that was blue with the red stripe of the federal police force. He left the room and went down the corridor to the front desk. The policewoman looked up from her computer, smiling sympathetically.

"She's resting now," Wyatt said. "I'm going to fetch her mother. I'll be back in about an hour, though it may take me longer. Traffic is unpredictable because of the crashes."

"We won't disturb her," the policewoman said.

Wyatt repeated his slight bow from the neck and went out into Goethegasse.

CHAPTER 21

Feng Yi piled his plate with scrambled eggs, bacon, sausage, and chocolate pastries. He took a flute of cava and sucked it down until the bubbles burned his throat. He filled it again from the bottle in the ice bath. *Champagne at seven in the morning,* he thought. *I love European luxury.* A blonde woman brought her plate to the buffet. She glanced up from the cheese board and smiled. Feng kept his eyes on her as he sank another glass of bubbly.

He bowled across the dining room of the Hotel Sacher, ricocheting off the tables where the trade delegates mumbled over their muesli and their little bowls of chopped watermelon. He rattled another table with his heavy hip. One of the American negotiators glanced up at him. Feng bowed low in apology. "General Feng, good morning," the American said.

He wasn't listed as military in the delegation handbook. Feng Yi was supposed to be a technical adviser to the negotiations. But the Americans knew his real position. "Engineer Feng, please," he said. "Computer technician, not soldier." He moved away.

"Is that guy wearing a toupee?" the American murmured to the Foggy Bottom stiff across the table from him.

Feng raised his hand to correct the tilt in his hairpiece. He reminded himself not to bow again as he stumbled to the table by the window where Minister Ma Wei and the other Chinese delegates slurped their oatmeal. There were seven of them. Only Ma had a smile for Feng. He reached for Feng's wrist. "We have work to do today. But first, eat your breakfast, you hungover pig. If you can keep from throwing it up, go over to the table just there near the door. I can see you won't be able to concentrate until you've talked to her."

The minister had noticed the blonde too. She had removed her thin cardigan. She wore a floral-print dress that left her shoulders bare. The blonde woman might have been German or Austrian. But she was tall. He guessed that she was Swedish.

Ma's communications secretary leaned forward, low over the table, the way he would have done had he been proposing a point of policy. "There are whores available in the hotel. Could she be a whore, Minister Ma?"

China's chief of international trade pouted, considering the comment. "Do whores buy the fifty-dollar breakfast buffet and eat it alone?"

The communications secretary stared at his plate, mumbling an apology for his stupidity.

Feng Yi didn't have to suck up to Ma—at least not the way the rest of the delegation did. The minister needed him. Feng controlled the most advanced cyberintelligence operation in the Chinese military. He didn't just break into computer systems and scoop up data as other cyber departments did. He figured out ways to wage actual war—with complete deniability. To keep the Americans busy fighting fires, while China focused on technological innovations that would bury the US economy and make the power of the Communist Party supreme in the entire world.

"I have been considering the plan that we dropped," Ma said.

Feng picked up a sausage from his plate. He chewed on it and watched the minister. He had worked almost three years to get everything ready for the operation. To develop the software. To make it undetectable. Then to train the engineers for their work at car companies across Europe and America. He had found them jobs in the auto companies. Ensured that each of them could infiltrate the code into the onboard computers, so that it would hit every new car made by the companies that produced 70 percent of all the vehicles on two continents. Then Minister Ma had called it off, because he thought it would destroy the trade talks. The old man had lost his nerve after the Darien crash. Now he wanted to reactivate the whole thing, just like that.

"I halted all the preparations at your order, Minister Ma," Feng said. "The Darien crash was caused by one rogue agent."

"Are you so sure of the others? Perhaps they all went rogue, all at once. Is this a betrayal?"

Feng had considered that. It was why he had ordered Wyatt to kill all the engineers as soon as his Detroit agent set off the Darien crash. Feng could still activate the big crash, if he needed to do so. He had modified the original plan. It took all-nighters of ingenious hacking in a miserable dungeon under the Chinese embassy to Austria and coding so clever it amazed even him. But he had gotten around the need for the engineers to install the crashware physically from within the car companies. He could do it remotely.

"The agents have not betrayed us," he said.

"Oh, yes. I meant them *too*." Ma's eyes glimmered with malice. Feng refused to respond to the minister's accusation. He held himself stiff.

"We didn't plan for the Darien crash, but we must turn it to our advantage," Ma said. "I want to be able to use the threat of further mass crashes, now that the Americans have experienced what we can do. For the last week, the American delegates have been unhelpful in these negotiations. The European Union people too. I can't go back to Beijing with the deal they are offering. I wish to break their newfound spine. Your operation will do the job. Can you do it?"

"I can make it happen."

Ma's tension left him now that he had what he wanted. He leered across the breakfast room at the Americans. "This morning, I will tell those bastards to give us a better deal, or we will bring their economies down. The Darien incident will show them I am not just talking."

"You still think that they will not take military action in revenge?"

Ma sniggered. "You have seen them, Feng. They can't even invade Syria to fight the Islamic State. They will find every excuse they can to avoid a military confrontation with China. I doubt that we will even have to do more than threaten them. They will collapse. Be ready."

Ma picked up his coffee cup in two hands and slurped. His eyes over the rim of the porcelain were like leeches. "Report to me at the end of the day."

If Feng activated the code, millions would perish. If not, only Feng would die. Hatred for the entire world filled him.

The minister nodded toward the table near the door. "You look tense, Feng. The woman is getting ready to leave. Go and have some fun with her. Get it out of your system. Then make sure you do as I command."

The woman rose. Feng hurried back to the breakfast bar. He poured two flutes of cava and headed for the door. He intercepted her as she passed the maître d's station.

"Madame, would you care to drink with me?"

She looked at him in surprise. Then she smiled. "Thank you."

He pressed the glass into her hand. "*Skol.*"

That surprised her too. "*Skol.* How did you know I was Swedish?"

"Swedish women are as beautiful as the land from which they come. And as free."

They went out into the lobby.

"I am free, yes." She spoke with her back to him, looking through the window into the gardens of the imperial palace. "But not when I am in Vienna. My husband is Austrian. He's very jealous."

"Your husband?" He scanned the lobby for some giant Teuton striding over to lay him out.

She moved toward the elevator. "He watches me almost all the time. I have a business meeting at the hotel this morning. The only opportunity I have to escape his close attention is when I go on a business trip away from Vienna."

They entered the elevator. The doors closed. He clinked his glass against hers. "I am an experienced world traveler. Where is your next business trip?"

She laughed, but she didn't answer the question. It was still just flirtation.

"What is your floor?" he said. "Mine is six."

She pushed the button for the sixth floor. He leered and fumbled out his cell phone. He took a quick photo of her. Later he would clip the head off the snap and pin it onto the body of an actress from a porn shoot.

On the sixth floor, he walked with her down the silent corridor toward his room. "I have five million dollars in banks around Europe and the Caribbean," he said.

"That's quite a lot of money. What is it that you do?"

"I work for a big organization, but I am the commander of a small and vital part of it. They can't do without me."

"What organization?" She sipped her champagne.

"Any time I want, I could disappear. The kind of work I do is not tied to a particular place, you see. I could be anywhere, with anyone."

Her smile wavered. He was coming on too strong. But the need to reveal his secret power was too great. "I can set up a team of hackers somewhere no one would find me: New Zealand or Namibia or—or Sweden." He took out his key card and opened the door to his room.

She stepped inside, glancing at her wristwatch. This was some kind of game to her. A shudder of disgust at this woman and all other women gripped Feng's guts. He considered a punch to her face. He imagined Minister Ma's rage at the embarrassment of an assault by one of his delegation. Each bubble in the champagne seemed to stab his innards. "I won't suffer Minister Ma's insults anymore."

"I don't speak Chinese. What did you say?"

He shut the door and spoke in English. "I said 'Screw Minister Ma.'"

"Who is Minister Ma?" She turned away and leaned over her champagne flute. He feared she was preparing to leave. When she came toward him, she held out the glass and gestured for him to take the drink.

Feng gulped down the entire glassful. She kissed his neck and cheeks. He went for her mouth with his, but she dodged away and bit at his ear. He snorted with pleasure. The light through the window glared. It was too intense for his eyes. He wobbled on his feet and leaned against her.

He grew to an enormous size and heard his voice as if it were a dragon bellowing before it consumed its victims in flames. "Feng Yi destroyed a man and left his servant to clean up the mess." He couldn't be sure if the dragon spoke aloud through him. Perhaps these words simply echoed in his head with no one to hear them except his desperate, lonely self. "Feng Yi is nuclear, he is radioactive. He is The One." The voice of the dragon became a seismic pulse that shuddered around him and blocked out his vision. Everything he heard was the thunder within him. He tried to fly on, to power through the air with his dragon wings. Colonel Wyatt would do his job. Everything would be arranged within a matter of hours. Feng would report to Minister Ma that the car operation was ready. Then he would return to this beautiful woman and leave the minister in the company of his pathetic sycophants, say good-bye to all the politics and the boot licking for good.

Then the room wheeled about him, and he spun downward, and his head struck something hard, and his dragon energy leaked out of him. He saw, as if through a veil, the Swedish woman kneeling beside him, cradling his head. The floor of his room was underneath him, and he was on his back. He passed out.

When he came around, he was naked on the bed and the Swedish woman was in her underwear, putting on her dress. He felt dreamy and high. Some dark part of his mind told him she had drugged him. Then the mellow afterglow overtook him, and he wanted to be with her and do it again.

"Tonight we will go away together," she said.

CHAPTER 22

McCarthy took his silver Mercedes sedan into the parking lot beneath Findel Airport on the edge of Luxembourg City. He glanced about him as he lifted the attaché case from the passenger seat and got out. He twisted quickly toward the sound of tires. A blue Fiat turned into a space two rows behind him, driven by a man with thinning hair in a navy suit jacket who was talking on a cell phone. McCarthy spoke under his breath as though cursing himself for his nervousness, locked his car, and headed for the terminal, walking fast.

In the Fiat, Todd watched the Irish banker go. He spoke to Kinsella on the cell phone. "Reckon he's going to fly?"

"Do you think maybe he went to the airport because it's got the nearest Starbucks?"

Todd smiled. Every question was a stupid question to Kinsella. "I'll keep you posted."

"If he *is* flying, get on the plane with him. He doesn't know who you are. I'll follow on the next flight."

McCarthy glided up the escalator to the departure hall. Todd weaved between the parked cars. "We don't know that he's flying somewhere connected to our case. He could be going to visit his mom."

"Then you'll have a nice trip to Dublin. Just follow the guy, for Christ's sake."

Todd scanned the departures board as he reached the top of the escalator. "No flights to Ireland. Maybe he's changing planes in London."

Kinsella growled impatiently and hung up.

McCarthy glanced over his shoulder and cut toward the LuxAir ticket counter. The ticket agent reached out a chubby hand for the Irishman's credit card. Within ninety seconds, McCarthy was tucking his boarding pass into the inside pocket of his suit and walking to the security check.

Todd showed his ICE identity card to the ticket agent. "Where's that guy flying? Name of McCarthy."

The ticket agent touched the trim goatee on his fleshy chin and turned toward a rear door in the back of the office. A woman with eyes hard enough to break your glasses tapped away at a computer there. Todd preferred to deal with the pudgy man. "I'll buy a ticket on the same flight. Or I'll have that flight grounded, and your boss will want to know who caused the hold up." He read the ticket agent's ID tag. "Do you want to be that guy, Florian?"

Florian shook the flab that hid his chin and ran his fingers over his keyboard. "One seat on the flight to Palma de Mallorca," he mumbled.

Todd dropped three one-hundred-euro bills on the counter. Florian stared at the cash. "I don't have change. People don't usually pay with—with money. Not in Luxembourg."

Todd watched McCarthy move through the metal detector beyond the check-in desks. The Palma flight was at the top of the list of departures. It was already boarding. "Keep the change, Florian. It's a gift from the Department of Homeland Security."

The ticket agent reached for the money nervously.

"If you see something, say something." Todd winked.

Florian withdrew his hand in surprise.

Todd jogged toward the security check and cut the line. The Luxembourgers didn't like that. They called out to him. The only word he understood was "Monsieur," which showed how little *they* knew—he wasn't looking for respect. He brushed off their complaints. "Yeah, yeah. Wheels up, pants down, guys." He showed his ID to the security guard and went past.

Down another set of escalators, McCarthy disappeared into the telescopic tunnel at the gate. Todd went after him. *Unless his mother retired to Spain,* he thought, *this guy has some other purpose to his trip, and that makes it a lot more interesting for me.*

At the door of the plane, Todd greeted the flight attendant politely and looked down the aisle. He flushed because he realized he'd made an error. The flight was full. McCarthy settled into his window seat in the front row, his legs constricted by the bulkhead. All the other seats were occupied by cheerful vacationers, excitedly looking forward to Spanish sunshine. Todd's seat was right next to McCarthy.

He sat gingerly beside the Irishman. McCarthy watched him closely. It wouldn't be the first time a suspect had read the signs that said law enforcement all over Todd. But those were street mopes who were accustomed to arrest, interrogation, and jail time. Nervously, McCarthy wrung his hands. Todd saw how smooth his knuckles were. McCarthy wouldn't know a cop until the cuffs were on.

So maybe it wasn't a mistake to buy this ticket after all. In fact, it was an opportunity. "Been to Palma before, sir?" Todd gave McCarthy his best simple-American-abroad smile. "I don't mind telling you, it's my first time."

The Irishman flinched, surprised by the down-home accent. "Palma? No, I've not been there before." He turned to the porthole. The plane drew back from the gate.

"What're you doing down there? Business trip?"

McCarthy glanced at the happy tourists in their T-shirts and the kids grabbing for their iPads. He touched the lapels of his suit and laid his hands flat on the attaché case across his lap. "Something like that, yes."

"*Something* like that? What're you, a criminal?"

McCarthy's eyes widened. The plane rumbled faster along the runway.

"I got you. Didn't I? I got you there." Todd nudged the Irishman's arm. "What's your game? I'm in real estate. I'm headed down to Palma to buy up land and develop it for vacation homes. Sorry, we're in Europe now. 'Holiday' homes. You in real estate?"

"No, no, I'm not."

"Banking? This is Luxembourg. You've got to be a banker, right? What do you do? I bet you hide rich guys' millions from the IRS. I nailed it, right?" Todd slapped the attaché case playfully. "What you got in there? About a million bucks?"

McCarthy yanked the case away and tucked it between his feet. He gestured to the flight attendant. "Whisky," he called. In a tone of profound desperation, he added: "Please."

The plane jerked into the air. The flight attendant's smile was a wince as she rolled her finger to signal that she'd be along with the alcohol as soon as they were at cruising height.

"Me too," Todd called out to her. Then he squeezed McCarthy's arm. "I'll take a whisky with you."

McCarthy couldn't resist a smile. An Irishman never likes to drink alone, and he always likes a man who drinks. Particularly when he fears for his life.

After the whisky arrived, McCarthy loosened up. It was a flight of less than two hours, but the Irishman seemed determined to put away enough scotch to last through a long haul to Australia. By the fourth measure, he had an arm around Todd. He pulled himself to his feet. "I have to piss, mate." He swayed drunkenly and dropped on top of Todd as he edged past him into the aisle. "Bugger me. Turbulence." He laughed. "Did you feel that turbulence just then?"

"Nearly shook me out of my seat, man." Todd joined in the merriment, so McCarthy wouldn't see or feel the agent's hand in his jacket pocket. Todd turned his wrist to slip the guy's keys out of sight. Then he touched his finger to the side of his nose, sharing the joke. "Right. That's what it is. Turbulence."

McCarthy locked himself into the toilet. Todd watched the green overhead light go on. Then he took the attaché case from under the seat. He flicked the keys through his fingers until he came to a small square one. With a turn in the lock, the key opened the clasps of the case. Todd lifted the lid carefully.

The case was half filled with blank letterhead from McCarthy's bank, ballast and camouflage for the real contents of the case. In the middle of the papers, Todd found a FedEx envelope. The edge had been torn away. Bloody fingerprints marked the waybill poking out of its plastic cover.

Todd glanced toward the toilet as he reached into the envelope. He drew out a plastic baggie. He turned the case on his lap so that no one else would see inside. He bent lower and examined the baggie. It was smeared with blood. At first he thought it contained a dead black rat. Then he saw what it was.

He shoved the baggie into the pocket of his jacket. He read over the FedEx waybill in a hurry. He couldn't see anything useful in it, but Haddad might be able to trace the sender, so he folded it unevenly in his shaking hands and stuffed it into his pocket. He pushed in the clasps on the case, turned the lock, and dropped the keys to the floor. Just as the toilet flushed, he stood the case in front of McCarthy's seat.

The Irishman called out for two more whiskeys from the flight attendant as he returned.

"We are about to start our descent, sir," she said.

"There's always time for another. Besides, me and my pal Billy here are never coming down, are we, sunshine?"

"Let's keep circling the airport until we run out of fuel or whiskey," Todd said.

McCarthy slid into his seat. Inadvertently, he kicked the keys against the side of the plane. "Look at that. I dropped these buggers." He jangled them and slipped them into his pocket. "Let's have that whisky, darlin' girl."

The flight attendant brought two more tumblers. McCarthy toasted Todd. The ICE agent smiled feebly. He ought to keep up the conversation. He had a lot of questions for the Irishman, but none that he could ask. Not outside of an interrogation room or a jail cell.

"You look a bit peaky," McCarthy said. "Whisky catching up with you?" He pulled out the sick bag from the pocket in front of him and unfolded it. Todd almost used it.

McCarthy picked up his attaché case and set it on his lap again. If it had been a nuclear device in the case, Todd would have been cool and directed. But the shock of what he had seen wouldn't leave him. Why did McCarthy have a scalp in his case?

Todd fumbled with the tumbler of whisky, dribbling some on his chin. The scotch burned in his throat and made him gasp. McCarthy hammered him on the shoulder, laughing. "Let's get together tonight, old fella. I'm at the Hotel Melia by the marina. Where are you staying?"

"No kidding. I'm at the same place. Want to share a cab?"

McCarthy lost a little of his vim. "Got to make a stop first."

"I'm okay to wait. Is it somewhere far? It'd be cool to see a bit of the city."

The Irishman stared out of the window as the airstrip approached. Beyond it, Palma's medieval cathedral spiked the sky on a rise at the edge of the water. When he looked back toward

Todd, he was wistful and his eyes were watery. "I don't mind telling you, I'm a bit fearful, mate."

"Are you okay? Are you sick?"

"I'm not talking about my health." He turned to the window, sniffing and wiping at his nose and cheeks, and then he was quiet until the plane landed.

Outside the terminal, the heat sucked the whisky right through Todd's pores and dried him up, so that his tongue felt thick and his head ached. McCarthy led him to the taxi rank. As they climbed into the cab, the Irishman pushed the door and started to get out.

"I can't do it," he said. "I have to go alone. I can't involve you in this, Bill."

Todd gripped McCarthy by the elbow. "We've shared a drink or two. It's not the booze talking when I say that it still means something to me. It's a bond between men." He made sure it sounded as though the booze was, indeed, running his mouth. "Something's worrying you, buddy, and I'm not going to ask you what it is, but I'm also not going to let you be alone in a foreign city. I'm going to watch your back, you hear?"

McCarthy swallowed hard, evidently moved, and settled back into the taxi. He leaned forward and spoke quietly to the driver. The driver frowned and uttered a couple of complaining sentences. McCarthy handed him a one-hundred-euro note. It did the trick. The driver shut up and took off.

"He's been waiting a while in the rank for his turn to pick up a customer," McCarthy explained to Todd. "We don't have far to go. Our boy felt a bit shortchanged."

"You made him happy?"

"Yes, I made him happy."

"Me too. I hate flying, but I just had a great time. You made me happy too, Dermot. You have a talent for it."

McCarthy murmured, "We'll find out in a minute, won't we."

The cab swung out of the airport. Instead of heading west into the city, it cut east into the shabby beachfront neighborhood of Can Pastilla. They rode through the dusty orange groves between the highway and the beach. The driver pulled over in front of a round building with a swooping roof. It could have been a basketball arena in a moderately sized city. The sign over by the ticket booth said it was the aquarium. Todd squinted at the sign advertising Europe's biggest shark tank. "You here to see the sharks, man?"

McCarthy's hands shook as he reached for his attaché case. He stepped out of the car. "I'll be back in just a minute or two, Bill. Probably best if you wait here."

Todd watched the Irishman walk at speed over the small plaza to the entrance of the aquarium. As soon as he was out of sight, Todd left the taxi and followed him. He bought a ticket and weaved through the vacationers and school groups and the staff dressed as mermaids and seals. A pirate on stilts gave him a playful slash with his plastic cutlass and waved a thumbs-up.

He trotted through the darkness of the tropical fish displays, illuminated only by the lights inside the tanks. If McCarthy saw him, Todd decided he'd make an excuse about an argument with the driver. But he picked up his target before the Irishman spotted him. McCarthy was into the daylight and moving toward the pirate ship playground.

Todd waited beside a pool of blue rays. McCarthy halted at the bar of a snack restaurant. The waitress brought him a beer. Todd clicked his tongue. The guy would soon be too drunk to make any sense.

Then he realized that McCarthy hadn't stopped for the sake of the alcohol. The man at his side carried an identical attaché case. He was four inches over six feet, with a deep tan and short white hair. His back spread out wide in the shoulders. He had an effortless power and authority that seemed to shrink McCarthy. Todd pulled out his phone. Keeping it low, as if he were reading a text, he took a few photos of McCarthy and the tall man.

The Irishman shoved his attaché case at the man, who took it smoothly and made the switch. They shared a few words that didn't involve much lip movement from the big man. McCarthy sucked down his beer and started away, but the man held him by the back of his jacket while he glanced inside the case and searched among the papers. His features darkened. Todd shivered. Even if the big man murdered McCarthy, he'd still have plenty of death to spare in that face.

McCarthy did a lot of shrugging and animated whispering. But the tall guy shifted his weight, drew himself up, and laid his hands flat on the attaché case with finality. The two men moved away toward the hall that housed the bluefin tuna tank. They passed within a few yards of Todd. McCarthy didn't see the ICE agent. He was squinting away the rivers of sweat pouring out of his brow.

"I do not know where it is." McCarthy spoke with the kind of emphatic whisper that's louder than much conversational speech. "It was in the bloody case. Jesus, God, Wyatt, I can't explain it. I had it on the plane."

"It ain't there now, hoss." The man McCarthy called Wyatt had an American accent, his voice deep and Southern.

Wyatt pushed the attaché case into McCarthy's chest and tried to take back the other one. McCarthy held onto it. "That's mine. You can't go back on this."

Wyatt let go of the second case. He didn't want a scene. "Did someone switch cases on you at the airport?"

"Couldn't have." McCarthy had sweated through his suit jacket. The silvery gray material was dark under the arms and down the back. "The case still has all the papers I put in there to—to add ballast."

"Then someone must've gone inside the case and taken it out," Wyatt said. The scalp seemed to scrabble like a live animal inside Todd's pocket. He ducked his head as Wyatt peered around the snack bar.

McCarthy turned a circle, staring about him, but he was blind with booze and panic and stinging sweat. "It has to be him, it has to be." McCarthy was looking straight at Todd. But he didn't see him. "The bloke on the plane. He had a few drinks with me. He took it, he must've taken it. When I went for a piss."

"Who is he?"

"Jesus, I don't know. But he's out front in a taxi, waiting for me."

"You brought someone here?"

"I didn't think it would—I thought it might—"

Wyatt gave McCarthy a look like he was something he'd just stepped in. He went into the bluefin pavilion and jerked his thumb for McCarthy to follow.

Todd wiped the sweat from his lip. He had to follow them inside. But McCarthy was looking for him now. He went carefully.

The giant tuna glided past him in the massive tanks. Up ahead, Todd caught sight of the tall American. Wyatt had his hand on McCarthy's shoulder, keeping hold of him in the crowd and the low light from the tanks. Everyone was moving swiftly, ignoring the tuna, heading for the shark display. A group of Chinese tourists cut across the stream of the crowd, stumbling and talking loudly. Todd lost McCarthy and Wyatt. He pushed through the Chinese and on into the shark wing.

Wyatt. He remembered the name now. Kinsella forced it out of McCarthy. Wyatt was the name on the account that received the profits from the Darien stock market play. The scalp linked that trade to the killings of the Chinese engineers. Which made Todd's situation even more dangerous.

A dozen sand tigers moved slow and menacing through the blue water. The crowd pressed to the glass and flowed down the stairs to the lower floor, where more of the predators glided in circles. Wyatt had given off the same deliberate aura of inexhaustible malice as the sharks. Todd steeled himself. He had to get on Wyatt's tail, no matter how dangerous he seemed. If the guy wanted the scalp, it was surely because he knew the reason the killer had cut away a strip of the flesh from the heads of the dead Chinese engineers. Todd needed that information. At any cost.

He didn't spot the two men on the upper floor of the shark tank. He made for the stairs. Then he heard the screams.

Children, women, and men bawling and bellowing and wailing. All transfixed by the blue water.

Todd followed their shocked stares. Inside the shark tank, a man in a dress shirt and undershorts came out of a dive at a depth of about twenty feet. His ankles were tied with a knotted pair of suit pants. His arms were wrapped behind him by a suit jacket that had been twisted to serve as a rope.

McCarthy wriggled toward the surface of the pool. He seemed to gape out of the tank at Todd with recognition. Then blood swirled from a deep cut across his belly. The scent in the water was enough to bring the sharks.

The screams of the tourists around Todd were deafening. Some ran as if the sharks might come for them too. Others watched in horror. More than a few recorded it on their cell phones.

McCarthy was dead in less than a minute, but the sharks were still working on him as Todd hurried away. He went down the stairs among the terrified tourists. He had to find Wyatt.

A ramp led toward the exit. Another short corridor went to a soft-play area for small children. Then Todd found a service door with the lock and handle kicked away. He pushed through it and went up the bare steps.

At the top of the stairs, he came to another busted door. He passed into a gallery that would have been used to feed the sharks and clean their tank. The water was murky with McCarthy's blood. The surface rippled with the distant traces of the feeding frenzy over his body. The gallery was empty.

Todd hurried down the stairs and back into the crowd. He headed for the entrance. His heart battered in his chest louder than the terrified bawling of the tourists around him. He knew what he had to do. He dialed Kinsella. "McCarthy is dead."

"How'd that happen?"

"Someone put him in a shark tank."

"Jesus. Who?"

"Wyatt. Got to be the guy whose name was on the crooked account. I'm going to send you a photo of McCarthy with him. I'll send it to Roula too. He's American. I heard his accent. Southern. Big guy. Looks military, or maybe law enforcement."

"You saw him put McCarthy in the tank?"

Todd came out into the heat and the glare of the sunlight off the Mediterranean. "What? No, I saw McCarthy in the tank. You think he jumped in for a nice cool dip?"

"I'm just clarifying, Bill."

"The American wanted the scalp. McCarthy was supposed to bring it to him. But he didn't have it."

"The scalp? What scalp?"

"I took it from McCarthy's attaché case on the plane. It's got to belong to one of the Chinese engineers. It's black hair, very straight. It's in my pocket."

"I'm getting on a plane to Palma right away. I'll be there to back you up."

"I couldn't locate the American after McCarthy went in the shark tank. But I heard McCarthy tell him about a guy on the plane. That guy was me. McCarthy figured out that I must've taken the scalp. He told this Wyatt that I was waiting outside the aquarium with a taxi."

She saw what he intended. "Bill, be careful."

"I can't find him. But maybe he can find *me*." He hung up.

The taxi driver was about to take a family of panicked vacationers away from the horror of the shark killing when Todd reached him. "Sorry, everybody. This guy works for me." He opened the rear door and lifted himself up, standing on the rim of the door frame. He looked about, making himself obvious. Wyatt was there somewhere, he was sure of it. He got into the taxi and shut the door. "Melia Hotel."

"What happened to your friend?" the driver said.

"He had a lunch date. Now go."

The taxi rolled toward the medieval city and looped around behind the marina on the wide Avinguda de Gabriel Roca. The tall palms cast their shade on the road, and the sun flickered through them as the driver picked up speed. The great white yachts of people twenty million times richer than Bill Todd languished on the quays beyond the seafood restaurants. The owners of the yachts were wealthy enough that someone out there might have a motivation for killing them. No matter what inputs you fed into the equation of an ICE case, it always solved to money and murder. Todd touched his fingertips to the baggie in his pocket and wondered how Wyatt intended to turn the scalp of the murdered Chinese man into money.

He tapped through to the photos of McCarthy and Wyatt on his phone. He e-mailed them to Haddad in New York and copied Kinsella. He dialed Haddad. "I just sent you—"

"I know. Noelle already talked to me."

"You're running a check on Wyatt? The guy in the photos?"

"I'm working on it, Bill."

"I meant to send them to Dom too. I just forgot. You know I was a bit—"

"I'll forward them when I can. We can't reach Dom just now."

"What happened? Is he okay?"

"Last we heard from him he was about to drive to Prague. Since then, nothing."

With Verrazzano out of contact, Todd was the agent with the most years of service behind him. It was time to give the team the direction it would've had from Dom. "Noelle's coming here to Majorca. She should go to Prague, instead."

"I don't think she'll want to do that."

"Maybe she can connect with Dom."

"I'll call her."

He paid off the taxi in the drive of the Hotel Melia and went into the dark wood and rich carpeting of the lobby. At the reception desk, a bony clerk in his late fifties lisped a welcome.

"I'm sorry, look, I have a reservation. But I don't have my passport." Todd did his best to seem flustered and tense. It wasn't hard. "I've been robbed. I was at the airport and—"

"Please, sir, let me set your mind at rest. I'm very sorry to hear about your experience, sir. Please don't worry. We will help you to arrange a temporary passport with your consulate and to get in touch with your credit card companies. Sadly, we are familiar with such situations. In the meantime—" The clerk gestured toward a welcome table with a tray of champagne flutes and a bottle of chilled cava.

Todd took a glass and had a long sip. *This is what happens to rich people when the shit comes down*, he thought. Someone gives them champagne. He reminded himself not to be on a government salary in the next life.

"Your name, sir?" the clerk said.

"McCarthy."

The clerk handed him his key card. Todd went to the elevator. Up in his room, he savored the silence of the expensive hotel. From the balcony, he watched the sun sliding into the Mediterranean. The red warning lights came on at the tip of the cathedral's spires, vivid in the darkening sky. On the avenue, the traffic light changed to red. A taxi rear-ended a Mercedes with a loud, terrifying percussion. Sometime after the sun came up, Todd wondered, was he going to hear that noise amplified ten thousand times?

At least he knew where some of the bad guys were now. "Right here in beautiful Majorca," he murmured. He set his champagne glass down on the nightstand and dumped the scalp beside it. He lay on the bed. It was more comfortable than any he had ever slept on. He put his hands behind his head and waited for the tall American to come kill him.

CHAPTER 23

The rental car sped along the highway that entered Prague from the west. Verrazzano came to in the passenger seat. For an instant, he thought it was morning and that it was time to get his niece up and dressed and feed her breakfast and hustle her off to school. Then a road sign informed him that the main rail station near Wenceslas Square was ten kilometers away, and a sharp pain in the back of his skull reminded him of the sleeper hold outside the lodge south of Bonn. German talk radio was blasting on the stereo loud enough to be heard over the wind through the open windows. He groaned. Tom Frisch drummed a happy paradiddle on the steering wheel and punched Verrazzano playfully on the shoulder. "And he's back. For a while, I thought I killed you."

"Why didn't you?" Verrazzano massaged his bruised neck. His brain felt thick and clotted from the momentary shut down of circulation.

"We're a team, Sergeant Major. We're going to nail Wyatt, you and me together. Man, you're as white as an English guy's ass."

"You've made a study of English guys' asses?"

"I kicked a few in my time."

Every fifty yards, they passed a concertina of metal and plastic that had once been a Darien or a car that tangled with one. The newsreader on the radio said the winner of Best Supporting Actress at last year's Oscars turned out to have been run down and killed by a Darien while crossing a street in Santa Monica. "I must've missed that flick. Didn't see a lot of movies in the detention center," Frisch spoke over the start of the next item on the news.

"—the famous author of thrillers remains in a coma even as his book hits number one on the bestseller list," the newsreader said, "after a Darien crashed into his Tesla on an interstate in New Jersey."

"I almost went into a coma when I read that guy's last book."

"As calls mount for military action against the terrorists behind the Darien incident, the UN will hold an emergency debate later today in New York. Secretary-General Ban Ki—"

"Well, I guess we can rest easy now that the UN is on the case."

"How'd you find me in Bonn?" Verrazzano said.

"In Washington, US Commerce Secretary Dick Bruce argued against military action in the Middle East, in a speech last night. Bruce criticized congressional pressure for the president to attack the Islamic State in revenge for the Darien crash—"

"You're a smart guy. You'll figure it out." Frisch took a cell phone from his jacket and tossed it to Verrazzano. It was his. "When I put you under, you'd just read the last text from your Agent Haddad. The screen hadn't even had time to lock. I got the address of the Bitcoin cashing place in Prague."

"Bruce urged world leaders to turn their attention to China, saying that he believed Beijing to be behind the Darien crash. That, according to Bruce, is where any military action should be aimed."

Frisch punched the off button on the radio. "I texted her back. Confirm this, I said. Give me that again, I said. I got the whole deal. See? I could've just killed you. I've got the information I need to get to the last Chinese engineer. But here you are, alive. I told you, we're a team, man."

Verrazzano turned his face to the window. He had to weigh everything he told Frisch, and he had to endure the stress of knowing that the man beside him could turn on him at any moment. "I'm not working with you, Frisch."

"One guy—no matter how good he is—won't stand a chance in hell against Wyatt. He's hooked up with the Chinese and moved into technologies that you and I could never comprehend. Any time I even think of Wyatt, I feel that ice in my belly, like I'm halfway dead. That's real fear."

Verrazzano watched the Prague suburbs flash by the window. A demonic image of Wyatt suddenly rose out of the tenements, swathed in fire and shooting red streams of pure death from his palms. The tires thumped over the ridges of tar between the concrete sections of pavement, a mirror for the ticking of Verrazzano's heart, counting down the approach to the next figure on Wyatt's path of death, the engineer Julie Jin. "It's hard to separate the fear and the hate," he murmured.

"You're a good guy. You won't go bad again."

Verrazzano turned sharply to Frisch in surprise. That was a mistake. The effects of the long unconscious spell made it feel like three punches delivered from different directions at the same time.

"That's what you're scared of, isn't it? The possibility you might still be nursing something evil in here." Frisch touched his chest, as he went down the off-ramp toward the station. "Some guys are so bad, they never come back. The worst thing they've done is the real them. Other guys make a mistake and they never forgive themselves. But you—you're not going back to it."

Frisch pulled over in a shabby street under a rail bridge. Even in Europe's loveliest towns, the central station was surrounded by neglected neighborhoods filled with cheap hostels for migrant workers and stores advertising cut-rate phone calls back home to Sudan or Sri Lanka. In Prague the atmosphere of hustle and sting extended from the station's taxi rank through the streets of flophouses and on into the popular tourist spots around the Charles Bridge. Frisch whooped with happiness as he climbed out of the rental car. The guy was entirely in tune with the lawless selfishness that defined almost every exchange in the Czech capital.

"Let's go find little Julie Jin, buddy." Frisch dragged Verrazzano out of the passenger door of the station wagon. Now he truly felt the effect of the stranglehold Frisch put on him in Bonn. It mumbled through Verrazzano's skull, reeling against the hemispheres of his brain, tripping over synapses, and clutching at his limbic system. Frisch ran him down the sidewalk with his hand under his elbow. "Julie's going to tell her story and we're going to figure out how to get Wyatt. We're going to finish this job together, man."

They walked along a street of cheap clothing stores, most of them closing for the night. A Romany woman and her child huddled in the doorway of a dry cleaner, whimpering and holding their hands out for change. Verrazzano halted. He reached into his pocket and took out a fistful of coins. He gave them to the woman. Frisch put his palm flat against Verrazzano's upper back. "Ain't you a sweetheart. You give me any funny stuff and I'll leave you in a doorway with your gypsy girlfriend—dead, you got me?"

They cut down a narrow street that ended in the bulbous dome of an Eastern Orthodox church. The traffic on the sidewalk was sparse. A few reedy African men sauntered home from their menial jobs. Another Romany woman bothered them for change. A single neon sign buzzed and flickered halfway along the block, showing a row of Chinese characters, a blood-red dollar symbol, and the words "Money Transfer" in English.

"According to your colleague Special Agent Haddad, that's the place we're looking for." Frisch checked his watch. "Soon be nineteen hundred. It's open late." He led Verrazzano to an old

Wolfwagen van across from the loan office. They stood in its shadow. "Now we wait."

The Romany came toward them. She tugged her shawl around her stout body and yammered through lips that wrinkled about a toothless mouth. Verrazzano reached into his pocket and came out with the last of his change.

"You're a regular Christian, ain't you," Frisch said. "Go ahead, give her the money."

Verrazzano closed his fist around the change and swung. His punch caught Frisch on the jaw. The weight of the coins doubled the impact. Frisch twirled and went down. Verrazzano kicked him in the ribs. He went for a stamp, but Frisch caught his boot just in time and twisted it. Verrazzano came down on his backside. The concussion jumped up almost as fast as Frisch and joined in the battering. Frisch grabbed Verrazzano's head and turned it sideways. He smashed his knee into Verrazzano's temple and let him fall.

The change tinkled from Verrazzano's hand onto the sidewalk. A charge burst down from his brain. He vomited into the gutter beside the Wolfwagen. The Romany scooped up the coins and hustled away.

"You got to pull yourself together, Verrazzano. You try that again and I swear it's the last thing you'll do. We may have to wait a couple days for this Chinese chick. But she could just as easily show up right now. Could be the loan office is about to close for the night. If she's smart, she'll come now, when there's no one about. No one to track her back to her family."

On his knees, Verrazzano looked along the ill-lit road. Would Julie Jin want to convert her Bitcoins and walk out into this neighborhood in the dark? "She could get mugged."

"I think she's got other worries." Frisch rubbed his knuckles hard on the top of Verrazzano's head, where the Chinese engineers had lost their scalps. Verrazzano flinched and gasped. Four African men walked out into the street to avoid him. Frisch spoke to them jovially. "Just another drunk English guy on a booze holiday."

The Africans had seen enough British tourists puking pilsner onto the cobblestones of the Old Town to pay no attention now.

Verrazzano wiped his face. He glanced across the street. The lights outside the loan office silhouetted a slight figure in a denim jacket and a baseball cap. The woman turned for a moment to scan the sidewalk. The red neon of the dollar sign caught her features. She was Chinese. She watched the corner up by the main street. Something there grabbed her attention. Then she went into the loan office and shut the door.

Verrazzano followed her glance. The man on the corner was barely visible, but he was there, crouching by a delivery truck. Then he was gone. One element of his outline was obvious to Verrazzano, even through the fuzz that gripped his brain. The man held a pistol. Verrazzano raised his hand, pointing, trying to speak. He choked and gagged again.

"Cool it, buddy." Frisch yanked him to his feet.

Verrazzano took himself back to a time when there was no danger and no pain. To the living room of his childhood home. He heard the piano and felt the keys under his fingers and watched his parents dancing and his brother and sister clapping along. He went there now, rolling his fingers through the trills of "The 'In' Crowd," mimicking the way Ramsay Lewis used to play it.

"It's her," he whispered.

Frisch got it. He glared at the door of the loan office.

"And there's also a—" The concussion filled Verrazzano's throat with bile and stopped his voice. "At the corner. There's a—"

Frisch bent over and took a short folding knife out of his boot. He flipped the scalpel blade out of the orange plastic handle and took a step into the street.

Verrazzano shook his head. "Don't. For God's sake."

"Now we found her . . ."

"It was you?" Verrazzano's thoughts raced and then crashed. "But you couldn't have."

"You're right about that, buddy. I didn't do a one of them. But Wyatt wants the scalps of these Chinese engineers, so I'm going to take him one."

"He'll kill you."

"He'll be glad to see me. He'll get me a new ID and put me to work again. No more detention centers for me, Sergeant Major Verrazzano." He put the H&K to Verrazzano's head. "No more *nothing* for you."

A silenced shot spat through the air, a ripping impact. Frisch fell without a word.

A man walked fast down the center of the street toward Verrazzano. The street light illuminated his scabbed face. The Krokodil called, "Frisch. Tom Frisch. Come out from there."

Verrazzano grabbed the pistol from Frisch's hand. The assassin thought he had killed the ICE agent. He *should* have been the one with the gun. The Krokodil had no idea that Frisch had turned the tables on him—that it was Verrazzano who had been about to be killed.

He struggled to take aim at the Krokodil. His brain couldn't put together a steady image. He saw two or three of him, all moving different ways in the twilight.

"Frisch?" The Krokodil sensed something wasn't right. "Wyatt wants to talk to you."

The door of the loan office opened. The small Chinese woman stepped out onto the sidewalk. She saw the Krokodil in the road, his gun at his side. Instantly she took off, running toward the church. The Krokodil chased her.

Verrazzano held onto the rear bumper of the Wolfwagen. He reached for the handle on the back door and tugged himself up.

Through the windows, he saw Julie Jin run around the corner. The Krokodil closed on her.

Every person who would die or lose someone they loved when the cars crashed, every kid who'd be crushed when their mother lost control of the wheel on the way to school, they all put out their hands and touched Verrazzano and soothed him, gave him focus. His head burst and his pain spattered the dark walls of the eighteenth-century buildings up to the fifth floor, but he was alive and he had purpose. He jogged down the street. After a few paces, he discovered that he hadn't fallen down, so he went into a sprint.

Around the corner, the street was empty. Then a motion drew his attention. A man vaulting a wall. Verrazzano followed. He hauled himself over the shoulder-high stone wall and came down in an old graveyard. The tombs reached out for him. *Not yet*, he thought.

Thirty yards ahead, the Krokodil checked his direction and went right. The ICE agent struggled after him. He struck his thigh on a leaning gravestone and tumbled over a long, low tomb. He scrambled to his feet.

In the darkness, the Krokodil's face was the only sign Verrazzano had to follow, patching and pale in the light from the clock face on the church tower. He went after it.

Then the Krokodil was gone. Verrazzano stopped and listened. There was the sound of waterproof fabric rubbing erratically against stone, and the Chinese woman screeching. She spoke some words of defiance, but quickly she switched to pleading. Then she was silent.

Verrazzano hurried toward the sounds. He was two rows of tombs away when the scene emerged from the dark. Julie Jin knelt, dead, her throat cut. The Krokodil ripped away her baseball cap and held her hair in his fist. It was barely long enough to get a hold of. His other hand took a knife to her brow. Blood ran down over her forehead as he started to scalp her.

Verrazzano lifted his H&K. "That's enough."

"Suck me, Frisch." The Krokodil's voice was like heavy sheets of paper ripping. "You want to go see Wyatt? Okay, I'll take you with me. But get out of my face right now."

"You shot the wrong guy." Verrazzano moved closer. "You saved my life."

The Krokodil spat. He kept his eyes on Verrazzano as he sawed farther along Julie Jin's hairline.

"Now it's time for me to save yours." Verrazzano made a swift step and kicked at the Krokodil's wrist. The knife flew from his hand and tinkled against a stone angel.

The Krokodil dropped the dead woman. He thrust his torso upward, held onto Verrazzano's shoulders, and bit into his neck.

Verrazzano dropped sideways, falling on top of the Krokodil, letting his weight crush him on a sharply angled tombstone that had been pushed out of kilter by centuries in the dirt. Any other man would have snapped with the impact of the stone against his lower back. The Krokodil didn't break, but he did open his mouth to let go of Verrazzano's neck.

Verrazzano rolled away and trained his gun on him. "We're the same, you and me. Wyatt did the same number on both of us. I know who you are."

"You don't even know who *you* are."

"Wyatt sent me out to kill people. Told me it was for the good of the United States. It turned out to be just to make him rich. I *know* who you are."

"Wait until your skin starts falling off. *Then* you'll know who you are. Because you'll see what's underneath." The Krokodil rose unsteadily, feeling his back. "Take a look at me. Imagine this happened to you. What would be under your skin?"

Verrazzano shuddered. The Krokodil smiled bitterly. "You think you know. But there's surprises for you there, no matter how

216

much you think you hate yourself." He pointed a finger at Verraz-zano's chest. "Only then, you can tell me you know who I am."

"I killed the Lebanese prime minister."

The Krokodil halted, confused by Verrazzano's sudden admission. "The who?"

"Prime Minister Rafik Karami was about to sign a peace deal with Israel. Wyatt told me the State Department had decided the peace would threaten US interests. I didn't ask why. I planted a bomb in Karami's limo and blew it up. Every time someone dies in Israel or Lebanon since that day, I get reminded of exactly what's underneath my skin."

"Better take another look, then, Sergeant Major." Coughing and clutching his chest, Frisch stumbled between the gravestones. He slipped onto his backside and leaned against a tomb. His hand covered the bullet hole in his chest, but air leaked noisily out of the exit wound in his back.

Verrazzano went to him. Special Forces training pushed soldiers beyond the pain and injury that would kill another man. They were deliberately dehydrated on long runs in full kit and half drowned treading water in their boots. They were tormented and terrorized by their drill sergeants, so that no one else would ever be able to do it to them. That training kept Frisch on his feet until he reached Verrazzano, when most men would have been expiring in the gutter back on the street. Even so, Frisch clearly didn't have much left. "I killed Karami. Not you."

The Krokodil edged toward the body of Julie Jin. Verrazzano lifted his H&K and held it on him. The Krokodil went still.

Verrazzano whispered to Frisch, "That's not possible. I saw the car pull away from Karami's home. I kept a visual on it until I activated the bomb. It went up in smoke. It was totally destroyed."

Frisch shook his head. "You blew up the limo, sure. You killed a few of the guy's staff. But Karami didn't take the ride. He wasn't in the car. Wyatt heard the prime minister's voice on a phone tap right after the bomb went off. So he had him killed at his home an hour later. He sent me. I killed the guy."

The ground in the graveyard seemed to tremble under Verrazzano's feet, as though the dead were disturbed to find him less of a murderer than he had supposed himself to be. "Why didn't he tell me? Why did Wyatt keep it from me?"

A siren sounded on the main street beyond the loan office. Verrazzano saw the lights on in a few apartments overlooking the graveyard. He noticed the silhouette of a stout old woman on the telephone.

"Let's go, Verrazzano." The Krokodil pointed toward the dead Chinese woman. "We take the scalp. We get you back with Wyatt. He'll explain whatever it is that Frisch is trying to tell you. The guy's lying for sure, anyone can see it."

Verrazzano stood still, knowing that Frisch told the truth.

Frisch tried to lift himself. "You don't need Wyatt to explain. Listen to what I'm telling you. In boot camp, they break you down to make you do what you're told. Even then, most soldiers shoot wide of any human target without even knowing it because they don't want to be killers. Wyatt understands that. It's why he never stops breaking you down."

"Come on, Verrazzano. Let's move," the Krokodil said. "You're going to die, Frisch."

Frisch wheezed and grimaced. "Wyatt let you believe you'd destroyed peace in the Middle East, Verrazzano. He figured you'd have to go all the way bad just to stop yourself from going suicidal. You'd be his guy forever."

The siren came closer toward the graveyard. Verrazzano ran his hand over his face. The concussion buzzed through his head. The Krokodil and the corpse of Julie Jin transformed into the prime minister and Maryam Ghattas, the woman he had murdered in front of her child to cover his tracks. So that she wouldn't expose him as the assassin of the prime minister. Except that he hadn't assassinated the prime minister after all. Wyatt could have stopped it at any moment. Could have told him he wasn't guilty. That he didn't need to kill Maryam Ghattas.

"Wyatt sent you to kill the Ghattas woman because she had sources that knew how Karami really died. She knew about Wyatt's deal with Hezbollah. She was going to blow the whistle on *him*. Not on you." Frisch choked and dribbled blood. He grabbed Verrazzano's arm. "Wyatt thought he owned you after the Karami hit. But—"

The police car pulled up on the other side of the graveyard wall. The blue light spun on the roof and striped the old stones of the church. Frisch's grip was insistent. "But you were too strong for him. You wouldn't go all the way into the darkness. Not like I did. Not like the Krokodil. Remember that, Verrazzano. You were too strong for Wyatt back then. And you're too strong for him now."

The Krokodil edged away, moving toward the knife he had lost. Verrazzano lifted his pistol. "Don't move."

"'Joy arises—'" Frisch's voice choked off.

"'Joy arises in a person free from remorse,'" Verrazzano said. Frisch's sweat glistened in the moonlight on his lifeless face. He was free. Verrazzano felt a curious sadness. So few people knew who he really was. Now there was one less of them.

"You still killed that woman in Beirut in front of her kid, Verrazzano," the Krokodil said. "You ain't clean, no matter what Frisch tells you now."

The voices of the policemen on the street were strained and muted. Verrazzano figured they were arguing about entering the graveyard without backup. He watched the Krokodil's ravaged features come in and out of the light as the clouds crossed the moon. He reached for his phone in Frisch's jacket. He needed to get in touch with the rest of his team. First he had to deal with the assassin lingering a couple of yards from him. The Krokodil had his eyes on the dead woman. He still wanted the scalp—that was why he hadn't made a more determined break, even with Verrazzano's gun trained on him. But he didn't want to be around when the local cops came over that wall.

"Don't even think about it." Verrazzano raised his pistol and advanced on the Krokodil.

One of the policemen called from beyond the tombstones. "Drop the gun."

Verrazzano glanced toward the street. A policeman climbed the wall into the graveyard. Another had his weapon trained on Verrazzano. "I'm a US law enforcement officer," he called.

"Drop the gun, I said."

The apse of the church shrouded the Krokodil in shadow. He ran quickly and silently out of sight into the darkness behind the building. Verrazzano went after him, but a shot cut the darkness and the silence. He felt heat in his shoulder, and he was spinning to the ground.

"Is he alive?" the cop shouted from the wall.

His partner leaned over Verrazzano and poked at his wound with his pistol. Verrazzano growled and tensed the muscles of his arm to cut off the bleed. "Ask me again in five minutes," the second cop said. He lit a cigarette and blew the smoke in Verrazzano's face.

CHAPTER 24

Feng Yi leered across the long cherrywood table in the Hotel Sacher's art deco conference room. Minister Ma had just told the American delegation that a particular body affiliated with the Chinese government—not one completely under his control, you understand—would crash every car in the Western world the very next day if the Americans didn't make the trade concessions he demanded. The US secretary of state's gigantic jaw trembled with rage. But he didn't threaten war. Minister Ma was right. The Americans had fought too many times in too many places during the last decade and a half, and their economy was too weak to sustain a conflict with the Chinese superpower.

"I have to tell you in no uncertain terms that we consider the proposition by the honorable Minister Ma to be highly unproductive." The American's response to Ma's threat was as animated as an accountant with a 1040EZ. He didn't appear to doubt China's ability to accomplish the devastating mass crash. Feng Yi felt the power to destroy the world rippling through him.

Minister Ma was blank and unreadable. Anyone who hadn't observed him in a negotiation before would have assumed he was thinking of something that had happened last night—something whose details he could only vaguely recall. But every cell in his brain was present, assessing each syllable from the American, calibrating and recalibrating. Feng, however, barely paid attention. He was measuring his chances of getting the Swedish woman naked that night. She had agreed to travel with him. He tapped through the alerts on his cell phone. European airports were opening, he read, though the Americans were keeping theirs in lockdown for another day. Everything was falling into place. The Swede would take him on the business trip she had planned for that evening—away from her jealous husband. He imagined posing her naked body and recording its movements with his camera. He would take thousands of pictures. He would manipulate and distort them to make them perfect in their power to arouse him. Her form was the basic ingredient he needed for the pleasure of digital editing and montage. When he had reworked the images, they would show her riding motorbikes naked and engaging in sex with famous actresses or cut open to show the computer motherboards in her belly. He didn't even have to persuade her to sleep with him—that was for men who failed to understand the possibilities of the web and of Photoshop. Women got it. It turned them on to display themselves to him, because he understood that there was no limit to pleasure, just as women's ecstasy was not restricted the way men's was to the insertion of the penis and the thrusting of hips and a brief moment of animal rapture.

Then Feng saw it. It interrupted his daydream as surely as a nudge from his neighbor at the negotiating table. Minister Ma's tongue flicked across his lips. It was an unconscious gesture of excitement that was as clear to Feng as if the old bastard would have jumped up and cried out. Feng came out of his reverie and snapped his attention back to the table. *What the hell did I miss?* he thought.

"Thus in light of the consequences presented to us by Minister Ma, we are reluctantly prepared to accept the three points the Minister made about patent regulations," the secretary of state said. "These shall be subject to further negotiation in the details during the working group stage, but for the purposes of statements to be made by the Chinese and United States delegations tonight, we can accept in principle the Minister's three points, and we will instruct our representatives on the working groups to move toward a full understanding on these points."

No way, Feng thought. He swiveled toward his boss. Ma was all stillness, except for his ankle, which jiggled hard under the table. It was happening. They had won. The Americans were caving.

"As a second concession, we are ready to agree to the two copyright policy adjustments raised by the Minister this morning in relation to intellectual property and the theft thereof by Chinese companies," the American said.

Minister Ma broke in. "Alleged theft."

"Alleged theft." The American had a pencil between the fingertips of his two hands on the tabletop. He was squeezing it as hard as he could without snapping it.

"The tariffs?" Ma said.

"The tariffs on the importation of Chinese steel." The secretary of state stared at his hands before he continued. "We are prepared to lower the tariffs from two hundred and sixty-five point five percent to a rate fixed at a more equitable—"

"Zero."

"Now hold on there."

"Zero tariff. Just as American steelmakers pay no tariff to reach Chinese markets."

"American steelmakers don't export to China because your domestic prices are—" The American realized this was no longer a negotiation. It was blackmail. "Zero percent tariff. Agreed."

Feng was three seats down from Minister Ma. He could smell the old man's pleasure. It drifted through the Chinese delegation like sex pheromones and made the minister's aides wriggle and twitch.

Then Feng started to sweat. If the American conceded, Minister Ma wouldn't want the crash operation to go ahead tomorrow. Feng would have to stop it. *Damn their weakness,* he thought, casting his eye along the table of senior US diplomats and Washington cadres. If one of them failed, the worst they could expect would be a transfer to the consulate in Kabul, or they might get stuck teaching political science at a university in one of those places in the Midwest where Americans come from but never seem to live. Fail Minister Ma and Feng would, at best, be kicked to death in the bunkroom of a *laogai* penal camp on his way to "reform through labor." More likely he'd confess in front of the cameras that he had betrayed the old pig and beg for the pleasure of a bullet to the head so that he might serve as a reminder to others of the importance of pleasing the great minister.

Ma beckoned to him. Panic caught Feng. He scuttled toward Ma and knelt beside his chair. The minister lifted his hand to his face to disguise the movements of his lips. "I have what I want from these Americans. Nonetheless I shall pass many hours here in further negotiations before I let them off the hook."

Feng pretended to show pleasure at his master's cruelty and diplomatic skill. "Minister Ma, you have scored a great victory for the People's Republic."

"I want to give you time to call off the operation." He surely saw the resentment in Feng's eyes. "If the operation is carried out, it will cost the People's Republic many billions of dollars. Billions that this clown"—he gestured toward the secretary of state—"has just tossed across the table to me. Don't throw them away as he has done. Are *you* a clown? Don't be a clown."

Feng bowed his head. "I will see to it, Minister Ma."

The minister laid his fingers on Feng's hand to delay him. "You think you're a big number, don't you? Look at you, crouching at my side, staring up at me. You are a dog that yaps noisily all the time to demand attention. I do believe that perhaps you even sweat through your tongue the way a dog does."

Feng realized that his mouth was wide open. He snapped it shut.

"When someone's computer goes wrong, they telephone a faceless drone at a call center," Ma said. "The poor drone helps them fix the computer. Then the customer hangs up on the drone and thinks what a waste of time it was, whether the computer was fixed or not. Do you understand?"

"I am the drone at the call center, and you are the one who called to get your computer fixed."

"Now I am hanging up the phone."

The power Feng had felt in his hotel room with the Swedish woman was gone. He was slack and limp. Minister Ma's aides glared at him. The Americans watched him with contempt. He lifted himself from his knees.

For a moment, Feng thought he might speak. Tell them that he would crash all the cars anyway, and there was no amount of American concessions that could persuade him otherwise. Instead he slouched toward the exit and went into the corridor. The bodyguards turned toward him, the robotic US secret service meatheads and Minister Ma's sleazy kung-fu practitioners with their ponytails and hair oil.

Screw them all. He would let the cars crash, and he would go to the airport with Maj and convince her not to return to her husband. He would hide himself in Sweden or Spain and fill the Internet with manipulated pictures of her body, and let Minister Ma take the rap for the failed trade talks and the billions of dollars' worth of lost opportunities. He went into the next room, where the Chinese delegation had its secure lines. The communications woman looked up at him.

"I need to make a call for Minister Ma." Feng picked up the phone and pulled Wyatt's number from his pocket. He dialed the code that introduced an additional element of encryption above the algorithms already set up by the communications experts. It was a code known only to him because he had written it and uploaded the scrambler to the delegation's system. Wyatt picked up at the first ring.

"I need you to call off the operation." Feng spoke in Chinese.

Wyatt responded in the same language. "You do not sound happy."

"What do you know about happiness? Are you in control of the remaining engineers? Are you able to get them a message that they must not go ahead with the plan?"

The line was silent. Then Wyatt spoke again. "I can see to it that the engineers do not carry out the plan. Are you certain? This is your wish?"

"Do as you are told," Feng bellowed.

When Wyatt's voice came down the line, it showed no reaction to Feng's anger and volume. This was the ultimate signal of the American's superiority. He didn't need to teach Feng a lesson, to demonstrate his power. He was utterly calm even when abused. "I shall do as you ask."

"I'm not *asking*."

"I shall do as you command."

"Make sure that you do."

"What else do you have to say?"

Feng wanted to weep. He wanted to tell Wyatt that no one loved him the way they should. He had taken thousands of images of men and women he had befriended and pasted masks onto their faces digitally, all because no face had ever turned to him with genuine love. "That is all. Report to me through the Silent Circle app."

Wyatt hung up. Feng tried to replace the handset in the cradle. He couldn't get it to fit. Twice it clattered onto the desk. The communications woman reached out and slipped it neatly into place, stifling a giggle.

Feng went to the lobby and jumped the line at reception. "I need to make a phone call. It's urgent. For the trade negotiations."

The middle-aged man in the brown round-collared jerkin behind the reception desk glanced toward the doors of the hotel. The antiglobalization punks waved placards and yelled their chants about the blood on the hands of the banks and the eco-fascism of Starbucks. The hotel worker was clearly going to be happy once the trade talks were done. He gave Feng the handset with a sigh. Feng dialed and waited. When the Swedish woman picked up, he said, "Let's go now to the airport. You are still in the hotel? Come to the lobby in five minutes. No, I don't have any packing to do. Five minutes, okay?" He handed the phone back to the reception clerk.

He went to the bar and sank a brandy in two swigs. He was finishing a second one when Maj found him. He wanted to weep into her breasts. But then he remembered that they were small, and anyhow, he was finished with honest emotion for now. "Let's go to the airport."

As they passed the reception desk, a woman with scarred cheeks was spelling out a name in her American accent. "F-E-N-G, first name Y-I."

The head of the European Union delegation was over by the door. A dozen reporters shoved digital voice recorders at him, and a handful of photographers jostled to the front of the press. "There has been a major breakthrough," the EU man said. "China and the US have agreed on some important issues, and I think in an hour or two we shall have a full agreement here."

Feng Yi scuttled into the revolving doors with the Swedish woman. He hustled along the sidewalk past the barricades. The antiglobalization people saw a Chinese man in a suit, so they decided he must be linked to the talks. They started up a chant that rhymed

Beijing and the *ka-ching* of a cash register. He ducked around the corner and came to the row of limos. He spotted Minister Ma's Red Horizon limo and his driver. He stepped in front of the parked car, perching against the rear of the next long, black vehicle in the line. Ma's driver glanced at him with contempt. Feng waved and smiled and took a quick photo of the license plate with his cell phone. Then he grabbed the Swedish woman's hand and climbed over the barricade toward the taxi rank across the street by the State Opera House.

As they reached the rear of the crowd, a short, bearded man in an old Russian army tunic and sweat pants pointed a finger and frowned, trying to put a face to a name. Then he snapped his fingers and said, "Maj. It's Maj, isn't it?"

The Swedish woman averted her eyes and moved past him. Feng glanced back at the confusion on the face of the man in the tunic. The protester shook his head, as though he were disappointed in someone. In Maj.

"You know that guy?" Feng said.

Maj skirted around the first taxi in the line and got inside without speaking. Feng craned to see over the heads of the protesters into the lobby of the hotel. The thin-faced reception clerk pointed toward the door. The American woman with the scars headed quickly back out onto the street. Feng Yi threw two fifty-euro notes at the taxi driver as he dived into the backseat. "Go to the airport. Very fast. I will give you four more of those."

The driver swung out toward the Ringstrasse. The American woman came onto the sidewalk, scanning the crowd. Then she saw Feng, and she ran toward Kärntner Strasse. She was heading for a taxi when Feng went around the corner.

He didn't need to know who she was. She was looking for him. No one called his name because they wanted to be nice to him. From Minister Ma to Colonel Wyatt to the American trade delegation, they wanted to use him or to hurt him.

Maj touched her finger to Feng's chin. He pressed the tip of her nose lightly and made a growling sound. "I have our tickets in my purse," she said.

"Where are we going?"

"Do you enjoy hot weather?"

"If it's hot, you will take your clothes off, right? So I like hot weather." He pressed his mouth to her ear. "Where are we going?"

"It's a surprise."

"Africa? Dubai? Greece? Come on, where?"

"Wait and see."

He glanced through the rear window of the taxi as they weaved along the Ring. He focused on all the cabs behind him, on their passengers. He didn't see the American woman with the scars. It was going to be all right.

CHAPTER 25

Jahn stared from her taxi into the taillights of the cars ahead and wondered which one was taking Feng Yi away from her. She guessed where he would go. She told her driver to take her to the airport. Feng was in Vienna for trade negotiations, but the EU diplomat in the hotel lobby reported a final breakthrough in the talks. Feng was done here. Done with Americans, at least—the man at the reception desk of the hotel had informed her that Feng's companion was a Swedish guest.

The terminal was packed with people stranded by the crash shutdown, all desperate to find flights now that the airports had opened again. Jahn sprinted down the long narrow shopping mall that connected the gates. There were imminent departures to London, New York, Rome, Zürich, and Bratislava. Jahn scanned them all quickly. The next flight was to Palma de Majorca, scheduled to leave soon from Gate 12. She pushed herself to go faster through the crowd. The Austrian Airlines flight flashed "Gate Closed" on the departures board. What was she going to do when she got there? She knew what she *should* do. But that would've been how she'd have handled it before. It was different now. She felt the weight of emotion and doubt and confusion, and it slowed her somehow even as she dashed between the travelers.

She burned down the last stretch of the concourse to the Palma flight. She was so tired. She hadn't slept since the Special Agent in

Charge woke her with the news of the mass crash on Monday. She had watched Verrazzano get a couple of hours sleep on the plane to Europe. But she had been in constant conversation with her husband in her head, ever since the Krokodil spoke his name at the rental car office at the Detroit airport, hissing that he knew where to find him. When Chris called from Beirut, he asked of her the very thing she had no right to give—his life for the lives of so many others. It was Verrazzano who gave her the resolution she needed. At the house south of Bonn, when she told him the story of how she got the ugly wound on her face, she sensed all *his* scars. She knew then that she must suffer the same way he had. She must reject the deal she made with her husband over the phone in the Jansen Trapp factory. She had betrayed everything she believed in for the sake of her husband. Everything but love. Well, love didn't count for anything when thousands of lives were at stake and you were a federal agent sworn to safeguard those lives. She had made a choice for which the entire world would condemn her—except Verrazzano. She sensed that he would pardon her if she ever had the chance to tell him what she had done. She wondered if she'd be able ever to forgive *herself*.

She reached the gate for the Palma flight. The Austrian Airlines staff were packing up their rolls of baggage labels and shutting down the computers. "Stop the flight," she yelled.

A young man in an Austrian Airlines vest flicked back his blond bangs and half-smiled. "The flight has departed, madam. May I see your ticket? We can reroute you through—"

"There is a man on that plane who is an important material witness in an international terrorism case." Jahn reached into her jacket for her FBI identity wallet. She showed it to the Austrian.

"Terrorism?" The blond man was quickly panicked. "He's a terrorist?"

Jahn tried to figure out what Verrazzano would have done. Then she thought of her husband again, and her determination melted into despair. She could have been the best agent in the FBI. Now she was barely even able to believe that she was one of the good guys.

"Are they going to blow up the plane?" The Austrian Airlines man's eyes were wide and innocent and horrified.

Quietly, Jahn said, "The person on board is a witness in a terrorism case. Not an actual terrorist."

"Then the plane is safe?"

"Well, yeah. But look—"

"Let's go and see the security chief."

"We don't have time."

"Do I look as though I have the authority to turn a flight around?" He waved the roll of baggage stickers, a badge of his menial status.

"Show me the passenger manifest."

The young Austrian flipped a couple of pages on his clipboard and turned it toward her. There was Feng Yi's name, and beside it under the next ticket number was a Swedish passport holder. Jahn dialed Haddad. "Feng Yi is on Austrian Airlines flight 8873 from Vienna to Palma de Majorca, Spain. He's in the company of a Swedish woman named Maj Sand. I couldn't catch them before they got on the plane."

"It's going to Majorca? Bill Todd is in Majorca," Haddad said.

"How in hell did he get there?"

"Bill can meet the plane and track Feng Yi."

"Okay. Keep me informed." She hung up. She pictured her husband in the torture rooms of Hezbollah. She had believed that if she saved him, she could heal him. But if she saved him this way, she'd be destroyed and he'd go down with her anyway. His voice came out of the silence. Not the brittle, dry whine she had heard over the phone from Beirut. It was the strong, loving voice that held her together when she was at her most despairing—back when he said, "There's no one like you, Gina. Don't ever change."

The Austrian held out his phone to her. "The head of security is on the line," he said.

She took the phone and hung up the call. "How soon could you get me to Palma?"

CHAPTER 26

The Czech patrolmen shut Verrazzano in the back of their squad car and left him there. Maybe they hoped he would simply bleed out and make a complicated situation less tricky. He used one of his socks to stanch the bleeding from the gunshot wound they had inflicted on his upper arm, then he ripped away the sleeve of his shirt and used it to bandage the gash in his deltoid. He thought about Frisch's final words. Verrazzano hadn't after all committed the terrible crime he had confessed to his wife and for which she had divorced him. He had not killed the Lebanese prime minister, had not doomed the Middle East to more years of war. For a moment, he thought that he could tell Melanie this news and she would forgive him. But it wouldn't work. She'd only think he was lying again. He couldn't go back to a time before his marriage died any more than he could return to the stairwell in Beirut before he killed Maryam Ghattas. Besides, Frisch hadn't absolved him of that.

The street filled with ambulances and forensics teams and plainclothesmen. Eventually a squat figure in a cheap leather jacket climbed out of the kind of battered little BŠZ that used to make Czech cars and lawnmowers so hard to tell apart. The plainclothesmen gravitated toward him. They gestured at the squad car. The short man walked purposefully across the cobbles, lighting a cigarette.

On Verrazzano's phone, Haddad updated him about the movements of Jahn, Kinsella, and Todd and of Feng Yi and his Swedish girlfriend. He tried to figure out the link to Palma. Everything was converging there. Wyatt killed the Irish banker at the Palma Aquarium. He felt the blood seeping into his bandage. Was he the shark right now? Or the chum, sinking through the murky water?

The Czech detective slipped into the back seat. He had Verrazzano's ICE ID in his hand. He pushed the button on the overhead light and examined it. "Verrazzano, like the bridge?"

The bridge across New York Bay was deliberately misspelled with a single *Z* by a sixties bureaucrat because the name of the Florentine explorer who first passed through the Narrows in 1524 looked too Italian. Verrazzano refused to acknowledge any connection to the bridge. "No, like the first guy to sail into Narragansett Bay."

"I thought that was Leif Ericson and the Vikings?"

"That's unconfirmed. Not historical fact. The Italians got there first."

"*Bravissimo* for them. Let's stick with facts, then. What happened here?"

"I was shot by Czech policemen."

"We have witnesses who'll say that's not what happened. We always do. So tell me what really happened, and I won't punch you on your wounded arm."

"Tell me who you are first."

The man scratched his bald scalp and exhaled enough smoke to make the cop car feel like a nightclub in 1972. "I am Sliva. The guy who has to sort out the crap from the shit here." He jerked his thumb toward the graveyard. "You want my rank and department? You'll find out soon enough if you don't cooperate fully. Now kindly explain why there is a dead Asian woman in the graveyard with bullet wounds to her chest and lacerations on her upper brow from a sharp blade. And continue from there to give me details of why there is also a Caucasian male a couple of meters from her who appears to have expired from a bullet that pierced his lung."

"I'm going to be straight with you. First you have to know that the stakes are even higher than they seem."

"For you the stakes are pretty high, that's for sure. But okay, I'm impressed. Go on." He took the window down a couple of inches and flicked his cigarette through the gap. He lit another, examining its tip thoughtfully.

"The dead guy in the graveyard is an American. He's a former Special Forces operative who has been helping me in an investigation. The Asian woman is Chinese. She's a witness and perhaps a suspect in the investigation."

"The investigation of what?"

"Of the mass crash of Darien motor cars last week."

"Names?"

"The American is Thomas Frisch. The Chinese woman is Jin Ju, also known as Julie."

"Why are they here?"

"In Prague?"

The cop gave a slow nod. "Start with that. Then why are they in the graveyard? Then you can get to why they are dead."

"Frisch abducted me because he knew I was coming to Prague to trace a Chinese computer engineer, Julie Jin. I believed Jin could lead us to the people behind the Darien crash. I knew Jin would eventually come to a loan shop on this street to convert a Bitcoin payment into cash. Bitcoin is a virtual currency—"

"This is central Europe, Special Agent Verrazzano. We have bigger mafias than you New Yorkers. I know what Bitcoin is. Proceed."

"Julie Jin arrived to collect her money. I intended to apprehend her as she left the loan office. The situation was complicated because Frisch was armed, and I wasn't. Right then we were surprised by a sudden attack from another source."

"What source?"

"I can only assume it was someone associated with the Darien conspiracy."

"He killed Jin and Frisch? Who was this guy?"

"I don't know." There was only so much explaining Verrazzano was prepared to do for someone whose officer had put a bullet through his arm.

"You don't know." Sliva's blink was long and disappointed. "Sure you don't. Who died first?"

"Jin. But Frisch was shot first. The killer thought Frisch was dead. He went in pursuit of Jin. I took my weapon back from Frisch and was holding the killer when your officers tried to get me to drop my gun. Then they shot me, and the killer escaped."

Sliva clicked his tongue. "Frisch was shot just down the street. There's a bullet lodged in a Wolfwagen van and blood on the cobblestones. But he died in the graveyard."

"He followed me there. He had great ability to withstand pain. He was trained for it. Any other man would've lain down and died where he was."

"A real American Superman. What happened to Julie Jin's head?" Sliva drew his finger across the point on his bald scalp where his hairline had once been.

"Some of the other Chinese computer engineers involved in the case have been scalped by their killer."

"Scalped? Like in the Westerns?"

"Julie Jin is the only one to die and *not* lose her scalp."

"Because you intervened just as the scalper was starting his work?"

"Because Tom Frisch showed up, still alive and holding a gun on the killer."

"I'm sure her husband will be deeply grateful to you and Mister Frisch. I'm serious. The dead woman has a crucifix around her neck. We do open casket funerals here. A scalping would have made for a pretty miserable time at the church."

The cop already knew Julie Jin was married. What else did he know? "She's Catholic?"

"I assume she converted when she married—" Sliva took a notebook from his pocket and flipped it open. "When she married a guy named Dusan Salac."

"A Czech?"

"Sounds like it. The name, I mean."

"I've been following the trail of Chinese engineers. They've been dying just as I get to them. Julie Jin was the last one. My trail is dead. Unless—"

"Unless Mister Salac would take time out of his grieving to enlighten you? Obviously there's something very basic you're not telling me. Something that makes this even more urgent than you would have me believe." He jerked his thick body across the back seat. He came close to Verrazzano's face. His breath smelled like Pittsburgh in the heyday of US Steel. "So if you want to question Mister Salac, stop treating me like an idiot."

"The Darien crash was only the first stage in the criminal operation."

"Ahh." Sliva let his bulk slip back across the bench seat. "What's the next stage? More crashes?"

"That's correct."

"But if all the Darien cars crashed on Monday, then—" Sliva's dark glower opened and urgency beamed out. "By Christ, there's another carmaker involved."

"More than one. Almost every car sold in the last year."

Sliva opened the door of the patrol car. "I bought my BŠZ when Axl Rose was in the charts. So I guess we'll be safe driving it. Let's go and see Julie Jin's husband."

It was a short drive to Jin's home in the Žižkov neighborhood. A patrolman perched against the hood of his squad car outside the apartment building, sharing his cigarettes with a girl. Even from a distance and at night, it was obvious that she was too young to smoke and much too young for a cop to have his hand up her skirt. Sliva pulled up behind the cop car and shunted its rear fender hard enough to jolt the happy couple. The girl's body jerked, and her cigarette lanced into the cop's cheek. He spun around and advanced angrily on the old BŠZ. He bent to talk to the driver through the window of the car.

Sliva opened the door forcefully, striking the cop on the head with the frame around the window. The younger cop's cap flew off and he staggered. Sliva stepped out. "Go home," he called to the girl. She skittered away, the lights in the heels of her sneakers flashing on the graffitied facade of the apartment building with each step. Verrazzano came around from the passenger side of the BŠZ.

"Gentrification." Sliva gestured at the faux ghetto daubings on the walls. "Real estate will be a thousand euros per square meter here soon enough. Very high class. Unlike this guy."

The younger cop was doubled over, one hand on his shaven head, the other on the hood of the BŠZ. He bled from a cut above his brow. Sliva gave him a wad of tissues from his pocket and a few whispered words that oozed contempt and headed for the apartment building's entrance.

A chain and a sign in Czech decorated the elevator door. Out of service. Sliva approached the stairs with reluctance. Julie Jin had lived on the fourth floor. By the time they got to the apartment door, Sliva was wheezing like a *sevdalinka* accordion at the end of an energetic folk song. Verrazzano walked lightly behind him, trying to fend off the sense that he was at a dead end. If Jin's husband couldn't give him a lead, he was stuck without any route toward stopping the crash.

Sliva entered the apartment without knocking. Verrazzano went in behind him. The hall was decorated with Chinese calligraphy and posters of Steve Jobs and Bill Gates. At the far end, a female police officer whispered to a sullen four-year-old whose features were Asian. A slim man in his fifties with delicate posture came out of the living room. His hair was swept to the side, falling over his brow. He pushed it back and stroked the beard that reached down to his collar bone. Then he spoke in Czech.

"English, please." Sliva jerked his finger at Verrazzano. "Your wife excited the interest of the Americans, Mister Salac."

Salac turned his sad eyes on Verrazzano. "What's so interesting about my wife to you? Except that she's dead."

Verrazzano glanced quickly along the corridor toward the child's room.

"Daniela doesn't speak English," Salac said. "Julie spoke to our daughter in Chinese. I speak to her in Czech. She won't overhear anything. So please explain why there's an American here."

Verrazzano had seen this aggression in the recently bereaved before. Some people fell apart when faced with death. Others reacted to investigators as a stupid inconvenience. "Your wife worked for a man named Feng Yi?"

"My wife worked for BŠZ." Salac's beard stuck out from his chest, as he lifted his chin angrily.

"Let's call that her day job. She was employed by Chinese intelligence. She was a plant."

Salac spoke to Sliva in Czech. The cop shrugged.

"Mister Salac asks me," Sliva said, "if he can refuse to talk to you. You see, he's old enough to have grown up under Communism. Despite these pictures of great capitalists on the walls, he'll do what I tell him because I'm the guy who could make him disappear in the night. Even if things aren't like that anymore."

"They're more like that than you'd care to admit," Salac said.

"The system is no longer like that." Sliva wagged his index finger at Salac and smiled. "But maybe *I* am."

"The photos of Jobs and Gates weren't put on the walls by Mister Salac," Verrazzano said. "They'd have been Julie's idols. She was the programmer. Mister Salac is a student of China in general and of calligraphy in particular." He stepped toward a wall-mounted frame that contained a sheet of paper three feet tall. The Chinese characters stacked in columns were a little more fluid than the rest. Where the others were unadorned almost to the point that they seemed to have been printed, rather than painted, this one showed signs of the movement of the brush around the edges of each stroke. "This is *Caoshu*, right?"

Salac inclined his head in assent. He wasn't about to be charmed by a little knowledge of Chinese art.

"I appreciate calligraphy because the whole point is that, when you write, the motion is as much a part of it as the information you're setting down on the page," Verrazzano said. "It fits what I've observed about the world around me."

"How so?"

"The message isn't only in what people tell you. It's about the time and the space in which they exist. It's about where and when you hear it, and about how you listen."

"So whatever I tell you, you won't believe me? That's what you're saying."

"I'll listen to what you say, but I'll watch how you say it and I'll pay attention to the reaction it triggers in me."

Salac turned to the Czech cop. "Is that how you work too?"

Sliva gestured at the *Caoshu* work in the frame. "It makes me hungry. It looks like the stuff they use to decorate my local takeout place."

"I came to calligraphy and to my wife through my love of China," Salac said to Verrazzano. "I still love China. So if my wife worked for Chinese intelligence—which I think is a crazy idea—I would still be rooting for them over some American government bastard any time."

Sliva turned his smile on Verrazzano. "This guy is covering you with shit. Luckily I am the final square of toilet paper." He slapped Salac hard across the cheek.

The slight man tumbled against the door frame. He slid down to the floor. His daughter wailed and jumped from her bed. The policewoman held her. Verrazzano knelt beside Salac. The man was out cold. Blood seeped through his beard.

Verrazzano lifted him. He pushed past Sliva into the bathroom. He ran the cold tap and sat Salac on the toilet seat. He checked his airway and splashed water on his face. The man came around. He jerked his leg involuntarily, kicking over the wastebasket, and slipped off the toilet seat. Verrazzano caught him. The wastebasket rolled noisily against a plastic bag filled with purchases from a pharmacy. The bag shifted and its contents spilled out—tampons, roll-on deodorant in pink with a flowery label, a tub of night cream, a tall aerosol of shaving foam, a Gillette Mach III razor, and a pack of replacement blades.

Salac focused blearily on the feminine products on the tiles and seemed only then to realize that his wife was gone. He wept and mumbled her name.

"You'll be fine," Sliva said. "I see you're planning on shaving that stupid beard. You'll get another little Chinese girl soon enough." He nudged the Gillette with his toe.

"I loved only Julie, you bastard. I don't want another 'little Chinese girl.'"

The detective lit a cigarette and dropped the match in the sink.

Verrazzano sat on the side of the tub and picked up the pharmacy items. He put the razor in the bag last. Salac had at least two years of beard on his face, yet he sent his wife out to buy the razor along with her creams and tampons. Maybe Julie Jin wanted her husband to get rid of his long beard. She decided to force the issue, perhaps. He set the bag down and righted the wastebasket.

Footsteps came into the hallway, heavy, shuffling, unsteady. The cop who had been set to guard the apartment came into the bathroom doorway. He took away the soaked tissues from the cut on his brow. Blood streamed down the side of his face. "You cut me bad when you opened the door, sir. I need to wash up."

Sliva stepped away from the sink and beckoned for the patrolman to enter the cramped bathroom. "Join the party."

Salac sobbed on the toilet. His daughter was silent in the corridor. Verrazzano folded his legs sideways to allow the cop to get to the sink.

The cop rolled up his sleeves to wash. His forearms were massive. The one closest to Verrazzano, his left, was tattooed with a girl's name.

"Who's Veronica?" Verrazzano asked.

The cop put his head under the faucet and sloshed water over his scalp. "That's my daughter, sir." He winced as he cleaned the wound. He took a white towel from the rack. He dried his head. Blood smeared the towel. The cop looked embarrassed.

Sliva took the towel and tossed it into the bathtub. The cop turned. On his other arm, the name Petr was tattooed.

"Your son?" Verrazzano said.

"One kid on each arm, sir." The cop smiled. "My wife's name is tattooed on my chest. Only when you put them all together do you get the whole of me. On their own, they don't mean anything. See? Because I'm only complete when—"

"We get it. Very clever," Sliva said. "What did you tattoo on your dick? A dotted line for the latest one to sign her name across it? Oh, but you like them too young to know how to write, don't you?"

"That wasn't what you thought it was, sir. The girl had asked for my help." The cop rubbed his shaven head nervously. "I'll get back to my post now."

Verrazzano listened to the cop's tread on the stairs. Sliva helped Salac into the living room. Verrazzano picked up the bag of toiletries. He glanced into the sink. It was pink with blood from the cop's head wound.

Something formed in that bathroom, a thought he couldn't absolutely grasp, as though he had just entered and detected the scent of a previous user. He ran over the prompts, the events and sights, everything that might have given him this sense that he was close to a point of understanding. He played it all out again—Salac's unconsciousness, bringing him around, the wastebasket, the pharmacy bag, Sliva's callousness, the young cop's arrival, his wounded scalp, his tattoos, the three names that made him whole, the towel, and the blood. What did it mean?

"On their own, they don't mean anything," Verrazzano whispered. That's what the cop had said. About his tattoos. As he rubbed his shaven head.

It was there. All of it in those few moments.

Verrazzano grabbed the pharmacy bag. He pulled out the razor, the replacement blades, and the shave foam. He ran to the door of the living room. Sliva was bent over Salac on the couch. The detective looked up.

"Take me back to the graveyard," Verrazzano said. "Right now."

He went down the stairs four at a time. He waited on the sidewalk for Sliva to join him. He drummed on the roof of the BŠZ. It was all there. Now he saw it all.

The tattooed cop sat in his squad car and averted his eyes. Sliva shambled into the night. "What the hell, ICE man?"

"Come on, let's go."

The detective took the old BŠZ onto Vinohradska. "Are you going to tell me why you're taking a razor and shaving foam to the graveyard?"

A trolley car jangled across the junction. Sliva veered ahead of it and yelled at the driver. "Just get me there in one piece," Verrazzano said. "Don't crash. You'll see what it's about soon enough."

When Sliva pulled up at the graveyard, Verrazzano jumped out of the car. The cops at the perimeter made to stop him, but Sliva called for them to let him through. Verrazzano vaulted the wall and weaved through the tombs. He glanced quickly at the plastic sheet that covered Tom Frisch's body. Then he went to the one shrouding Julie Jin. He pulled it away.

A photo technician made a protest in Czech and reached for Verrazzano's shoulder. Sliva bellowed at him, and the tech drew back.

Verrazzano stared at Jin's face, bloodless but for the brow where the Krokodil had begun to scalp her. Like all the other Chinese engineers.

He covered the strip of short hair from her brow to the crown of her head in shaving foam from the can Jin had bought at the pharmacy. He ripped the razor out of its packaging.

Sliva came to his side. "This had better be good, ICE man."

Verrazzano braced Jin's head in his left hand and with his right stroked the razor back from her brow. He wiped the foam and hair off the razor onto his jeans. Then he made another stroke.

"Mother of Christ, how am I going to explain this to the coroner?" Sliva's sweat glimmered in the spotlights of the crime scene techs.

Verrazzano worked at Jin's hair. All the engineers had been scalped. The killer needed something from them. From their scalps. The Krokodil had lied when he said it was just his psycho passion. The scalps were the reason for the killings.

The dead woman's hair was fine and soft, but it gummed up the razor. He flicked off the disposable head and fitted a second blade from the replacement pack. A few more strokes and he saw the first letters. On her scalp. Her head had been shaved and something had been tattooed into her skin so that it'd be hidden when the hair grew back. He tried to figure out what it was. A neat section of scalp on the very top of her head in the center, three lines of letters and numbers, square brackets and arrows, colons and semicolons. He rubbed away the shave foam.

"Is that computer code?" Sliva said.

It was the kind of operating code that filled Julie Jin's head. But this was *on* her head. Verrazzano took a photo with his phone and sent the image to Haddad.

On their own, they don't mean anything. The scalps were a set; he was sure of it. Whoever was killing the engineers needed all five of them to have the complete code. The code that, when it was input to a car's computer, would make the disaster happen. Send every new car in Europe and North America hurtling toward a collision. But now they didn't have all the scalps.

Verrazzano sat on a flat tomb and stared at Jin's head, at the lines of blue code. Had he stopped it all? Had he beaten Wyatt?

A warm wind picked up, coming through the streets of old tenements from the River Vltava. The sheet covering Tom Frisch rustled. It was as though the dead man moved. Or spoke. Verrazzano heard him. He had to agree with Frisch. This wasn't over.

His phone buzzed in his palm. He picked up. "Roula," he said. "The photo I sent you. What does the code mean?"

"Is that someone's head?"

"It's a tattoo on the scalp of Julie Jin. The code, Roula?"

She hesitated. He imagined her making sense of the borders of the image, seeing it as the skin of a dead woman. Then she said, "It's a bytecode, a set of instructions for a software interpreter. See, it's numeric and—"

"To put it in layman's terms?"

"It tells a computer what to do. It's written this way, rather than in human-readable source code because bytecodes can be used on different hardware and different platforms."

"Does that mean you have to run it to figure out what it does?"

"I have to reverse translate it to make it human-readable. But I can see from a quick look that it's connected to the auto-crash software. Look at the middle of the second line. That's the date of execution, and it's July fourth."

"That's tomorrow." A chill passed through Verrazzano. If he had stopped this attack, he was just in time. If he hadn't, then he had no time left. "Without this code, can they activate the bug?"

"Only if they have a copy of this code."

"Assuming that there was different code on each of the engineers' scalps, the bad guys have four-fifths of the code they need. They don't have the final scalp, the final code. So they're stuck?"

"They're stuck."

"And the cars aren't going to crash."

"I guess not. Who was taking the scalps, though? The Chinese would surely have had the code themselves, somewhere central."

"The engineer who died here in Prague had bought shave foam and a razor. She was going to shave her head to reveal the code. I think she'd have read it in a mirror and activated it on July fourth."

"Why not just do it from China?"

"They'd have needed to hack into every major car company's system at the same time. Instead they put engineers inside who could each input a little bit of the whole code."

"I see it. Each of them together would beat the security of the car companies, and then their individual sets of bytecode would mesh over the different hardware systems of the car manufacturers. So maybe the killer is just trying to stop them? It could be another intelligence organization."

Verrazzano closed his eyes. He knew the deaths weren't caused by any white knight. The Krokodil was working for Wyatt. "Think of the short sale on auto stocks that Bill and Noelle uncovered in Luxembourg. Someone's in this for the money. It's not an intelligence operation."

"But now they're stuck."

Verrazzano wasn't counting on that. He rubbed at his jaw. "Did Jahn get anything else out of Vienna?"

"She's on a plane to Palma now, following Feng Yi. Before she took off, she got an ID on the Swedish woman who accompanied him onto the flight. Her name is Maj Sand. I can't find anything more about her, except that she's listed on the website of a drug treatment clinic in Stockholm as a counselor for addicts."

The Krokodil was still taking his drugs. His blighted skin revealed that much. But he might have taken counseling, might have been in Stockholm and met this woman. It was possible, of course, that she was unconnected to the assassin, but Verrazzano had to let the worst case play out in his head to figure out how he could counter it. "Is Bill going to tag them when they get to the airport in Palma?"

"That's his plan. What's Feng Yi's game now? Has he gone rogue?"

"Possibly. But I think he's been lured to Palma." Verrazzano scanned back through the diagram he built in his head of leads and possibilities. He reached the house in Detroit where he had found the first Chinese engineer dead. The victim's wife, pregnant, weeping in her bedroom, recalled that her husband said the trouble started "when the big man took off his wig." What did that mean? Was Feng Yi the big man?

"Lured? By the guys who've been killing the engineers, you think?"

The big man. "Because he has all the codes. All the secrets. Everything they need to activate this big crash."

"Oh, my God. But we've blocked their stock market play. They won't make any money, even if they do pull this off."

"Maybe there's another short sale that we don't know about. Or someone else is paying them to do it. Maybe money's not even why they're in it, after all. Tell Bill to be careful. The Swedish woman is working for the most dangerous man you could imagine."

"The Krokodil?"

Verrazzano was silent a moment. Todd was up against much more than that. The Krokodil was only as lethal as Wyatt's left hand. "Tell Bill not to lose them. But warn him to keep an eye out for Wyatt. I'm going to get on a plane to Palma as soon as I can."

CHAPTER 27

Bill Todd's trip from his hotel to the airport in Palma took almost as long as it did for Feng Yi to fly from Vienna because he had to work hard to be sure the man who killed the Irish banker in the shark tank wasn't on his tail. He took a bus from his hotel and got off under the palms at the busy intersection of Avinguda de Jaume III and the Passeig de Mallorca, where the detritus of the Darien crash had been shunted and piled in between the tall palms. He crossed the dusty nineteenth-century flood culvert and headed into the alleys of the medieval town. At least there were no Dariens there to pressure him with the enormity of his job. He hurried past the cathedral and down the steps to cross the Parc de la Mar. He hailed a taxi on the broad avenue by the beach. He scanned the traffic behind him as the cab pulled away. He was pretty sure he was clean, but he couldn't be certain. The road was just too crowded and the lights of the speeding vehicles weaved and ducked like two dozen boxing bouts in a single ring.

By the time he spotted Feng Yi and the Swedish woman at arrivals, Todd was sweating hard. He chided himself for focusing on his worries about a tail. *Stick to the job of watching the Chinese suspect*, he told himself. He tried to stay alert to the potential threat behind him while also trusting that he had done a good enough job of evasion back in the old town. He followed Feng,

skirting the groups of loudmouthed English tourists and their sullen, tired children.

The Chinese man walked politely at the side of the Swede
most of the way through the terminal. He spotted a Wi-Fi zone
and snagged a spot on the end of a metal bench beside a crowd of
excitable teens and wilted business travelers. He brought a tablet
out of his shapeless blazer and set to work. The Swede stood at
his side, biting her nails. Todd worked around behind them. He
saw a picture of a limo on the screen of Feng's tablet. The limo
had been photographed on a city street, somewhere classy and
classical, Europe for sure. As Feng opened up another interface,
he spoke to the Swede with a big smile. He tapped in a few pieces
of information and a couple of lines of code before he submitted
it. He put the tablet back in his jacket and rose from the seat. He
drew a finger across his neck and rocked backward. His laughter, shrill and cruel, cut through the babble of conversation and
the public address announcements in the terminal. The Swedish woman shared in the laughter. Her smile was quite genuine.
Feng high-fived her. They went out into the late-night heat.

Feng and the Swede joined the line for a taxi. Todd allowed
a few passengers to take the spots behind them, then he hid himself at the back of the line. When Feng's turn came to climb into
a cab, Todd cut out of the line and walked quickly to the fifth
taxi in the waiting lane and climbed inside. The driver started
to protest. Todd flashed his ICE ID. It would mean nothing spe-
cific to the Spaniard, but it would at least suggest that this wasn't
just an impatient tourist in the rear of the little SEAT hatchback.
The driver shrugged and pulled away. Todd pointed at Feng's taxi.
"Stay with him, okay?" Another shrug from the driver, and they
went toward the highway ramp.

Todd checked the road behind him. Some kind of fight had
broken out at the taxi rank. Tourists spilled onto the roadway.

Maybe his success in cutting the line had prompted others to try the same thing. A Mercedes pulled out of the taxi lane and took the same direction on the highway as Feng and Todd.

He watched the Chinese man's outline in the rear window of his cab. Feng was talking, gesticulating with his fat hands. The Swedish woman nodded her head. There had been something conspiratorial about them at the airport, and their behavior in the taxi confirmed it for Todd. He couldn't say quite why, but the man and woman seemed like business associates after a long negotiation, a deal done and plans laid. The taxi left the highway at Son Malferit and took the road along the seashore, back toward the cathedral.

Todd checked the road behind his cab. The Mercedes was a few cars back in the next lane. A plane flew low over the road, its engines blasting, on its way in for a landing. He craned his neck to watch its path.

Feng's taxi looped around the marina as far as the Embarcadero where the ferries left for Barcelona and Valencia on the Spanish mainland. The cab pulled into the bus stop, and the passengers got out. Feng tossed some cash to the driver and took out his cell phone. The woman lifted her foot and rested it on the bollard. She edged her skirt up to show him her leg. He took a photo and laughed his shrieking bray. He fiddled with the phone and showed her something. She slapped his shoulder playfully.

They walked past a seafood restaurant by the ticket booth for the ferries and toward the private quays. The dock was lined with gleaming white pleasure cruisers that'd be way too small for a billionaire but plenty big enough for someone with ten million in the bank.

Todd paid off his driver and hurried into the cover of the bus stop. Across the busy avenue, the Mercedes pulled up outside a tapas bar. The passenger stayed in the cab. If it was the shark tank killer, Todd wondered whether he could back himself to win. Well, if he lost, he wouldn't have to pay out on the bet.

He cut around the far side of the seafood restaurant. Feng and the Swede were on a quay running parallel to the shore, about one hundred yards from Todd. The man was a couple of yards ahead of her, eager, gesturing for her to move faster and laughing.

Todd glanced back to the road. The Mercedes was gone. He had missed the passenger's exit. He scanned the traffic for a tall American crossing between the racing vehicles, but he saw nothing. Maybe the shark tank guy was behind the bus stop. Todd took a step toward it.

"You're clean, Bill."

He spun toward the voice. Noelle Kinsella wasn't looking at him. She stood at the corner of the seafood restaurant, lifting up onto her tiptoes to keep Feng Yi in view.

"Jesus, Noelle. You were in the Mercedes? I thought you were—"

"The shark tank guy?" She ignored his anxiety, still scanning the quay for their targets. "My flight landed just before Feng's did. Don't worry. I was just checking you to be sure you weren't tailed."

"Why didn't you tell me?"

"So that you could spend your time gaping in my direction and letting everyone know I was keeping an eye out?" She beckoned to him. "They're going to that yacht out on the end of the quay."

Todd rubbed the sweat from his eyes with his sleeve. He had been on his own with the knowledge that the tall, deadly American was in the same city for twelve hours. He was glad to see his partner. "Should we get closer?"

"Once they're on board. But not yet." Kinsella went to a thick, low palm tree and peered through the fronds. Feng gestured to a

150-foot motor yacht with wonder. "Did you figure her out? The Swede?"

"I'd have said Feng was counting on some action once they get to the boat. But I don't know."

"Spill it."

"It's more than just a sex thing between them. There's some kind of understanding."

"Sex isn't an understanding?"

"At the airport, he sent some kind of file from his tablet. I couldn't tell exactly what. It had to do with a car, though, and when it was done, she was satisfied somehow."

Feng helped the Swedish woman up the steps onto the motor yacht. They went into the living quarters through the rear deck. The door swung shut behind them.

"When's Dom getting here?" Todd asked.

"His flight leaves Prague about now. Our sweet little friend from the FBI is arriving soon too." Kinsella sneered.

"I told Roula you should go to Prague. To help Dom."

"Dom can manage without me."

"But I can't?"

She watched the yacht. The lights came on in the forward cabin. "You're my partner, so I came here instead of Prague."

He smiled.

The low whine of an outboard engine sounded over the traffic from the avenue. An inflatable dinghy came around the prow of the motor yacht and swung about to the swim deck at the rear of the boat. A tall man climbed out into the glow of the single blue night-light, tied off the dinghy, and went up to the deck of the yacht. In the shadow of the canopy, he glanced around the marina.

Todd saw the face. "It's the guy who killed McCarthy." He pulled himself back against the wall of the restaurant.

"You're sure? Wyatt? He's hard to see from here."

"I've spent the last day waiting for him to kill me. I recognize the son of a bitch."

Wyatt went into the cabin and shut the door behind him. Todd reached into his shoulder holster and started for the quay.

"Hold it, Bill." Kinsella grabbed his arm.

"We've got to go in there. Feng's our only lead. Wyatt's going to kill him."

"We don't know that. They could be working together. Wyatt didn't exactly look like he was sweating it. If we go over there now, he's going to see us coming a long way off. If he's who you say he is, the boat will either be gone or we'll be dead before we get to the gangway. We need to let this play out, and we need backup."

Todd holstered his weapon. He kept his hand on it for a long moment, then he let his arm drop.

"We have to alert the ICE agent in Madrid, Bill, and have him liaise with the police here in Palma—"

"Liaise. Will you listen to yourself? You actually said *liaise*."

"We're ICE agents, Bill. We're not James fucking Bond. You want to jump on a Jet Ski and paraglide through the window of the yacht in a tuxedo, you joined the wrong organization."

"Okay, okay. You're right." He kicked a palm tree and cursed.

"Putting your faith in procedures isn't working for you, huh?"

"This is real big stuff, Noelle."

"Then put your faith in Dom Verrazzano." She shifted her attention to the yacht. "That's my plan."

CHAPTER 28

One of Vienna's favorite desserts, a Bundt cake called a *Gugel-hupf,* was created for the Emperor Franz Josef to eat during afternoons with his mistress. At the Club Rex, Minister Ma enjoyed the company of a naked woman and a slice of that same delicacy. Unlike the staid old ruler of the Austro-Hungarian Empire, Ma dipped the sweet sponge into a wide martini glass and sucked the vodka out of the cake.

He lay on the cushioned floor in his private room and watched the Ukrainian woman dance in the red neon lights, each movement repeated a hundred times by her image in the mirrored walls. She piled her peroxided hair on the crown of her head sensuously and gave the Chinese minister the kind of smile that suggested she was worried her teeth might pop right out of her mouth if she relaxed her jaw.

Ma leered at her. This was how the foreign delegations had danced for him at the trade talks that day. Briefly he superimposed the face of the secretary of state on the writhing whore. Then he rode the woman, imagining she was one of the new cars that Feng Yi's computer virus had hijacked, savoring the wildness of her movements, letting her power shoot him out of control.

He could still smell the woman, the cheap perfume and the pungent sex, when his communications director opened the door for him to climb into his Red Horizon limousine out on

Lindengasse. He touched his fingers to his nose and inhaled as the car rounded the corner to Mariahilfer and headed past the art museum toward the Burgring. The dark hulk of the old palace hid the great paintings of centuries past. Ma smiled. The models had all been whores, and the painters had been their johns. Now their works were examined for brushstrokes and composition by the pompous, fat bourgeoisie. He would make them look again, when he led the Communist Party—when he led China. They would see that beneath the velvet smocks and the petticoats, their art was decadent and syphilitic, just as their economies were diseased. They would feel his mastery.

The communications director took his cell phone out of his jacket. He read a text and frowned. Minister Ma turned away. He was all bliss, and the men who worked for him only ever saw problems.

The limousine picked up speed and ran a red light. The driver's shoulders lifted, his grip on the wheel noticeably tighter. Ma watched through the plastic shield that separated him from the chauffeur. They weaved through the late-night traffic, faster and faster.

"Minister Ma," the communications director said. He proffered the phone. "I do not understand this text."

"Not now." Ma moved forward, perching on the edge of the bench seat. He opened his mouth to speak to the driver. The car sped still faster through the junction by the State Opera House, narrowly missing a garbage truck clearing away the day's tourist mess. Ma looked to the left and saw his hotel recede out of sight.

"Where are you going?" he called. "Tan, what are you doing?"

"I can't stop." The driver's voice was strangled and panicked. "Minister Ma, I can't control the car."

They raced up behind two ranks of vehicles at the next red light. The driver swung the limousine away from the waiting cars, south into Schwarzenbergplatz. A taxi pulled out abruptly from the curb. The driver screamed and cut left. The communications director fell across the bench seat and crushed Ma against the door. Ma pushed back and cursed. The director's cell phone dropped into Ma's lap. The limo jumped onto the wide pedestrian area down the center of the square. The cobbles were crowded with young people strolling in the mild summer night, gathering around guitarists to sing songs and watching Pakistani men try to sell bright-pink light sticks.

"Stop the car, you fool," Ma yelled.

"Minister Ma, the car is accelerating like the Darien cars the other day."

Ma picked up the communications director's cell phone. He raised it to hurl it back at his underling.

Before them, General Schwarzenberg rode a gigantic bronze horse atop a huge granite plinth. The hero of the Napoleonic Wars stared ahead, watching the great battles of the nineteenth century unfold. For a moment, Minister Ma realized that, of course, the general's brave regard would actually have been a witness to the extinction of thousands under his command. *Here comes one more death*, he thought, as the car hurtled between the screeching young Austrians toward the mass of stone. The driver let go of the wheel and dived across the front seats.

The car hit a low bollard, and Ma's arm, holding the cell phone, jumped up in front of his face. The text message on the cell phone read, "You are the drone. I am hanging up now."

Ma recalled the insult with which he had humiliated his computer expert. The massive plinth of granite rushed up at the car. Ma filled his lungs and bellowed. "Feng, you bastard."

PART 3

CHAPTER 29

The Spanish police created a perimeter with plainclothes officers. They wanted to empty the marina, but Kinsella persuaded them that a clear out would alert the suspects on the yacht
to the presence of the cops. So when Verrazzano arrived from the
airport, he found a dozen local policemen loitering undercover
along the quay and behind the seafood restaurant, which was serv-
ing an early breakfast to a group of middle-aged German vacationers with skin burned by the sun to the vibrant tone of the
lobster in the salad on their plates. Kinsella showed him the yacht
where Feng Yi had spent the night with Wyatt and the Swedish
woman. "Wyatt is dangerous," she said.

You don't know the half of it, Verrazzano thought.

Todd came to him accompanied by a Spaniard who hunched
nervously and twitched his neck. "Hey, Dom. This is Comisario
Cruz. He's commanding the squad from the local police department and he—"

"I cannot handle this situation," Cruz said. "Your ICE agent
in Madrid told me this was an interdiction connected to a computer software case. Now it's about the Chinese government and
the Darien crash and the man who went in the shark tank at the
aquarium. We need backup."

"You have twelve officers here," Verrazzano said. "Any more
and the people on that boat will know we're coming."

"See? You want to board the yacht. My officers aren't able to do that. I mean, they can try. But it's not what they know how to do."

Verrazzano saw what might be at the root of Cruz's agitation. "What *do* they know how to do?"

"We are from the *Brigada de Investigación Tecnológica*. How do you say it in English?"

"The cybercrimes unit?"

"Is correct."

Kinsella slapped her hand against her hip. "Harrison messed up. I told him all the details, and he sent us a bunch of computer geeks."

"Comisario Cruz, we don't have a lot of time," Verrazzano said. "We're going to move right now, before the people on that boat realize we're here. And you're moving with us."

"I will go to explain to my men."

"Do it quickly."

Cruz hurried to the edge of the quay and hid himself behind a palm tree, speaking to his officers through a microphone on his lapel. Kinsella handed Verrazzano an earpiece, a receiver, and a mic. He reached up to fit the earpiece and grimaced. He switched it to his other hand and plugged it in.

"You're hurt?" Kinsella pulled the lapel of his jacket to get a look at his wounded shoulder.

"Not as bad as my dad was hurt when the Islanders moved to Brooklyn." Over the earpiece, the comisario's voice came through in impatient Spanish.

"How're we going to do it, Dom?" Kinsella said.

A taxi pulled up at the bus stop in front of the restaurant. Two of the Spanish cops approached it, gesturing for it to move on. But the rear door opened and Jahn stepped out. She brushed off the Spaniards and hurried toward the ICE agents.

"Before everything kicks off, you'd better look at this, Dom." Todd pulled a FedEx waybill from his pocket. "It's from the packet the Irish banker had in his attaché case. Inside was a scalp. The waybill was sent from a FedEx office in Cologne, so I'd guess the scalp belonged to the fourth engineer."

Verrazzano took the paper. The Irishman's Luxembourg address was written in a shaky hand. Printed beside it, the location of a FedEx office on Klarastrasse. He remembered the street. It was where he had found Turbo dead, with Jahn standing in the middle of the road looking hopeless.

Jahn reached them. She grabbed the paper. "The hell is this?"

"It's nice to see *you* too," Kinsella said.

Jahn read the waybill and stuffed it in her pocket. "What's the situation?"

"We have the three suspects on the yacht at the end of the quay. Support is from a local cybercrime unit."

"Cybercrime?" Jahn glared at Kinsella accusingly.

"We have to board the yacht right now. Bill, wrangle these Spanish cops to keep the perimeter. See that Agent Jahn is issued with intercom hardware. Let's go, Dom."

"I'm going to do it," Verrazzano said, "with Gina."

Kinsella stared from Verrazzano to Jahn. "Dom, what the hell?"

"There's another suspect at large. The guy who's actually been doing the killings."

"The one with the rotten skin?" Todd said.

"The Krokodil. If we, all four of us, go to board the yacht, we'll have no one but the computer nerds between our backs and a very deadly assassin."

"We don't know that he's even in Palma," Kinsella said.

"I won't take the risk. Noelle, I need you and Bill to secure the end of the quay and make sure that the Krokodil doesn't slip past the Spanish cops. Whatever happens over there"—he pointed toward the yacht—"I want you to maintain the perimeter back here. Things blow up over there, you do not, repeat *do not,* come running in. It could be a distraction intended to draw us all toward the yacht."

Todd shrugged his acceptance. Kinsella clicked her tongue.

"Go tell Comisario Cruz how it's going to be, Bill." Verrazzano took Kinsella a few yards away from Jahn.

"What the hell's going on here, Dom?"

"You have to let me play something out, Noelle."

"I should be going with you."

"There's no one I'd rather have with me boarding that boat than you. But it isn't going to be that way." She opened her mouth to question him. He turned away and spoke to Jahn. "Gina, let's move."

Kinsella moved closer and spoke quietly. "There's something you're not telling me, Dom, and that's okay. I'm going to do this your way. But when it's done, I don't care what you write for the files—you're going to tell me the real story. All of it."

"No secrets. It's a promise, Noelle."

"In that case, take care. Get on now."

"Gina, come with me."

Jahn ran her finger down the scar on her face, her nerves telling in her movements. For her, this was more than just an arrest they were about to make.

It was for Verrazzano too.

They walked side by side onto the quay, measuring their pace in case someone was watching them from inside the yacht. If they were very lucky, the people on the boat would still be sleeping. But Verrazzano had never once seen Wyatt asleep, and he didn't expect to catch him napping now.

Jahn went into a slow jog. "Let's move, Dom. We've got to get on that boat."

Verrazzano caught her arm. His eyes were hard. "It's a dangerous operation, boarding the boat."

"Okay, so it's a risk. Let's go."

"You're mighty keen to get on board. Are you expecting to meet someone?"

"Meet? What the hell are you talking about?"

"You sent the scalp to the banker in Luxembourg."

"That's nuts."

"I found you on the street outside the FedEx office. With Turbo dead. There's no way the Krokodil had gotten there before you. I was tracking him. He couldn't have done it."

"You don't know what you're talking about."

"Tell me the truth, Gina. Or I'll bring Kinsella over here and board the boat with her, instead."

"No." Jahn strangled her shout. She glanced at the boat, anxious that she may have alerted the people on board. "For God's sake, I have to do this."

"How did Wyatt get to you?"

Her shock seemed to double. Her eyes searched him, terrified, wondering how he knew.

"Who does Wyatt have on that boat?"

She spoke in a murmur. "My husband."

The Special Forces soldier she had thought was dead. Wyatt had found him and made him a hostage—and made Jahn work for him to save her husband. Verrazzano watched the first glimmer of the rising sun on Jahn's scarred face. The scars her husband had tended and soothed until an operation in the Middle East took him away from her. Now Wyatt had given her the chance to get her man back, one sacrifice from her to repay the many sacrifices he had made in the military. All she'd had to do was kill one Chinese computer engineer. Verrazzano saw the force that had overcome Jahn's sense of duty. It was love that made her betray her mission.

"I'm going to stop Wyatt right now." He put his hand on Jahn's shoulder. "And we're going to go get your husband."

She stared at him in surprise. Her eyes teared up.

"Doing right isn't really important until you've felt what it is to do wrong," he said. "Let's go make this right."

She wiped the back of her hand across her eyes. "How're we going to handle it?"

"It's a big boat, but not so big that we have to split up. We'll go up on the aft deck and into the master cabin. Then we flush right on through until we find whoever's in there."

"They could come out of a hatch farther up toward the prow."

"Once they're out in the open, we don't have to worry about them. Inside the yacht they've got Wi-Fi and, maybe, the codes they need to activate the big crash."

"Wait, they don't have the codes. You got the tattoo on the head of the engineer in Prague. Without that, they can't activate the crash. They also don't have Turbo's scalp. Agent Todd intercepted it. They needed five scalps. They've got three."

He put his hand against her shoulder blade with a gentle pressure, and they moved off. "Gina, we're going in. Focus on that."

They passed two of the Spanish cops on the quay. One of them perched on a bollard set up to prevent vehicles driving into the water. The other kicked aimlessly at a cleat, his toe poking the knot that tied off a thirty-six-foot sailboat. They glanced at Verrazzano with all the confidence of naked middle managers addressing the board of directors.

The chugging of a heavy diesel engine at low speed sounded beyond the next dock. Through the earpiece Verrazzano heard Comisario Cruz demand to know its source. The cop on the bollard squinted between the boats. A forty-foot power boat with shiny gold bodywork rumbled toward the sea.

"The Spanish cops are going to screw it up," Jahn said. "If we *do* force our suspects off the boat, these guys will either let them get away or they'll shoot them dead."

They were fifteen yards from the motor yacht when the noise of the diesel swung suddenly toward them. The high prow of the power boat emerged from beyond the row of docked yachts, lifting from the water, the engine thundering. Behind the windshield, the Krokodil spun the helm.

Loud voices in Spanish yelled through Verrazzano's earpiece. He called into his microphone, "Noelle, keep those guys cool back there. *Mantened donde estáis.* Everyone stay where you are."

The cops at his side drew their weapons and made for the yacht. Verrazzano shoved them backward. "It's a diversion. *Ved el barco, no mirad la lancha.* Everyone watch the boat, not the motor launch."

The powerboat's engines caught and started to drive past the big yacht. The Krokodil left the helm. He jumped onto the prow and leapt for the yacht. He scrambled through a hatch beyond the forward mast.

"What's he doing?" Jahn said.

The powerboat kept going, its engine at full strength even with no one at the helm. It bellowed and stamped over the water toward the rear of the seafood restaurant on the quay.

"Noelle, get those people out of the restaurant," Verrazzano shouted.

Kinsella rushed toward the seafood joint, waving her arms and yelling. A few of the sunburned Germans pointed toward her. One or two even stood up. But they were still there when the powerboat nosed through the plate glass windows and smashed its hull into the quay. The Germans screamed, and the ones that could still move got up and ran. Through the chaos of the panicked tourists, the bawling of the Spanish cops on the earpiece, and the impotent clamor of the powerboat straining against the quay, Verrazzano heard the purring of the motor yacht's engine. "Move, Gina. They're running." He sprinted for the boat.

The Krokodil was back on deck, ducking along the gunwales, slashing a K-bar through the ropes, cutting the motor yacht loose from the quay.

Verrazzano leveled his H&K. He squeezed off four rounds. The Krokodil sliced the final rope and rolled under the bullets, into the wheelhouse and out of sight. The motor yacht moved off.

Throwing himself from the quay, Verrazzano caught the stern and hauled himself aboard. Jahn made the leap. Her legs slipped toward the churn of the engines. He grabbed her wrists and lifted her. She came onto the poop deck as the boat powered forward. She stumbled into him. He felt the force of her heartbeat against his chest. The boat moved out into the marina. The quay behind them was in chaos. Over the earpiece, he heard Kinsella calling out. "Dom, Bill and me are coming to back you up."

He bellowed into his microphone. "Noelle, remain in position. I want the quayside cleared. The Spanish cops will have to handle the evacuation of those tourists. You and Bill are all I have between me and the Krokodil. I believe he's somewhere on the quayside to your rear."

Jahn flashed a surprised look at him, shocked at his lie. The Krokodil was on the boat with them.

"Hold your position, Noelle. I repeat, hold your position." He pulled the mic off his jacket and tugged the earpiece away. He tossed them into the water. No one, not even Kinsella, would hear what he and Wyatt talked about. He could count on Jahn's own secrets to keep her quiet about anything she learned on the boat. She tugged the communications rig off her jacket and threw it aside too. "It's just you and me," she said.

"And a couple of very dangerous guys."

They entered the luxurious salon and went through to the dining room and the galley. The engines rumbled them farther from the quay toward the marina's entrance and the open sea. The shouts and screams and sirens receded behind them. Then they heard a slap, and a man cried out ahead. They picked up the pace.

They passed the open doors of the yacht's four bedrooms. Each of the cabins was empty. At the entrance to the owner's quarters, Verrazzano signaled for Jahn to throw the door open. She gripped the handle and stared at it. Verrazzano whispered, "It's time, Gina."

She yanked the door open. Verrazzano spun inside. He held his weapon high.

In the center of the room, Feng Yi was tied to a chair by his wrists and ankles. He was shirtless and shoeless. Blood streaked his fleshy torso and pooled around his feet. His nipples had been peeled away. His detached toenails lay on the boards of the deck. The scent of his urine and his soiled pants was strong in the enclosed space. Wyatt stood over him in a black T-shirt, his feet a yard apart, a hunting knife in one hand and a set of pliers in the other. His hands glistened with gore. Behind him on a rolltop desk, a MacBook flashed a connection to a page running computer code down the left side of the screen, waiting for the missing inputs from the dead engineers' scalps. The Krokodil wasn't in the room. Jahn entered behind Verrazzano. She covered every corner with her pistol, but Verrazzano locked onto Wyatt.

"Where's my husband?" Jahn shouted.

The Chinese man wailed in pain. Wyatt jammed his pliers into the back pocket of his jeans and laid his big hand over Feng's mouth. "Hush now," he whispered. "General Feng, the cavalry has arrived."

Feng struggled to free his head from Wyatt's grip. He turned his myopic eyes toward Jahn and Verrazzano. His voice was shattered and torn. "Please."

"I figured it wouldn't take long to get what I needed out of this guy," Wyatt said. "I was wrong. Turns out, he isn't just a nasty little Chinaman. He's also an awful tough little Chinaman."

"You're wasting your time." Verrazzano gestured toward the laptop. "Even if Feng talks, you won't make any money from instigating a massive car crash."

"You figured out my short play on the stock market?" Wyatt's smile lingered. He slapped Feng's cheek gently. The man winced.

"Your stock play is blocked."

"You're sure that's the only trade I put on?"

"It doesn't matter. You won't be able to activate the crash codes. It's too late."

"It's never too late, son. You sure as hell know the truth of that."

Jahn stepped to Verrazzano's side and spoke in a strangled rush. "We've got the scalps of the last two engineers, Turbo from Cologne and Jin from Prague. You can't do this thing now. You're missing two parts of the code."

Wyatt glanced at her tenderly. "Honey, I know how to make a guy talk. I'm just getting started on fat boy here."

"You're done torturing him," she said.

"Your husband is in the prow of the boat with five kilos of plastic explosive strapped to his skinny neck." Wyatt lifted his hand and showed a remote detonator in his palm. "If you want to see your husband alive, you'd best take care of Agent Verrazzano here. Meanwhile, I'm going to work on the honorable General Feng."

Jahn turned her weapon toward the ICE agent.

Wyatt took the pliers from his pocket. "Go ahead and disarm him, Special Agent Jahn?" He waved the detonator.

Verrazzano didn't look at Jahn or the gun that was pointed at him. "Do what you have to do, Gina."

Wyatt wiggled his fingers over the button on the detonator. "Maybe you want poor old Chris blown up, Agent Jahn, so you and Verrazzano can be together. He's a free agent, after all. His wife kicked him out when he told her all the bad stuff he'd done working for me. Right, hoss? You confessed to sweet little Melanie because you didn't want any secrets between you, but instead she decided you're a murderer and she hates your guts. That's the price you paid for all the sacrifices you made for your country. At least it means you can be with Gina. You'd be an awful nice couple."

Verrazzano spoke quietly. "I said do what you have to do, Gina."

She hesitated, then she spun away from him toward Wyatt. "You can push that detonator. You can blow up the boat, and me with it. But you don't get to torture this man, and you don't get to kill thousands of people."

Wyatt shrugged. "Makes no difference. After all, Dominic's going to join me. Ain't that right, son?"

Verrazzano understood why the Krokodil hadn't intervened yet. Wyatt wanted to have him alone with Jahn. To bring him back onto his team. It was no risk, after all. If Verrazzano didn't accept, the Krokodil would come in and kill him.

Feng Yi coughed and spat. He lifted his head and craned his neck toward Verrazzano. "I have five million dollars. You can have it all. Please help me."

Verrazzano had a deal to strike that morning. But it wasn't going to be with Feng. He moved forward and laid his hand on Feng's head. He yanked the man's toupee away. Feng bawled as the pins tugged against the hair around his ears and at the nape of his neck.

"Well, damn me." Wyatt stared at the bound man's bald head. It was tattooed with lines of code—the commands that would activate the huge malfunction in the onboard computers of every new car. The characters spread from an inch above Feng's brow back toward the crown of his head. Turbo had remembered what Feng told his engineers: *It's all in your heads. But if you screw it up, it'll be on your heads anyway.* The code was split between all the engineers, a few lines tattooed to each of their heads. But if one of his computer engineers was lost or decided to revolt against the operation, Feng's fail-safe had been written under his own hairpiece.

"No, you idiot," Feng said. "You have given him the codes."

"Special Agent Verrazzano, I congratulate you." Wyatt's face, brown from the sun off the sea, showed calculation like the fast darkness of a shoal of fish racing under the surface. "You're my next generation, son."

Verrazzano had wondered if Wyatt would still exert his old power over him. But now he spoke with absolute certainty. "It's over, Wyatt."

"What're you going to do? Kill me?"

"First things first." Verrazzano pulled Feng's head back and put two bullets through the tattoos on his scalp. The slugs ripped into the computer code and smashed Feng's brain.

"Goddamn it, son." Wyatt punched Verrazzano hard. He aimed for his jaw. Verrazzano dodged enough to take it on his cheek. The bone exploded at the contact from Wyatt's heavy fist. Verrazzano knew it would only be a fracture and it wouldn't render him unconscious as a jaw shot would have done. He tumbled onto the bench along the side of the cabin. Jahn came to him, training her weapon on the colonel.

Wyatt scrabbled his fingers over Feng's wrecked scalp. The dead man flopped across the chair. Wyatt pulled at the scraps of flesh, trying to piece together the code. He hammered his hand down on the dead man's shoulders in frustration. "Son, you have messed it all up again."

Jahn grabbed for the detonator. Wyatt closed his fist and back-handed her. She went down in front of the forward door.

A series of fast steps came from the direction of the prow, and the Krokodil entered. The door struck Jahn's head as he opened it. She rolled away groaning. The Krokodil held a Belgian submachine gun and pointed it at Verrazzano. The P90 had its action and magazine behind the trigger where the stock would usually be. That made it no wider than a man's body and easy to maneuver in the cramped space of the cabin. Over his shoulder, the Swedish woman gasped and covered her eyes at the sight of the dead man. Then she took her hands away and Verrazzano noticed something turn in her face. He had seen it before, innocents robbed of everything they thought was true and left with an explosive hatred. Sometimes it stayed with them forever. Others could resolve it with one desperate act.

Wyatt waved for the Krokodil to hold back. He slapped the chubby cheek of the Chinese man, angrily. "Goddamn it. I was going to turn this bastard and make him work for us."

"You mean, work for *you*," Verrazzano said.

"You're smarter than that, son. Jesus H. Christ, stop listening to Tom Frisch and trust *yourself*." He came close and rested his hand, bloody from the man's smashed skull, on Verrazzano's shoulder. "Everything you ever did for me was done on the orders of Washington. Everything I did was for Washington. Including this here operation."

Something in Wyatt's anger rang true. Verrazzano pictured the traces of the colonel's operation, mapping them toward Washington instead of Beijing. "You're not working for the Chinese?"

"Sure, I was. Double-crossing them. The Chinese called it all off, boy. My man back in DC wants this crash thing to go down anyhow. He wants the White House to finally accept that diplomacy won't work with China. China needs to be dealt with by force."

"Who's *your man*?"

Wyatt grinned. "You think *I'm* scary, son? My guy is the devil himself. I'm not going to give you his name. I care enough about you to want you to never even think of going after him."

The Krokodil's boots shuffled on the varnished floorboards. The Swedish woman brought herself very close behind him. "Shane, we have to go now. This isn't right. You have to get away. Come with me." He shrugged her off.

"Who is it?" Verrazzano said to Wyatt. "Who's behind this?"

"It's a black op, for Christ's sake," Wyatt said. "There *is* no proof. It's completely deniable."

The Swedish woman spoke, her voice louder than it needed to be, pushing her words out despite her nerves. "You must help Shane, Colonel Wyatt."

Jahn crawled toward the door that led to the prow. Groggy from the blow to her head, she muttered, "The detonator. Dom, the detonator."

"Who ordered the operation?" Verrazzano said. "I want a name."

"You must get him help for his addiction," Maj said. "This was your promise. You must pay for his treatment. Or he will die."

"Your boy has a job to do, sweetheart." Wyatt turned briefly to Maj. "When that's done, he'll be taken care of."

The Swedish woman shook her head. "Shane, he's going to make you keep doing these things until you're dead."

"Maj, leave it alone." The Krokodil's voice was hesitant. He moved the barrel of the P90 away from Verrazzano toward Wyatt. The ICE agent prepared to jump him.

Maj touched her lover's raddled face. "I'll take you away from him and cure you."

Wyatt chuckled. "There's no cure for what he's got, honey. I don't mean the drugs and the gnarly skin. Your sweet little boy there is a killer, and it's all he's ever going to be good at. Take that away from him, and he'd be nothing but scabs and scars, inside and out."

Verrazzano leapt at the Krokodil. He snapped the submachine gun out of his grasp and head-butted him on the bridge of the nose. He twisted as they landed on the floor of the cabin and held the Krokodil in a half nelson. Maj screamed and pounded his shoulders. Verrazzano took out his handcuffs, hooked the chain behind the leg of the heavy bench, and snapped the cuffs on the Krokodil's wrists.

Jahn got to her knees and caught Maj around the neck, dragging her away.

"Help him." Maj raised her hands toward Wyatt, pleading. "How can you let this man do this to him? You were like a father to Shane." She delivered a sharp backward head-butt that caught Jahn on the nose and sent her back to the floor.

The Krokodil glared at Wyatt, lips tight, wrists jerking against the handcuffs. Verrazzano went toward the colonel. "I'm taking you with me too."

Wyatt laughed softly. Then he frowned. Verrazzano followed his glance.

Maj held a Beretta subcompact. Her eyes were teary, but her arm was steady, and the gun was aimed at Wyatt. Verrazzano cursed. The pistol must have been in the Krokodil's vest.

Verrazzano stepped toward the Swedish woman. In the instant that Maj's finger strained against the pressure of the trigger, Wyatt threw Verrazzano to the floor, out of the line of fire. Verrazzano went down. Two bullets struck Wyatt in the chest. He collapsed against the expensive paneling of the cabin.

Verrazzano grabbed the gun from Maj. Jahn scrambled across the floor. She peeled back Wyatt's fingers and lifted the detonator away. Blood gushed onto Wyatt's shirt and ran with the camber of the deck toward starboard. He made a tiny motion of his head, signaling Verrazzano to come close. "I did that for you," he whispered. "Now get me revenge. I told the truth. About the dark op."

"Then who is it? Who's behind this?" Verrazzano knelt at his side.

"That one knows."

Verrazzano followed Wyatt's glance. The Krokodil stared at his dying master. Profound loss crossed the man's face. Then it receded, as if the scabs and infection smothered it. Maj wrapped her arms around his shoulders and kissed his brow.

Wyatt's face froze, and the blood stopped pumping out of his smashed carotid. "Dinner at Odin's table, old man," Verrazzano whispered. He took the detonator from Jahn. With a flick of his finger, he deactivated it. "Go find your husband." She went through the bulkhead toward the prow.

Verrazzano took the Swedish woman by the arm. He pulled her to the stern. Maj struggled against Verrazzano's grip. "I won't leave him. Shane is good. I can save him."

"I'm the only one who can do that."

The Krokodil closed his eyes briefly, a signal to Maj that he accepted his fate.

At the swim deck, Verrazzano put Maj in the dinghy. He heard a big launch coming after them from the marina. The Spanish police had finally mastered their panic, or Kinsella and Todd had commandeered a boat. The engine was less than one hundred yards away, but the dinghy was shielded from view by the yacht. Verrazzano yanked the cord on the outboard and set Maj's hands on the wheel. She sobbed and wavered. But the wheel gave her something to hold onto. He untied the line. She swung the dinghy away from the yacht and headed into the half-light toward Punta de Sant Carles.

The voice of Comisario Cruz came over the loud-hailer from the police launch. "People on the boat, come out and show yourselves."

Verrazzano went back below decks. Through an open cabin door, he saw Jahn embracing a man who was weeping hard. Back in the owner's quarters, he unlatched the handcuffs and guided the Krokodil up to the bridge and around to the bow rail.

"If Maj hadn't killed him, I'd have done it," the Krokodil said. "He went too far."

Verrazzano waved to the police launch. At the bow, Kinsella's shoulders dropped in relief when she spotted him. The launch came around. Todd went up and down the deck to be sure the panicked Spanish cops didn't open fire.

"I'm going to jail for a year," the Krokodil said. "Then I'm going to die."

Verrazzano glanced toward the point where the Swedish woman's dinghy had disappeared. He read the last traces of her wake, white against the morning sun on the water. He had thought he was tracking Wyatt, to confront him about the car crash conspiracy, to do what a law enforcement officer did, to put a stop to something and tie it up. Instead he discovered that the filth was really everywhere, deeper and more complex and unforgiving than he had ever imagined. That was Wyatt's message to him in the end. It had all been a long training for this moment. A Washington power broker wanted war with China, and he would surely find another way of getting what he wanted now that Wyatt was gone. Verrazzano sensed in himself something tougher and darker than he had known before, something tenacious and unforgiving enough to stop the man who wanted war. The Krokodil shuddered because he saw it too, on Verrazzano's face—saw how far he would go.

Jahn emerged from the wheelhouse. At her side, a thin man with pale skin and a long beard came squinting into the sunlight, his face still wet with tears. Her husband held her hand in both of his. She smiled at Verrazzano, and there was a question too on her face. He shook his head. She was clear.

The police launch bumped against the gunwales of the yacht. The Krokodil stumbled with the impact. Verrazzano caught his upper arm to steady him. He pulled him close. "You're not going to jail to die, and you're not going to die of your addiction. You're going to lead me to the Washington guy who set up Wyatt's dark op."

"How in hell would I know who that is? You think Wyatt told *me*?"

Verrazzano opened his mouth to speak. Then he halted. He ran it through his memory again, the moment when Wyatt had demanded revenge for the betrayal of his black op and glared across the cabin at the Krokodil and said, "That one knows." Special Ops had trained him to challenge every step in his logic, to identify the lazy thinking that could cost his life. He traced the angle of Wyatt's eyes. Something wasn't right. Then he caught it. The old man had been looking just to the side of the Krokodil. At the Swedish woman.

Verrazzano shaded his eyes to stare at the boathouses on the Punta de Sant Carles. Maj's dinghy drifted empty by the quay.

The Spanish comisario wailed over the loud-hailer, begging for information so loudly that Maj could probably hear him as she disappeared into the city. Kinsella and Todd leapt onto the yacht. The bell in the cathedral tolled for early Mass. Traffic noise drifted over the waves.

"Dom," Kinsella called out, "what the hell happened here?"

Verrazzano went to the rail. The water was just catching the southern light that turned it from nighttime gray to azure. The dinghy was a quarter mile distant. He kicked off his boots, tied the laces together, and strung them over his shoulders.

He plunged into the sea. Under the surface, the space around him was as silent and cool as his soul. He came back up. On the deck of the yacht, Jahn watched him with her husband at her side. The Krokodil gave Verrazzano a small nod of understanding.

Verrazzano struck out for the shore.